ALL WRAPPED UP IN A PRETTY LITTLE BEAU

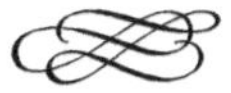

MARIANNA FORREST

TANGLEWOOD PRESS

CHAPTER 1: DECEMBER 20TH

lright, eyes forward. The time has come. One, two, three...
Eldan Noelle growled as he pushed himself up from his warm bed. He forced his eyes open and stared bitterly at the darkened windows. Life was calling out to him, telling him it was time to get ready for work, but that meant he would have to leave the warm nest that was his bed. The heavy quilts wrapped around his body only made it that much harder.

Dear Lord, why couldn't I have been born in the Bahamas? Or Texas? Hell, I'd even take Florida at this point.

Eldan glared at the windows a while longer before a faint snuffle came from the corner of his room. Mr. Hopson, his Flemish Giant rabbit, slept peacefully in his kennel. Next to him, Honey Bun, a French Lop, looked almost like a stuffed toy. The rabbits' muffled snores taunted him; they were a constant reminder that it was *way* too early for this shit.

But before he could grumble about how he woke up before his alarm *again*–

"*Have a holly, jolly Christmas–!*"

Eldan jolted and slammed his fist down on the snooze

button, but he only succeeded in knocking the clock to the floor. The song continued without a care in the world. In fact, it got louder. He groaned and flopped back onto his pillow.

It was mocking him, damn it.

It was saying he wasn't fast enough, not strong enough. Now, that stupid song was stuck in his head, which was far worse than any other punishment he could've been forced to endure.

He slid off the bed to the floor in defeat and grabbed his clock. With the press of a button, the dreaded song came to an end, and he slammed the clock back on the nightstand. Admittedly, with *a little* more force than necessary.

Usually, he woke up bright-eyed and bushy-tailed, but this time of year always threw him for a loop. When the mornings brought overly merry songs and ice falling from the skies, it became harder and harder to leave the sanctuary of his bed.

That, and he *definitely* wasn't a below-freezing temperatures kind of person. He pulled his quilt tighter around his body and grumbled into the warm fabric before he pushed himself to his feet to see what fresh hell waited for him outside.

Yep, as Eldan had predicted, it was snowing. Great. Fantastic, even. He could see the glittering flakes of evil dancing against the light of the streetlamps. Eldan let out a frustrated groan, and he bunched up the quilt so he could get the show on the road.

One look at Mr. Hopson's kennel told him the sleepy little rabbits truly didn't give one damn about all the racket he made earlier. It was downright unfair how easily sleep came to those rabbits. He tore his gaze from the sleepy little bunnies, trudged into the hallway, and headed down the stairs.

As he walked through the house, his friends' blissful

snores were a friendly reminder that he shouldn't be a complete asshole and stomp down the corridor like he planned. Jenny and Quentin were kind enough to let him stay here while he finished up his last year at college, despite being stretched-thin grad students themselves. Now was one of those rare times he could return the favor.

Easier said than done, though. Chills ran through his body with every step on the hardwood floor. He really needed to find another pair of slippers. His last pair met their end a few days ago at the supremely flawless fluffy paws of Mr. Hopson.

Had to be my absolute favorite pair of slippers too—

Eldan froze, and a shiver ran up his spine as he stepped on something *disgustingly festive.*

Oh, what the fu—

He'd know that feeling anywhere. Tinsel. He squinted in the darkness of the hallway and saw gleams of gold and silver tinsel winding in a messy trail down the hallway that led to the living room.

And the tinsel trail was only the beginning. As Eldan got further into the living room, he noticed a scattering of wrapping paper, ribbon, and boxes. The TV was on, lighting up a small area around it, and on the couch lay Quentin, surrounded by Christmas candy wrappers.

Eldan groaned and sidestepped the boxes. He *was* going to give Mr. Hopson a stern talking-to, but since it was actually Quentin behind this mess, he wouldn't bother. No, what he needed was some coffee. Right this very instant.

And maybe some blockers. He went over his mental calendar and sighed. His next heat would be here soon—what a joy.

Suddenly, goosebumps prickled across his skin, and he was hit with an overwhelming premonition that something jolly was going to pop up on the screen. Call it a sixth sense, if you will. But before he could lunge for the remote—

"Ready, Rudolph?" the TV taunted him.

Eldan grabbed the remote, but the buttons weren't responding no matter how hard he pressed them. He fumbled the remote and realized it was far lighter than it should've been. The battery compartment was empty, devoid of any spark of life.

What sort of fool would do this? Quentin, that's who. Eldan braced himself as the commercial played out, then he tossed the remote on the couch with a huff. Yeah, it was turning out to be a great day so far.

"Your bedside manner needs some work."

Eldan turned around and saw Quentin smiling stupidly at him. He waved the remote toward Eldan before tossing it on the coffee table.

"You are sleeping on a couch. Couchside manner is not a thing." Eldan grumbled.

"I don't think you understand the meaning of bedside manner." Quentin rose and stretched, popping a kink out of his shoulders before surveying the mess around him. "Oh, damn, I'm good."

"At what?" Eldan sighed. Better to let Quentin get it out of his system so he could drink his coffee in peace.

Quentin pointed to the darkened corner of the living room. Eldan squinted and saw a vague triangular shape.

"And what is *that*?"

"It's called a Christmas tree, Eldan." Quentin pulled out his phone and pressed an icon on the screen. The tree lit up in a horrifying display of multi-colored lights and tacky ornaments.

It took every ounce of willpower in Eldan's body to refrain from hissing and shrinking back into his quilt.

"Oh, hush, and just look at my work."

"I'm looking, and it burns." Eldan squinted at the tree and scoffed. "I didn't think you were gonna put it up this year."

"You wish." Quentin rose from the couch and stared at his work proudly. "Yeah, I wanted to surprise Jenny…"

Eldan gazed up and down at the atrocious thing taking up the entire corner. "Well, she'll definitely enjoy it."

He wasn't being sarcastic for once. Jenny loved Christmas, and when the first days of December passed, and the decorations weren't up yet, anyone could tell her mood was dropping. Jenny had a face that could tear your very soul apart when she was sad. Yeah, she would be thrilled to wake up to this tacky thing.

Eldan, on the other hand, was horrified beyond measure. That thing was probably gonna stay up all the way through January to make up for lost time.

"Don't give me that look." Quentin snorted. "I don't say a word when you pull out all those rabbit villages and throw them around the house."

"At least the villages aren't tacky."

"Not tacky?" Quentin grinned. "To each his own, I guess?"

Eldan let out a string of curse words and tried to make his way back toward the kitchen. "It's too early to deal with you. Coffee first."

"You work with coffee all day. How can you stand to drink it all the time here?"

"Quentin." Eldan took a deep breath. "Hear me, and hear me well. I live life by a very specific motto."

"And that is?"

"Coffee is easier to deal with than people."

Eldan left Quentin in the abode of the damned that was the living room and rushed to start his coffee. He only had a few precious minutes free of anything jolly before he had to go to work and, by God, he was gonna enjoy them.

COFFEE WAS, IN FACT, NOT MUCH EASIER TO DEAL WITH THAN

people. It was just one thing after another. Eldan flexed his hand, testing the limits of the bandages wrapped tightly around it. Today he confirmed, once again, that spilling hot coffee on delicate skin hurts. Definitely not recommended.

He must have pissed off fate—between the holly-jolly moments and the not-so-jolly customers, it had been a rough day so far. If one more person claimed they knew the manager and they were promised a free coffee, he wouldn't hold back. He would sass them like there was no tomorrow. That was a guarantee.

Eldan was torn from his thoughts as the man at his register *finally* decided what he wanted. It was the same thing he always got.

Yes, thank you, Mr. Tall Skinny Caramel Chestnut Vanilla Brulee. We'll be sure to heat it to precisely 192.5 degrees and, don't worry, I will personally make sure there is absolutely no foam in it before I serve it to you. Sure thing. Eldan grumbled. Always the same wait, always the same thing.

After passing Mr. Brulee's order along to his co-workers, Eldan's gaze settled on the display cases. He was too tired for this shit. Nightmares tended to do that to a guy. How else would you describe the moment when the sexy, muscled *dreamboat* in your slumber suddenly morphs into Frosty the Snowman?

And no, the muscles didn't transfer over. They got lost in transport.

"Eldan, you awake?" a voice called out behind him. "Why are you glaring at the Christmas cookies like they insulted your honor?"

Eldan turned and threw an uninterested look over his shoulder. Guess you could only glower at the sugar cookies for so long before someone spoke up. Now, his boss was watching him expectantly.

He knew he wasn't in trouble. Yeah, the Bossman, old Louie Johnston, usually poked fun at Eldan's immense distaste for Christmas. He was the one person who could actually get away with that tomfoolery.

Only because he paid Eldan to put up with it.

"They. Exist." Eldan shoved a new tray of cookies into the display case.

"Well, they're fixing to not exist." His boss pointed out the window before he cleared his throat. "Attention baristas, this is a Code Caramel. I repeat, Code Caramel. This is not a drill!"

Every worker that was out on the floor stopped and looked out the window. Some of them knew what was coming. Others, like the hires who were unfortunate enough to join the team just a few short days ago, had no idea.

As his co-workers scrambled behind the counter, Eldan took a deep breath.

"Get ready!" Louie's face was beaming. "Here they come!"

Eldan braced for impact moments before the doors swung open. A cacophony of screams and squeals drowned out the horrid Christmas music, if only for a moment, as a large crowd of exhausted parents and their lively miniatures burst through the door.

Now the real fun began.

"This is just wonderful." Louie beamed. He joined Eldan and the others behind the counter, ready to help manage the new crowd. "Ever since that toy shop opened, business has been booming."

"Yeah, I love being judged by teddy bears and nutcrackers all day every day." Eldan grumbled. "Look at them. They watch us from behind the safety of those painted windows. And the tree? It *spins*. Absolutely fantastic."

"I knew you'd come around." Louie laughed before he barked out another order.

Every time Eldan looked out the front windows and across the street, he saw that den of horrors. Crispin' Cringle's Christmas Shop. When he started working in

Louie's shop four years ago, it was a dry cleaner. A quiet, calm, somewhat bland, dry cleaner. But one day it just up and shut down. Now, in its place?

Hell. Year-round Hell.

Eldan's eyes drifted one last time to the shop across the street. Even now, he could see the owners of Crispin' Cringle's, all dressed up in their costumes. They were the spitting image of the Clauses, with the jolly disposition to match.

It was an absolute nightmare, like that ugly yellow SUV that just rolled by. Who the hell decorates their car that much? It had these horrifying antlers and red nose, a wreath, *and* it was covered in tinsel?

The day couldn't end fast enough.

WHEN ELDAN'S SHIFT FINALLY ENDED, AND HE STEPPED FROM the shop, he buried his nose in his oversized scarf. He tucked his free hand under his arm and grasped a cup of coffee tightly in his other. Even one moment outside in the cold was hellish, and the flurries falling to the frigid streets didn't help.

His ears perked at the sound of music nearby. It wasn't the usual crackle of a distant radio playing Christmas songs, but something else. He strained his ears to locate the source, so he could flee in the opposite direction if need be, but he gave up after a few moments. It wasn't like he was going to stay outside for long. It was too cold to even be alive right now, and there was *snow* in his hair, damn it.

Eldan mussed his hair with one hand and took a long drink of his coffee as he fell in place behind a group of people at the crosswalk. There were a lot more people out today than usual. *Probably last-minute Christmas shopping.* He found himself squished between bodies and shopping bags as more people piled closer to the crosswalk.

Eldan tapped his foot impatiently and kept his eye on the light. He could hear the faint *ting* of a bell ringing down the street. No doubt, another poor sod in a Santa suit collecting spare change for the needy. He burrowed deeper into his scarf. Yeah, it was for a good cause, but every time he saw a Santa suit, his soul died a bit.

The crowd around him seemed to be getting a bit antsy as the seconds passed. Indistinct whispers and giggles reached his ears. What was taking this light so long? And was that music getting closer?

Pinpricks of dread crept up Eldan's neck, and his body tensed. People were pulling pieces of paper from their shopping bags and pockets. He craned his neck and saw that it was sheet music.

You've gotta be kidding me.

"O, come, all ye faithful…" A sole young woman started singing near him. Suddenly, it made sense why there were so many more people than usual.

"Joyful and triumphant–"

Oh, hell no. I gotta get out of here.

Eldan was on a time crunch now with approximately ten seconds to leave the area, or he would be trapped by a flock of crazy, once-concealed carolers. One last glance back up at the light told him leaving wouldn't be so easy. The little bastard of a sign was still denying him safe passage across the street. He would have to figure out some other means of escape.

Okay. Eldan took a deep breath to calm his nerves as the singing grew louder. *Just bolt for the closest opening, then straight home.*

Eldan took a step forward and started pushing through the congregation, cradling his coffee close to him. That little cup of joe was his only lifeline right now. One wrong move, and it would be bye-bye warmth.

Every time Eldan thought he was free, another person moved to block his escape. Of course, the *one* time he forgot his earbuds at home, there was a damn flashmob of carolers waiting for him. What had he done to deserve this?

The crowd was indifferent to his struggles. They were too focused on their performance to care about one person pushing through their ever-growing circle. Their euphoric and powerful voices drowned out even the sound of passing traffic.

After he pushed past what seemed to be the hundredth person, Eldan finally saw an opening, and he made a mad dash for it. Freedom was finally in sight, and he wasn't gonna let it get away.

When he popped free of the crowd, he let out a low grumble and hugged his arms close to his body. He made it out alive. Now, all he needed was a thirty-minute session with his little snuggle bunnies. Maybe even forty-five and a chocolate–

Eldan dragged his eyes from the sidewalk a moment too late. Lost in his thoughts, he ran right into some unfortunate soul, and now, the poor coffee that he tried so hard to protect lay in a pitiful little puddle at his feet. He felt warmth seeping through his clothes, and large hands firmly gripped his shoulders.

"Are you okay?"

No, I am not okay, damn it. Eldan groaned and shook his arms, flinging droplets of coffee. His nice gray jacket would have stains for weeks. "No, it's fine, I just…"

Eldan suddenly remembered that normal human beings made eye contact when talking to each other. He was staring intently at the coffee splattered all over the stranger in front of him. Eldan's gaze went higher. And higher.

Jesus, how tall was this guy? And had he even moved

when they ran into each other? The stranger sure felt like a wall of muscle when they collided.

When Eldan's gaze finally reached the man's face, he felt his chest tighten. He really *was* a wall. A hot wall. A hot, rugged alpha wall with a magnificent beard, broad shoulders, and golden-amber eyes that reminded him of warm honey apple tarts and brandy.

And then it was all ruined by the sight of a Santa hat. The offending frippery of a headdress sat right at the top of the mountain he had once lovingly dubbed 'Mount Him-A-Lay-Yes.'

Eldan cried a little bit on the inside.

"Can I get you another coffee?"

Eldan chewed his lip and shook his head. The closest coffee shop was the one he worked at, and the thought of being dragged back to work to get another coffee was not his idea of a good time.

He just wanted to get home to his snuggle bunnies. Eldan took a step back and crossed his arms. "No, don't worry about it." He tried to brush past the alpha and–

A choked noise escaped Eldan's lips as he took a step forward, and his scarf was ripped off. He spun around and saw that his scarf had gotten caught on one of the alpha's shopping bags. Yes, even his favorite scarf was against him today. He'd have to up his session to five hours to recover from this betrayal.

Eldan reached for his scarf with a mumbled apology before a tremble ran through his body. And it wasn't the cold wind this time. No, his body was suddenly warmer, almost as if–

That scent...

Even though the alpha had tensed a bit, the look in his eyes hadn't changed. Still friendly, still outgoing. On the other side of the coin, Eldan was motionless, locked in a moment that seemed to run a million miles per hour in his own mind.

And when it was finally over, and the world started moving again, he realized he needed to get the hell out of there.

Nope, nope, nope. He quickly grabbed his scarf and took off down the sidewalk. Too quickly.

Eldan slid forward, flailing his arms, and trying to catch something, anything, that would stop him from meeting a similar fate as his coffee. In a perfect world, he would have been able to stop before he embarrassed himself anymore.

But it was not a perfect world, because fate had different plans. Eldan came to a stop only when he slid into a preoccupied Santa ringing a bell on the corner.

"Watch where you're goin', ya cockmuppet!" The disgruntled Santa shook his fist at Eldan. "Damn 'igit. Mama not teach you how to walk right?"

"Right back at you, asshat!" Eldan threw a bird at the man and grumbled as he gathered his scarf up again. He heard people whispering all around him, and he just wanted to leave, but that smoking-hot alpha was making his way over. The stranger stretched out his hand and helped Eldan to his feet.

"You sure you don't want another cup of coffee?" A playful smile graced the alpha's lips.

"I'm sure." Eldan took off slower this time and disappeared into the crowd. He hurriedly wrapped his scarf around his neck and buried his nose in the fabric again. Sure, he didn't need it right now since his entire body was flaming hot but, damn it, he wasn't going to let anyone see he was out of sorts.

As he headed down the street toward Quentin and Jenny's, he slipped into his thoughts again. He had to be wrong. It was a trick of the nose. Maybe the car exhaust was fucking with his sense of smell. Or maybe he had finally gone insane. Yep, that had to be it. He had gone too long without a session with Dr. Hopson, and now he was imagining things. That alpha couldn't be–

Eldan came to a stop, and his gaze dropped to the sidewalk.

Was it really my imagination?

∾

"And so, Dr. Hopson, that's why I came to you today." Eldan lazily played with Mr. Hopson's paw. "Can you believe I didn't maim anyone?"

Mr. Hopson let out a little huff, stretched, and flopped his head down on the mattress with a yawn.

"I know, right?" Eldan scooted closer and buried his face in the giant rabbit's side. "You're the only one that gets it."

Eldan heard a scuffle behind him. He rolled over just in time to see Honey Bun knock a few things off his dresser before bolting from the room. The sound of shattering glass made him bolt up. Eldan could only hope the little troublemaker didn't cut himself.

"You see what we have to deal with, Dr. Hopson?" Eldan flopped back into the furry pillow before pushing himself up and out of bed. After a quick inspection of the Lop's furry body, Eldan grabbed a small broom and dustpan near the kennel and started cleaning up the glass.

Okay, maybe it was time to clean out his room a little bit. He had collected a ton of knick-knacks over the years, and they were scattered over every available surface.

He stooped to gather everything that fell, feeling more than a bit worried for Honey Bun. The little guy loved to climb and get into trouble. "Must've been a cat in a past life." Eldan muttered. "Maybe I should invest in a few memory foam pads for him to crash land on. Helmet included."

Said Lop was peeking around the corner of Eldan's doorframe, watching his every movement.

"Thanks for redecorating, Honey Bun," Eldan mumbled to the Lop, who hopped in excitement and took off down the stairs. "Yeah, that's fine. I'll just clean up here."

Eldan grumbled to himself as he started piling things back on his dresser. He found his hairbrush, an unfortunately almost-empty cologne bottle, and at least three dollars in change. The glass scattering the floor obviously wasn't from the still-intact bottle.

If it wasn't the bottle that broke, what...

Eldan's heart dropped as he realized what was missing. After making sure there wasn't any glass left on the floor, he stooped down and looked under the dresser. He saw a vague shape in the darkness. He carefully grabbed the last item and stared for a moment.

Oh, Mary...

Or rather, an old, worn picture of Mary, taken a few years ago. It was barely held in an old, mangled frame by the remaining shards of glass. Eldan fished the photo out and tossed the frame in the trash.

Mary had been his best friend, his mentor, his long-lost sister from another mister. A twinge of pain heated his chest the longer he stared. Every time he saw her face, all the memories came flooding back. Echoes of laughter, cheers, even tears. They went through it all together. After all, she was family.

But life had taught Eldan that everything can change in an instant.

This was the last photo he had of her, taken when she finally decided to teach him how to knit. Or rather, when she decided to take him to the class she went to. She sat in her favorite chair, with a well-crafted infinity scarf draped over her lap. Her silver hair fell to her shoulders in fluffy curls, and her weathered hands rested on Eldan's shoulders as he proudly held up his first knit animal.

A small bunny.

He still had that bunny. Eldan raised his gaze to his bookshelf, and saw the rough-and-tumble knitted animal sitting on the top shelf, just where it should be, surveying its kingdom. A smile played at the corner of Eldan's lips before he turned back to the faded picture.

Mary. God, I wish you were here. You would not believe the guy I met today.

Eldan hung the photo on his dresser mirror and flopped back onto his bed. He buried his face in Mr. Hopson's side again. A small weight hit his side, and Honey Bun crawled up onto Eldan's back.

"Et tu, Honey Bun?" Eldan raised his head. "Why do you treat me like this? Is this all I am to you? A lounge chair?"

Honey Bun settled into the small of Eldan's back and rested his head on Eldan's butt with a quiet huff.

"You're a courageous soul, Bun."

Eldan flopped back into Mr. Hopson's side. He had almost fallen asleep when a knock startled him from his moment of peace. He raised his head and saw Jenny standing in the hallway, her dark hair sprinkled with snow.

"This is a private session." Eldan sighed and buried his face again.

"The open door says otherwise." Jenny smiled and leaned against the doorframe. "So, what's got you in a funk today? You know we're always here if you want to talk."

"That's what I pay the rabbits for," Eldan mumbled into Mr. Hopson's fur. "Though, the one back there is still in training." He motioned to Honey Bun with his thumb.

"Fair enough, but Quentin and I come with a side of takeout if you change your mind." She grinned and held up some bags.

Eldan gave her a sidelong glance from the comfort of his furry pillow. "Continue."

Jenny put the bags on Eldan's dresser and sat on the bed next to him. "So, why are we in the office of Dr. Hopson today?"

"Life is pain. I curse my nature. The real question is: to drink or not to drink?" Eldan pushed himself up on his elbows. "Also, super-hot alpha guy."

"So, heat, huh?" Jenny grinned.

"Lord, I wanted to climb that mountain so bad…" Eldan flopped back into the fur. "You would not *believe*."

Jenny was silent for a moment as Eldan grumbled on about the holidays, festivities, and hot alphas.

"Ah, you grumble and grumble about the holidays, but it ain't all bad." Jenny rubbed Mr. Hopson's back. "At least your mom cooks a great Christmas dinner."

That much was true. His Ma cooked a brisket to die for every year. It was Eldan's one solace at this time of year because he knew the season was almost over when he smelled that mouthwatering dish. It was so close he could almost taste it.

"Yep. Hoo-ray." Eldan groaned and went limp. "One last big meal with the family and then the holiday is over. I can't wai–"

Mr. Hopson shifted beneath him, and Eldan jerked back as pain burned on his cheek. Jenny had found 'the spot' and triggered the rabbit's maximum overdrive.

"You did that on purpose." Eldan cupped his cheek and glared at his friend. He was pretty sure he had a paw-shaped red mark on his cheek now.

"Maybe." Jenny giggled. "Can't have you moping around all afternoon. Your food will get cold!"

Eldan cradled Honey Bun on his lap. He'd launched the poor Lop when he sat up so suddenly, and Honey Bun needed an apology cuddle.

Jenny stood. "Now, come on down. We have a nice dinner ready to be consumed. That is, if your 'private session' is over." She winked and grabbed the bags from the dresser.

Eldan let out a small sigh and nodded, prompting her to leave the room.

"Well, guys, same time tomorrow?" Mr. Hopson shifted and stretched, letting out a little yawn and squeak.

"Yeah, yeah, I'll bring the treats tomorrow."

To Mason Shepard, the best part of waking up was the view he had heard so much about. As he threw back the curtains of his hotel room, the snow-covered Boston Commons greeted him with a glittering smile. In the streets below, people were already going about their busy days, heading on without a care in the world.

"In other news, we're cooking up some very special Christmas magic here at The Urban View. Stay tuned for the story of how owner–"

The report droned on, simple white noise filling the over-spacious room. As he dragged his suitcase to the bed, he couldn't help but feel a bit giddy. He was finally here. Finally, he was going to be able to experience Christmas in Boston! Sure, he'd heard the holidays in New York were generally preferred, but Boston's old town charm never failed to pull him in.

Only wish they could've come along, too...

Not a moment later, a buzz on the nightstand caught Mason's attention. He dragged his outfit of the day from his suitcase and stashed the case back in the corner before grabbing his phone from the nightstand. A quick glance showed his Oppa's face on the screen.

Well, speak of the devil.

"Hey, hey, Oppa." Mason smiled into the phone.

"Morning." Oppa's voice was light and cheery. "Why don't we FaceTime? I need to see my little Plum's face."

"Your little Plum isn't decent right now." Mason flicked on the light to the bathroom and set the phone on speakerphone before running some water in the sink.

"Ohhh…Fine. I got a bone to pick with you anyway."

Mason shook a bit of water from his face before drying it with a soft towel. "Uh, oh, what did I do now?"

"More like what you didn't do. You didn't call us last night to let us know you got in safe! Do you have any idea how worried we were? Why I oughta…If I wasn't stuck here in Montana–"

"I did call. *Some people* go to bed too early."

"Hey, 9PM is not too early," Oppa protested. "What were you doing out that late anyway, mister?"

"Don't you know?" Mason began pulling off his pajamas and folded them on the sink. "I'm a certified crinimal. And, before you say anything, yes, that exact pronunciation."

"A crinimal?" Oppa gasped, not missing a beat. "My own son?"

"Yeah, and on a side note, if you see any reports of a serial glitterist in the greater Boston area, don't worry about it."

"You truly are my son." Oppa snorted. "Now, what's the plan for today, Plum?"

"Oh, Oppa, there are so many things to do here, I have no idea where to start." Mason went over his mental map, remembering all the shops he saw as he explored. "I might check out a few of the shops today. You know, get you and Appa some nice, new things."

"Are you maybe hinting at a brand-new set of pots and pans for little ol' Oppa? I mean, I wouldn't protest that."

"I don't know a soul that would, pumpkin. I think people would kill for your food." Mason perked up as his Appa's voice came through the speaker. "Hey, Son."

"Hey, Appa, how are you feeling?"

Appa let out a low whistle. "Fever's been gone for a couple days, and your Oppa hasn't felt bad at all, so I think this household is flu-free."

"I wish you both could've come with me." Mason slapped some cologne on his neck and sighed. "I know you wanted to visit again so badly."

"I know, boy, but I wasn't going to risk getting you sick on your vacation."

"And I knew Oppa wouldn't leave you at home alone." Mason chuckled. "He'd have been worried sick."

"Of course, I would've been! Have you seen the disaster this man is in the kitchen?" Oppa laughed. "Speaking of… have you seen that retro diner we recommended?"

Mason laughed nervously and did a little dance as he tugged on his pants. "Can't say I have, Oppa. I spent the first afternoon here walking the streets, getting a feel for the place."

"Well, the last time your Appa and I made it up to Boston, we were stunned. They have *the* best food. I daresay you should take all of your meals there while you're in town."

Mason zipped up with a grunt and let out a staggered breath. "Oppa, if I go too crazy, none of the pants I packed will fit."

"Eh, pants are for the weak anyway," Appa whispered under his breath, earning what sounded like a light smack from Oppa.

Mason tugged an old sweater over his head and fixed his hair before he turned on the FaceTime call his Oppa wanted so badly.

"There's my boy!" Oppa brightly smiled before he squinted. "Oh, my word, you still have that old sweater?"

"You made it for me. Why would I not have it?" Mason panned the camera up and down so they could see how well he cared for it.

Oppa wiped an imaginary tear from his eye. "You always were my favorite little hatchling, you know?"

"I know." Mason grinned as he walked out of the bathroom. The TV was blaring a news report about an upcoming parade. Today, to be exact.

"Oh, you gotta go to that parade! You'll love it!" Oppa pointed to the screen, and Mason turned the phone around so he could see the report.

Appa wrapped his arm around Oppa's waist. "You better listen, son. That parade is your Oppa's favorite part of the whole 'Christmas in Boston' package."

"Duh! That's where we met! Of course it would be my favorite part." Oppa laughed and looked back at the phone. "Anyway, make sure you see the sights for us. And go to that parade."

"Don't go too crazy without us." Appa gave the screen a stern look. "We know we're leaving you unsupervised, but that means we trust you."

Mason put on his best smile. "Who, me?"

"Yes, you! And don't forget to try out the food at that diner. You remember the name?" Oppa cut in.

"The Roaring Ridgemont Eatery, yeah?" Mason snuck a glimpse outside, his excitement for the day growing.

"Exactamundo." Oppa nodded. "Love you, Plum. Have fun, and be safe. And be sure to keep in touch. I want to hear all about your adventures."

"Love ya'll, too." Mason smiled warmly before he ended the call. He gave himself a once-over in the mirror, turning his head this way and that before he nodded.

Now...jacket, gloves, scarf...nah, no scarf. What else should I take?

Mason's gaze landed on the bright red Santa hat hanging

on the headboard. Excitement flitted through his body at the sight of it, and he grabbed it and tugged it on. Now, he was ready to walk the winter wonderland.

~

WAS IT STRANGE TO SAY THE STREETS WERE CALLING TO HIM? Mason felt as if every historic building, every backroad, and every park had its own story to tell, and he was the only one that could hear them.

Or maybe it was the mind-blowing amount of festivity. It truly felt like he was walking through a Hallmark movie.

Living in a small town in southern Texas was great and all, but nothing really prepared him for the day he left his little sandbox behind and entered the great unknown. The sights, the sounds, the smells—it was all a totally different experience from that tiny town in the middle of Hell's backyard.

But the real reason Mason was in Boston was for one thing. Snow. And it was coming fast. He pulled out his phone and checked the weather, grinning when he saw the meteorologists reporting a good few inches of snow. The best part was the storm would be there just before Christmas.

Mason could picture it now. It was gonna be a perfect, magical snowstorm. Light, fluffy snow, perfectly piled into mounds for impromptu snowball fights in the streets. Maybe followed by a steaming cup of hot chocolate and a–

He came to a stop. Usually, after a snowball fight and hot chocolate, there would be a quiet moment with a lover. A peaceful end to a hectic day, holding your loved one close. At least, that's how it went in the movies.

But I don't–

Mason sighed and started moving again. As much as he wanted life to be like his favorite Hallmark movies, there was still that last little bit missing. Call him a hopeless romantic, but he was waiting for a very special someone.

And a little nagging feeling told him that someone was right around the corner.

Maybe I am going crazy. Mason took a seat on a bench under an awning.

He looked up and watched the people hurrying by, a rushing current of shopping bags, bulky winter coats, and hot drinks steaming in familiar-looking cups. He eyed a cup that someone near him was holding and recognized the logo.

Now that I think about it, that guy had a cup with that logo.

When Mason accidentally ran into that guy on the streets yesterday, he had felt so bad for the stranger. The look in that man's eyes when his coffee hit the ground had been absolutely heartbreaking. He wanted to scoop the stranger up and run to the closest coffee shop and tell him it would all be okay. But the poor guy ran—or, well, slid away from Mason before he could.

That poor guy didn't deserve to be called all the rude names that Santa was calling him. That Santa gave the suit a lousy reputation.

What the hell is a cockmuppet, anyway? he pondered.

Mason let out a sharp breath and shook his head. His thoughts wandered back to the grumpy guy. Okay, he wasn't gonna beat around the bush, that man was gorgeous. Despite his dismissive attitude, he had an innocent, almost tragic, look about him, and it had drawn Mason in like a curious cat to a Christmas tree.

Also, that hair was to die for. It had looked so soft and fluffy, and it took every fiber in Mason's body not to ruffle the poor guy's hair right there on the street.

Maybe that shop is nearby.

"Excuse me, ma'am?" Mason got the attention of the woman near him. "Where did you get that drink?"

"Oh, this?" The woman held up the cup. "It's from Hot

Shots Barista over on Cane Avenue. I go there every day. They've got the best coffee this side of Boston!"

He pushed himself up from the bench and gave her his best smile. "Thank you so much. I'm dyin' for a hot drink right now."

It was only a half-lie. Sure, he couldn't feel his face right now, but the real reason he wanted to find this shop so badly was simple. Because maybe, just maybe, he'd run into that guy again. Maybe fate would see fit to give him another chance.

Cane Boulevard...why does that street sound so familiar?

"Mommy, look, it's snowing!"

Mason turned at the sound of a child's voice and noticed a small family down the street from him. The little boy was holding his mother's hand and pointing to the sky. Sure enough, there were small, delicate flakes dancing down to the streets.

The little boy's childlike glee was contagious, and Mason found himself smiling up at the flurries, just like the kid. The stares of passersby landed upon him, but he didn't care. This was his moment, and he would enjoy it.

Just so long as his face didn't get frostbite.

Mason was dragged back to the real world when a frigid wind whipped down the street and cut through him. Yep, his face was still numb. Maybe he should've brought his scarf after all. With a final push, he started down the sidewalk. According to his phone, Cane Boulevard wasn't too far from here. Not much longer, and he'd be enjoying a warm drink and the sight of the falling snow.

～

CANE BOULEVARD SOUNDED SO FAMILIAR BECAUSE THAT'S where it all began. Yep, it was around this time yesterday that he ran into that cute omega. Hell, the coffee stain was probably still there on the sidewalk, it was so recent. No time to go check, though. If he was out much longer, he'd have icicles hanging off his beard.

Which is exactly why a choir of angels sang out when Mason saw Hot Shots across the street, cozy as cozy could be. A beacon of light in the darkness, that little coffee shop called out to him, drawing him in and promising an ice-less respite.

When Mason finally stopped admiring the outside and wandered in, he couldn't help but stop and stare. The small shop was decorated simply, but it was perfect.

Who would have thought a building could be so welcoming?

A small tree, covered in tinsel, ornaments, and candy canes, stood proudly in the corner next to a window, and carefully wrapped gift boxes sat on the bedazzled skirt around the base of the tree. On the other side of the shop, he noticed display cases full of baked treats and bags of coffee mixes. He had to get his hands on some of those gingerbread men, for sure.

"Toasted White Chocolate Mocha for Nicholas!"

Mason froze. *That voice...no way.*

He turned his attention to the workers behind the counter, where he caught sight of a familiar bunch of fluffy hair. He pinched himself and took another look.

Is this real? Am I dreaming? Mason felt his emotions swell. *Is this the moment where I run into the man I thought was gone forever? A lost chance at love found again due to fate's loving guidance?* He chuckled to himself. *Okay, maybe I've watched a few too many Hallmark movies recently.*

Mason came to a halt, justly horrified at the thought that just ran through his mind. He mentally slapped himself and took a deep breath.

Good Lord, Mason, get ahold of yourself! There's no such thing as 'too many Hallmark movies.'

Meanwhile, back in the real world, Mason composed

himself. It was the grumpy guy, all right. Mason would recognize that hair anywhere. He did a little fist pump, ignoring the stares of the other customers. Fate favored him today, and that was cause for celebration.

Okay, deep breath, Mason. First, hot chocolate. Second, see if I can get him that coffee he needed so badly the last time we met. Mason puffed out his chest and headed up to the counter. *Here we go.*

Just a few more steps and–

"Hey, Eldan?"

The grumpy guy tossed a look over his shoulder toward another co-worker, a young woman with short, blonde hair. "Yeah?"

"Louie wanted to talk to you before you go!" she shouted over the clamor of the barista line. "Something about ideas for upcoming holidays!"

Eldan? Mason grinned. *Eldan...from the valley of Elves, I think it means...*

That name sounded right for the peculiar little omega behind the counter. Special. Intriguing. Well-suited for him and his dreamy, almost mystical presence.

"Sir?" Eldan's disinterested voice pulled Mason from his thoughts.

Oh, shit. He's seen me. Act natural, Mason.

Mason raised his gaze to meet Eldan's, and a spark of recognition rose in the omega's dark blue eyes. If that wasn't enough to confirm Mason's suspicions, the flush on the poor barista's cheeks sure did.

Yep, he definitely recognizes me. Mason grinned.

"Are you going to order anything, or are you just gonna stand there staring?" There was a bitter, almost embarrassed edge to the omega's voice. "If you're not ready, please step to the side."

"Nah, I'm ready." Mason stepped up to the counter and gazed down at Eldan. "If you are."

"Obviously," Eldan huffed. "Now, what can I get you? We're running a special on our custom-made coffee mixes. We hold tastings of the most popular customer-made brews every day at 2PM."

"Just a hot chocolate, please."

Eldan's eyes narrowed. "That's it? No toffee nuts? No caramel sauce? Not even a disturbing amount of whipped cream on top?"

Mason tapped his chin. "Maybe one of those peppermint speckled cookies?"

"There is no maybe, just yes or no." Eldan pursed his lips.

"Yes, bestow upon me your best peppermint speckled cookie!" Mason's voice boomed in a theatrical tone, drawing stares from the other customers. "That is, if you see fit, dear friend."

"What the–?" Eldan's voice was a sharp whisper now. "Alright, already! Go sit down!" He shooed Mason away from the counter.

"But what if I want it to go?" Mason smiled down at the flustered barista.

"Then I'll make it to go!" Eldan gritted his teeth.

Mason grinned and locked his hands behind his head. "You know what? I think I'll stick around for a bit. It *is* super cozy in here."

"Fine, just–" Eldan buried his face in his hand. "Go somewhere that isn't blocking my line. Please." He waved his hand dismissively and looked away.

"Can do, Captain."

Mason made his way to the table next to the Christmas tree and pulled out his phone. The parade would be starting soon. Maybe he could invite his favorite flustered barista to watch it with him.

As he looked over the parade route on his phone, Mason couldn't help but snicker. The irony that he would've brought Eldan back to his workplace for a replacement coffee wasn't lost on him. No wonder Eldan was so against it.

Mason's ears perked as he picked up on some chatter behind him. A few sets of curious eyes watched him from behind the display cases, and Eldan wasn't at the register anymore. Instead, he was working a machine, tossing a few ingredients together. Other employees were glancing between Mason and their grumpy co-worker.

Eldan, on the other hand, was avoiding looking in Mason's direction at all costs.

Which made it all the sweeter when he slipped up and glanced quickly back toward Mason. The alpha gave him his best smile, and Eldan bit his lip with a scowl before returning to his work.

When Mason put down his phone, the click of heels got his attention. One of the other employees had brought his hot chocolate over for him instead of calling his name. He was a young omega, judging by his scent, and he had a nervous look about him.

Mason glanced at the name on his tag. *Okay, Brandon. What'cha got for me?* Mason braced himself. He knew what was coming, but there was no need to be rude.

"So, you're new in town?" Brandon asked.

"Visitin' from Texas," Mason drawled. "I saw one too many tumbleweeds tumblin' across my lawn and decided I wanted a change of pace this Christmas."

The server keened and fidgeted in place. "Well, if you ever need someone to show you around..."

"I appreciate it, but one of my greatest joys in life is finding new ways to get lost and found." Mason took a quick drink, hoping to change the topic. And boy did it change.

This is– Mason hoped he wasn't moaning. That would be awkward.

"Who made this?" Mason held up the mug.

"He did." Brandon pointed at Eldan, who was back on the

register. "He swapped with Miriam because he wanted to make that one himself." He rocked back and forth on his heels. "Just let us know if you need anything else."

"Will do."

The server left and started talking to his co-workers behind the counter. They were looking Mason's way again, and he lifted his mug and gave them a smile.

Mason took another drink and melted. It was a creamy, silky, hint-of-spicy cup of deliciousness that probably could've been served to royalty. And it was extra chocolatey. He looked into the brew that was left and noticed small, half-melted chunks of chocolate in the bottom of the mug.

Ah ha...I see... Mason smiled and set the mug back down on the table. *Just look at you, breaking the rules for lil' ol' me.*

Eldan was doing everything in his power not to look Mason's way again. Instead, he stared at the baked treats in the display cases, particularly the peanut butter turtle cookies.

Mason knew that look. It was the look of a man who desired some hot, fresh cookies on a cold day, and he was ogling those cookies like it was an addiction.

Maybe he could use a little pick-me-up.

CHAPTER 3: DECEMBER 21ST

I can't believe this. Eldan groaned. *There must be hundreds of cafes and coffee shops in Boston, and he steps into this one. Why do you hate me so, fate?*

Eldan gazed at the corner where the alpha sat. *Look at him, sitting all tall and perfect. I can almost tolerate the presence of the Christmas tree behind him when he sits near it.*

Almost.

"Look at that guy! He's got my stamp of approval…"

"Fine as hell…"

"I'd let him fill my stocking!"

The excited whispers of his co-workers carried across the barista line. Eldan felt his eye twitch. They weren't exactly being subtle. If they wanted to gossip, they could've at least had the decency to go back to the breakroom instead of being useless up front.

"Looked like he knew Eldan…"

Eldan barely refrained from spinning around and telling them what was what, and that was only because he was holding a couple of cups of hot coffee. His hand throbbed at the thought of getting even a single drop on his already-injured flesh.

Eldan grumbled and called out the order. When he sent the customers on their way, he threw a look over his shoulder at his co-workers. They were still watching him, expecting some juicy details. With his hands free of any dangerous liquids, he turned around and took a deep breath.

"Listen, I don't know why he's here. No, I don't know how long he's staying. And, regardless of what you may think, I especially don't know *him*." Eldan crossed his arms.

Unfortunately, that wasn't enough to satiate the gossip-hungry crew.

"You never make anyone's drink special!" one of the younger employees pointed out. "And then all of a sudden, you pull Miriam from the line and ask her to take over the register? Something seems a bit fishy, man!"

An older employee nodded in agreement. "Yeah, you're very by-the-book. When you trained me, I swear you measured every ingredient out." She chuckled.

Eldan felt his cheeks heat up, and he turned away. Since when did they start paying so much attention to him? So he added a few extra bits of chocolate to the alpha's drink. Big deal. Eldan had only spilled scorching-hot coffee on the alpha's rock-hard body yesterday. He needed to make it up somehow.

Another co-worker came out of the small baking area with a tray of fresh cookies and passed it to Eldan. At least one thing was going right on this bothersome day. A tray full of turtle cookies? Yes, please.

Eldan began cleaning out the display cases. Anything to keep his focus off people for the last five minutes of his shift. Admittedly, his gaze lingered on the freshly made peanut butter turtle cookies a bit longer than he planned. He bit his lip before he pulled out an old tray and slid the new one to the front of the case.

"I gotta thank you for that drink. It was the best hot chocolate I've ever tasted."

Eldan jerked back and scrambled to steady the tray he was holding. Who dared to scare him like that? He furrowed his eyebrows and looked up and saw the hot alpha smiling at him with his stupid smile.

"How do you always manage to materialize in front of me like that?"

"You're always lost in thought." The alpha scratched the back of his head sheepishly. "But that's okay."

The alpha's voice was a bit softer, with a hint of… adoration? Eldan felt his chest tighten a bit. He ducked his head and averted his eyes. Now he was gonna have to add some peppermint schnapps to his own hot chocolate when he finally got home.

Don't make eye contact. Don't touch him. He sucked in a shallow breath and held it. *Don't even breathe.*

"Looks like that parade is passing through here." The alpha was looking outside. Sure enough, the floats were slowly cruising by, and more people were lining the sidewalks to watch. "You have a good spot in here to watch it."

Unfortunately, Eldan, as a human being, had to breathe again at some point. When he did, he realized he suddenly felt way too light-headed, and this alpha smelled way too good. It felt like he was slowly going mad, like his body was about to turn against him and seek a 'stocking stuffer.'

Eldan nodded quickly at the alpha before he focused on the cookies again. "Yeah, guess I do. Did you need anything else?" His voice was almost a whisper. He cleared his throat and felt his ears heat up.

"I need a big ol' bag of those cookies." The alpha pointed at the tray of fresh ones Eldan had just put in the display.

"And how many cookies are in a 'big ol' bag'?" Eldan grumbled.

The alpha flashed a teasing smile. "Let's try a dozen or so. How's that sound?"

Okay. Eldan took it all back. This alpha was no longer just a mess of mind-blowing alpha pheromones. He was an *infuriating* muck that muddled his thoughts *and* made him want to never leave home again.

"'Or so' is not a form of counting." Eldan crossed his arms.

"Okay, so let's do thirteen." The alpha grabbed his wallet. "How much do I owe you?"

"So that's…" Eldan punched some buttons on the register. "Fifteen seventy-five for the hot chocolate, the peppermint-speckled cookie, and the thirteen peanut butter turtle cookies."

"Not gonna charge me for the extra bits of chocolate in my drink?" The alpha grinned and quirked his eyebrow.

Fuck.

His life ended here. The *one* time Eldan added extra stuff to a drink, the dude picked up on it like it was nothing. He knew he should've shaved the chocolate a bit more. Maybe it would've melted before he found it.

"There was no extra chocolate," Eldan grumbled. "Now, $15.75, *please.*"

"Alright, sure thing." The alpha laughed and handed over the cash. "I wouldn't mind getting the recipe for it, though."

"It's just hot chocolate. Nothing more, nothing less." Eldan bit his lip. That was a lie. It was his personal recipe he used at home, minus the peppermint schnapps, of course. He couldn't do that at work. "Sorry to disappoint." Eldan handed the alpha his change and the bag of fresh cookies. "Have a good one."

"Yeah, you too." The alpha smiled and held the bag of cookies close to his body. "See ya later."

Eldan had already turned around and covered his nose and mouth with his hand. His mind had gone blank, and he was way too hot. He tugged on his shirt collar. *Fuck it, I'm going home two minutes early.*

Eldan pushed past his co-workers and slinked back to the breakroom, pulling off his gloves and undoing his apron.

"You look disappointed." A voice said behind him. Louie sat at his desk eating lunch. That explained why the others hadn't come back here to gossip.

"How's your leg?" Eldan veered off topic, hoping to get the spotlight off him.

"Ah, you know how it is. It's been bugging me a bit more than usual today. I'm telling you a big storm is coming. Bigger than what those weather people are saying." Louie rubbed his leg before leaning back in his chair. "Now stop trying to change the subject. What's got you so down and disappointed?"

"I don't know *what* you're talking about." Eldan opened his locker and hung up his apron. "I'm going home, so I'm far from disappointed."

Louie almost choked when he laughed. He pointed his fork at Eldan."Don't you lie to me. I watched that entire encounter."

"What?"

"Don't you worry, I'm not upset about the extra chocolate or anything. I know you don't do that a lot." Louie leaned back in his chair. "Never, actually."

"So why were you watching?" Eldan narrowed his eyes. "Did I do something wrong?"

"No, nothing of the sort." Louie took another bite and swallowed. "I heard whispers when Susie came back here."

"Who?" Eldan wracked his brain. *Was that the woman with the short, blonde hair?*

Louie sighed. "You know what, that's just sad. We really need to make you some friends around here."

"Not my fault they never stick around long." Eldan slammed his locker shut and pulled his coat on. "Listen, I know you wanted to talk about the upcoming holiday plans, but can it wait until tomorrow? I have an appointment."

"Thought you said you were going home?" Louie quirked an eyebrow. "Got an appointment with a bottle of whiskey?"

"Close." Eldan pulled on his warm gloves. "Dr. Hopson."

"Ah, yes. Dr. Hopson. He who hails from Hopson Hills." Louie chuckled. "As for tomorrow, I vaguely recall giving you some time off, starting the moment you leave today."

"Huh? I didn't ask for any days off, though." Eldan walked over to the schedule hanging on the wall and flipped through it.

"You didn't, but you've worked a lot recently, and I know you still haven't gotten any Christmas shopping done."

"And who said I was gonna shop this year?"

"Don't pull that with me. Listen, I know that, no matter how much you may hate this time of year, you always go out and get gifts for your family." Louie tossed his lunchbox under his desk. "And those rabbits of yours, too."

"Why is everyone suddenly an expert on everything I do?" Eldan reached into his coat pocket and pulled out some Chap Stick. "And why is my life suddenly so interesting to everyone?" He rubbed his lips together, enjoying the minty tingle on his lips.

"I'm just sayin'." Louie glanced at the cameras around the shop. "Anyway, I gotta get back to it. Have to get that supply order in tonight." He squinted at a picture on the screen. "Just be sure to relax on your vacation, all right? Maybe make some friends, dear boy!"

"Yeah…" Eldan grumbled under his breath. "I'm out of here."

"Good luck!" Louie yelled after Eldan.

Good luck? What the hell? Eldan squeezed out from behind the counter and braced himself for the cold. He pulled on his scarf and bunched it around his neck before he pushed the door open. Already, there were a ton of people on the sidewalks, and he had a brief flashback of yesterday's events.

Eldan shoved his hands in his pockets and prepared to push through the crowd.

That is, until a familiar scent made him pause in his tracks.

That alpha. Eldan furrowed his eyebrows. *Why is he still here?*

Sure enough, there he was, sitting on the bench next to the door. That was why Louie shouted at him before he left. He saw the alpha still sitting outside on the cameras.

Louie, you bastard. Eldan groaned. The alpha had a stupid hat covering his stupid hair, so Eldan didn't recognize the back of his stupid head before he left the shop.

Okay, maybe that was a little mean. The alpha's self was… fine, but Eldan couldn't deal with all the festivities much longer. Eldan turned and tried to slip away, hoping to get away before the alpha noticed him. He'd take the long way home if he had to but–

"Hey, Eldan!"

Eldan froze. *Maybe if I don't move–*

"Eldan?" The alpha's voice was right behind him now, low and hopeful. Eldan couldn't hide the shiver than ran down his spine.

Shit, does he know? I swear I put on blockers today. Eldan gave himself a quick sniff. *Yep, still good.* He turned and looked the alpha in the eyes.

No. No, he didn't know. Eldan saw it in his eyes. That low voice wasn't seduction mode. That was just good ol' home-grown disappointment. Now that Eldan had acknowledged him, the alpha lit up.

"Glad I caught you before you headed off." The alpha looked a bit sheepish. "Was wondering if I could interest you in a batch of freshly made peanut butter turtle cookies?" He held out the white paper bag.

"I don't care that I just sold those to you. I've always been told it's a bad idea to accept food from strangers." Eldan ducked his nose behind his scarf and glared at the wall. Was it just a lucky guess that he picked out Eldan's favorite cookies? The glaring confidence in the alpha's eyes said otherwise.

The alpha held out his free hand and smiled. "Well, to start, my name is Mason. Mason Shepard. And I believe I owe you an apology."

"For what?" Eldan side-eyed Mason. "I'm the one who ran into you."

Mason paused, but recovered with a chuckle. "Nah, we'll call that a tie. Anyway, you made the best hot chocolate for me, and now it's my turn." He opened the bag a little bit and swayed it around slowly. "I saw you eyeballin' these cookies pretty hard in there."

Eldan grumbled to himself. This man must have a death wish. Really, he should say something to preserve his dignity, but those cookies were rapidly chipping away at his resolve. Before Eldan knew it, his hands were around the bag, and Mason was beaming again.

"A little bit of an apology for breakin' your heart last time we met."

"Let's say that you did 'break my heart.'" Eldan took off his glove, reached into the bag, and grabbed a gooey cookie. "Do you always buy cookies for broken-hearted strangers?"

"If it would help them feel better, yeah, I'd do it every day." Mason laughed and sat down on the bench. "And I hope you don't mind my saying, but you seemed like you need those today."

"Yeah, I suppose so." Eldan sat down on the bench next to Mason and nibbled on a cookie. His gaze drifted over the roving crowds. Perhaps, in the spirit of goodwill, he could put up with the festivities for a few minutes now that he had sugar.

"So, we even-steven?" Mason turned and smiled softly at Eldan.

Eldan swallowed and pursed his lips. "Maybe."

"Maybe?" Mason's eyes widened. "How soon we forget our own sayings. I thought you said it was either yes or no? Does that mean you want to spend more time with me?"

Mother–

Eldan cradled the bag of cookies close to him and covered his mouth as a bit of cookie went down the wrong way. Mason's cocky gaze shifted to worry, and he moved to help Eldan just before the omega stopped coughing.

Fucker.

"Don't you sass me, boy," Eldan sputtered.

Mason let out a bellowing laugh. "Boy? I'm at *least* ten years your senior!" He wiped a tear from his eye. "So?"

"So, what?" Eldan nibbled on another cookie.

"Am I right?" Mason threw his arm over the back of the bench and crossed his leg. "I gotta be close, right?"

Eldan played dumb. Mason's jolly attitude had to have a limit, and he was about to test just how far that limit ran. "About what?"

"Aww, don't wanna talk about it? Okay, I'm guessing." Mason leaned a bit closer and studied Eldan's face. Eldan only hoped his cheeks weren't as red as they felt.

"Twenty-four."

Eldan didn't say anything. He just shrank back into the bench and continued nibbling on a cookie.

"I was right!" Mason grinned.

"Yeah, so?" Eldan looked away and closed the bag. If he ate any more cookies, he'd regret it later.

"I'm exactly ten years your senior." Mason smiled smugly and leaned back into the bench. "How about that?"

"That's very interesting," Eldan deadpanned as he glared at the sidewalk.

Mason's attention was grabbed by the passing floats, which gave Eldan ample time to sneak a peek at the alpha. Honestly, Eldan couldn't believe he was still here, especially with a huge parade going on mere feet away, but he couldn't help feeling drawn to the alpha.

Eldan nipped at the last bit of cookie in his hand as he watched Mason from the corner of his eye. How could one man have it all? Tall, muscular, a proud owner of those trademarked 'hold me close and love me' arms. He had laugh lines on his cheeks, and his eyes glowed in the afternoon sun like warm, spiced brandy. Not to mention his beard was magnificent.

How many years did it take to raise that majestic beast?

"You must like bunnies."

Eldan felt heat rising on his neck. Did he have his entire life story written on his forehead? "What makes you think that?"

"You nibble on your food like a wee rabbit."

And there was that stupid smile again.

Fuck it. I need this.

Eldan quickly opened the bag of cookies again and shoved a whole cookie in his mouth just to spite the alpha. Mason burst out laughing as Eldan painfully realized the gravity of the situation he was in. He didn't remember the cookies being this chewy.

God, I need to have a word with the new guy about the amount of molasses in these. Apparently, he heard 'dump the entire jar in' instead of 'measure it out.'

It took Eldan a while to work through the ooey-gooey cookie, and he could still hear Mason rumbling on in the back of his mind. Eldan's jaw was hurting something fierce now.

"So, I was wondering if you wanted to go check it out with me?"

Eldan coughed and sputtered. "What?"

"That new shop over on Ember Avenue. Or, at least, this article says they're new to the area. I don't know, since I'm not from around–"

You've got to be kidding me. Are you really this clueless?

"In case you didn't notice…I don't…enjoy Christmas." Eldan slowly spelled it out.

Mason gaped, trying to process what Eldan said. "But why not? It's wonderful! There's all the food, gifts, meeting with family–"

"The excessive amount of glitter, the rabid mobs, the horror that is fruitcake…" Eldan mumbled. "Not to mention the cold embrace of snow."

Mason was quiet for a moment. Unsure words formed on his lips but were never uttered. "That's one of the best parts —the feeling of wrapping up on a cold day and waking up to a steaming cup of hot chocolate by the fire. The songs, the decorations…"

Eldan followed Mason's gaze to the floats rolling by. Atop the largest one, Santa and Mrs. Claus sat, waving at the people below. Elves danced down the street near the float, passing out candy.

"The magic." Mason turned and smiled at Eldan with a twinkle in his eyes.

All at once, Eldan felt a pain tugging at his heart. That look in Mason's eyes–

No. No, no, no, no.

Eldan gripped the paper bag tightly in his hands, crinkling the once-crisp paper. He bit his lip and rapidly blinked to hold back the burning in his eyes. He had to get out of here.

"Don't you understand? Not everyone is like you." Eldan stood. His eyes snapped shut, and his eyebrows furrowed. "I. Hate. Christmas!"

When Eldan finally opened his eyes, the pain hadn't gone away like he hoped. No, the crushed look on Mason's face broke his heart even more. Eldan could scent the pain wafting off the alpha, and heat flared through his own body. He couldn't stay. He just couldn't.

The eyes of nearby parade-goers were scrutinizing Eldan's every move. It was almost like they were saying, 'How *dare* he say such horrible things?'

Time seemed to stand still as Eldan stared at Mason. Despite the look in the alpha's eyes, he didn't lash out. No, Mason simply sat in disbelief, almost limp against the bench.

Don't look at me like that... Don't.

Eldan felt his muscles go weak, and he hugged his arms close to his body. When heat started building in his stomach, he quickly realized his scent blockers were starting to wear off.

I gotta get out of here.

"I'm..." Eldan choked. "I'm sorry."

Before Mason could respond, Eldan took off, leaving him on the bench. As Eldan hurried back home, he wiped the tears from his eyes. He prayed to everything that was holy that Quentin and Jenny weren't home to see him completely messed up.

When Eldan finally made it home, he immediately rushed to the office of Dr. Hopson and buried his face in the rabbit's side. Mr. Hopson simply rolled over and let it happen, and Eldan took a deep breath.

"Dr. Hopson?" Eldan mumbled into the rabbit's fur. "I'm in trouble. Deep, deep trouble."

The rabbit squeaked, almost as if he understood.

Eldan bit his lip. "You ever find someone that's completely irritating, but you find you can barely drag yourself away from them?"

Eldan felt a weight against his side. He looked over and saw Honey Bunny nestled against him.

"Hey, Bun." Eldan ran his fingers through the Lop's soft fur. "I know. I'm warm right now." He flopped back into Dr.

Hopson's side. "So? Any words of wisdom for your broken patient?" Eldan cradled the rabbit's large body as best he could.

"Seems to me like you're in deep shit, Eldan!" A high-pitched voice pierced the quiet in the room. Eldan's head bolted up, and he eyed Mr. Hopson in awe.

Laughter echoed from the doorway. "Dr. Hopson! Watch your language!" Quentin stepped into the room, and Mr. Hopson rolled over to let Quentin rub his belly.

"Haven't you ever heard of knocking?" Eldan sat up and crossed his arms.

"You leave the door open all the time, dude. That's basically an open invitation for me to harass you at my discretion."

Eldan didn't have the energy or the willpower to get up and evict Quentin, so he just flopped back on the bed and groaned.

Yep, heat time is now.

"What's wrong, Bro?"

What isn't wrong? Eldan turned to his side and hugged his pillow. "I met someone today. Someone who loves Christmas more than anything in the world."

"That's a daily occurrence. Almost every person around here claims that." Quentin smiled. "My beautiful wife included."

"No, he's…" Eldan trailed off. "He…"

Eldan hugged the pillow tighter and stared at Mary's photo.

"He reminded you of her, didn't he?" Quentin asked.

"Yeah. That look in his eyes when he talks about the 'magic' of the holiday…" Eldan squeezed the pillow and doubled over. "…I can't go through that again."

"I know, man. I know." Quentin stared at the photo a bit longer. "So, you met a guy who really loves Christmas. He's just a stranger, right? A tourist who'll leave come New Year? Why is that such a big deal?"

Might as well settle in for the long haul.

Eldan raised his head from the pillow and sighed.

"Because I think he's my Fated."

CHAPTER 4: DECEMBER 24TH

"And that'll be $47.98, please!"

Eldan grumbled as he handed over the last of his cash. That was that. He had just hit the limitations of his wallet. No more.

"Thank you!" The cashier handed Eldan his receipt and smiled brightly. "Merry Christmas!"

"Yeah, you too," Eldan grumbled with disdain. He was *so* ready to get out of there. Everyone was *way* too merry.

Eldan heaved a sigh of relief as he stepped from the shop and saw that only a few families still wandered the large corridors. Finally, the mall was blissfully quiet. He sank down into a nearby bench and let the bags on his arms slip across the empty seats around him.

One last check...

Eldan quickly started rifling through his bags, making sure he had gifts for everyone. God forbid he forget to pick something up for his sisters or their kiddos. He'd never hear the end of it.

Here's Ma's, Holly's, Carol's, nieces, nephews, Quentin and Jenny...and, of course, my little snuggles bunnies. Eldan held up some packages of rabbit toys and treats. Maybe these offerings would stop them from eating any more of his things.

Shit, I should get another pair of slippers while I'm here.

With a groan, Eldan pushed himself to his feet before loading the bags back on his arms. Eldan looked at a small map nearby. *...Just past the fountain.*

Figuring out where the store was and actually getting to the store were two entirely different battles. Everywhere Eldan had gone shopping, he'd been pushed, shoved, jostled, and called names, and, frankly, he was tired of it. Now, he was doing everything he could to avoid everyone.

Even now, the few families that were still in the mall seemed to be between him and his slippers. A few bored kids were playing in the corridors while their parents picked up last-minute gifts. Eldan noticed a couple of little boys crawling around on a huge throne set up near the fountains.

Even Santa has gone home, huh? Eldan held his bags closer to his body as a couple more kids ran past him. *Figures.*

"What do you think Santa's gonna bring you, Tyler?" A little boy rolled around on the large seat. "I hope I get that dinosaur arena thing we saw on TV!"

Tyler looked up from his spot on the ground. "The one with the big Tyrannosaurus and Stego?"

"Yeah!" The little boy beamed. "And it has armor for them, too!"

"Lame! The one with the Carno and Anky is way cooler!" Tyler shouted.

The first little boy raised his voice to match. "Nuh, uh! My Tyrannosaurus could beat your Carno any day!"

"Your Tyrannosaurus would have to catch it first!" Tyler stood and clenched his fists. "Everyone knows Carnos are the fastest dinos!"

Eldan rushed past the throne just as the boy on it tackled Tyler. He didn't have time to referee. No, he just wanted to get his slippers and get home. Less dinosaurs there.

Okay, almost there. Eldan glanced down the corridor and sighed in relief. *Hopefully, they still have some decent deals on slippers.*

"Hey! What's up, Dad?"

Eldan's ears perked up as a man with his family down the corridor talked loudly into his phone. *And, of course, he's right next to the store I want to visit.*

Eldan grumbled and hoisted his bags close to his body. Two kids held the man's free hand and jacket, quietly watching Eldan as he got closer.

"What's wrong, Pops?" The man's voice lowered. "Are you okay?"

"*Storm...from the Lakes...saying to shelter in place–*" The raspy voice from the phone sent chills down Eldan's spine.

Suddenly, the slippers weren't important anymore. Eldan turned and headed back toward the exit, only to find it blocked by a few families.

Great. Eldan groaned as he placed his bags on the floor. *Just what I wanted to deal with.*

"You can't even see the cars from here." A young woman with a toddler in her arms squinted, staring out into the blizzard. The two little boys that were playing on the throne stood near her, grasping her long coat.

"Are we gonna be stuck here forever, Noma?" Another little boy holding a tall woman's hand looked up with wide eyes.

The tall woman quickly crouched to his level and ran her hand through his hair. "No, Baby. We'll be able to get out in a few minutes once this calms down. Don't worry." She stared outside for a long moment before she picked him up and balanced him on her hip. "We'll be home with Nomo soon."

A small part of Eldan wished that were true, but he knew better. He'd lived through many storms, but nothing quite like this.

"Came outta nowhere." An old man sighed.

"Looks bad. I wonder how many people got caught out in that?" Another man wearing a beanie stared outside with a frustrated sigh.

Eldan crossed his arms and tapped his foot, letting his mind wander to the alpha that totally wasn't from around Boston. If he got caught out in this storm…

I wonder if he's okay?

A sudden heat spread through Eldan's body, and he shook his head.

What the fuck? Of course he's okay! He could probably plow through ten feet of snow, easy! Eldan watched the strangers chatter among themselves for a moment before he reached down and grabbed his bags. *Might as well find a quiet spot and–*

"What a storm!" a voice behind him bellowed.

Eldan's head jolted up. *Oh, hell no.*

"One of the worse I've ever seen," an old woman spoke up. "And I was going to start my cooking when we got home!"

"We won't be stuck here that long, right?" Another young man threw a worried glance at his mate. "Surely we'll be home soon?"

"Wouldn't count on it." The man's mate held up his phone to show everyone the radar. "All those tiny storms over the Lakes merged into this monster."

The man wearing the beanie let out a low whistle. "Damn, you've got to be kidding me! How did the forecasters miss this?"

Now's my time to exit, stage right. Eldan prayed to everything that was holy that his bags didn't crinkle and make any noise that would give him away. He took a few uneasy steps and–

"Eldan? Is that you?"

Fuck. You have got to be kidding me.

"Hey, mister!" Eldan flinched as a little girl with red hair pulled at the hem of his sweater. "That guy is trying to talk to you!"

Eldan gritted his teeth. "I know. Trust me, I know." He slumped his shoulders in defeat when he heard Mason stepping up behind him.

"But maybe I'm mistaken." Mason's voice was quiet, like he was afraid he was going to be scolded. "If you were Eldan, you would've turned around and given me an angry glare already."

Eldan scowled before he turned around. "Out of all the stores in Boston..." He pursed his lips. "Why are you always–"

"There it is. So, it really is you." Mason took a deep breath and whispered, "I'm happy to see you again, you know."

"Suppose I can't stop you if you feel that way." Eldan let his bags down to the floor and pushed them against the wall with his foot.

Damn it, does he ever get angry? If he were a normal person, he'd have words for me after what I said a few days ago.

Eldan crossed his arms and looked up at Mason. The alpha's eyes were soft, still full of hope. Hope for what, though? That they'd be friends after everything Eldan said?

Maybe it was just that. Eldan bit his lip. The longer he found himself under that intense, hopeful stare, the more he felt like a piece of human garbage.

"Did you see the radar? They're saying it's looking pretty rough for the next few hours." Mason gazed outside.

"Wonderful," Eldan huffed.

"Were you heading home? You look like you bought a lot of stuff." Mason motioned to the bags against the wall.

"No, my original plan was to hunker down here. You know, take in the sights, camp out in the food court for the night, that sort of thing. It's my favorite thing to do when I'm surrounded by..." Eldan shuddered. "Holiday which must not be named."

Mason chuckled nervously. "About that…"

The music on the loudspeakers overhead came to a stop.

"Attention, shoppers." Static crackled on the old speakers. *"Due to the sudden onset of inclement weather, the city of Boston has issued a mandatory shelter-in-place order until the storm passes. We will provide you with food, water, and blankets for the duration of your stay. Thank you for your cooperation."*

The loudspeakers clicked, and the music resumed. Voices of disapproval rose from the small crowd.

"What? Seriously?"

"But I've got to get home to wrap everything…" The woman with the toddler sank onto a bench as her two sons climbed up next to her.

The man in the beanie groaned in frustration. "Are you kiddin' me? I was supposed to be meeting my girlfriend back home for dinner!"

Mason stepped up and took a deep breath. "Hey, hey, it's okay, everyone! At least we're safe and warm in here, right?" He looked around the crowd, and some of them nodded. "See? We just gotta make the best of things while we're here."

A few people agreed, and everyone started to calm down. Eldan simply leaned back against the wall and watched.

Amazing. Guess that's the power of an alpha, huh?

Eldan jumped as his phone buzzed in his pocket. He fished it out and turned his back to the group of people gathering around Mason. His ma's face and number flashed across the screen, as well as a notification for two missed calls from her. With a sigh, he pressed the screen and held the phone to his ear.

"Sweetie? Baby? Are you safe? Where are you?"

"The Whos have taken me hostage, Ma," Eldan whispered weakly into the phone. He rested his forehead on the cold wall, as if that would keep him sane.

"Who's the Whos?" Eldan could practically hear her grinning through the phone.

"Are you really gonna make me say it?"

Eldan's mom snickered. "So, the mall? That's the only place you'd be today, right?"

"Yeah, I'm at the mall." Eldan sighed. "What about you? Are you safe at home? What about Holly, Carol, and the kids?"

"We're all fine. You were the only one unaccounted for."

Eldan heard pots and pans clattering in the background. No doubt, his mom was already getting started on the food for tomorrow.

"Just as long as you're safe." She said.

"Ma, I don't think you understand the gravity of this situation." Eldan furrowed his eyebrows. "I am trapped. In a mall. *Surrounded* by Christmas decorations. There is *constant* Christmas music playing. The Whos are probably gearing up to *sing*, Mother."

"It'll be a good experience for you!"

"Ma, please."

"Hey, if you can't beat 'em, join 'em. Stay safe and have fun, sweetie!" She made a kissy noise in the phone. "Love you, baby!"

Before Eldan could respond, he heard the phone beep. He pulled it away from his ear and saw the screen had gone blank. His own mother had just hung up on him. The world was indeed a dark place.

Eldan sighed before putting his phone back in his pocket and turning around to lean back against the wall. Mason was still talking with everyone. That damn charismatic charm drew them in and held them tight, that much was certain.

"So, you know what this means, right?" Mason crouched down and talked to the kids. "We're gonna make this a Christmas Eve to remember."

"How?" The kids watched Mason's every move.

Mason motioned to the long corridors. "How about a little race?"

A few of the parents nodded as they watched their kids' eyes light up. One of the store owners, who was nearby listening in, stepped forward and pointed to his sled display.

"Yeah, it could work. Just put some layers of felt on the metal prongs, and they'll slide across this floor as if they were on ice!"

"And I have these." Another store owner held up some straps and buckles. "We can use these for harnesses. Just like the sled dog races!"

"Alright!" Mason took a few straps and held them up. "Anyone who wants to pull a sled, get suited up!"

As a few people stepped forward, Eldan hung back. The kids were chattering excitedly, watching the adults get suited up for the race. Eldan sighed and pulled out his phone before heading to a nearby bench. If he was going to be trapped here, he was going to listen to his own tunes, damn it.

Or so he thought. Only a few short songs later, Eldan heard a constant clanking over his music. He dragged his gaze from his phone and saw a few people suited up and ready to race, but Mason was struggling to get a strap properly tightened.

This. This is why we can't have nice things. Eldan pulled an earbud out and pushed himself up from the bench. The faster he helped, the faster this whole race nonsense would end.

"Aw…do you want to join in?" Mason grinned as he saw Eldan coming over.

"Hell no." Eldan grabbed the strap Mason was having trouble with and tightened it just a little too much, and Mason made a choking noise. "I have better things to do."

"Well, if you change your mind–"

"I won't." Eldan slid the strap into the last buckle and straightened it up.

Mason leaned forward and whispered, "*If* you do, I'll gladly take you for a ride."

Eldan swallowed and backed off, trying his best to ignore the heat that flared up in his stomach. "I won't."

∽

"AND COMING IN HOT, WE HAVE TEAM FROSTY IN THE LEAD! Team Nutcracker is right behind them with Team Rudolph in the rear! Looks like that shiny red nose wasn't built for speed, folks!"

Eldan tried his best to look disinterested, but more often than not, he found his gaze slipping from his phone back to the race.

"It's gonna be a close one, folks!" The old man announcing the race leaned forward with his fake microphone. "Who will take home the glory tonight?"

The kids in the race cracked the reins, and the sleds started moving faster and faster. It was a close race between Mason and another alpha, and she was neck and neck with him!

"Team Frosty is looking a bit frosty! They appear to be losing a bit of ground to Team Nutcracker!"

Eldan leaned forward in his seat. Mason was slowing down and looking more than a bit winded. *What are you doing? You're so close!*

"I've seen this before," a man next to Eldan whispered to his mate. "Classic move. Just watch."

Eldan focused back on Mason, and time seemed to slow down when he caught the alpha's gaze. A wide smile grew on Mason's face before he puffed out his chest and took off with an extra burst of speed, barely crossing the finish line before his competitor.

"And they've done it, folks!" The old man jumped from his seat. "Team Frosty takes the cup! What a knockout! And only a second behind them, Team Nutcracker finishes second! But where is Team Rudolph?"

The old man announcing looked back at the fountain. "Uh oh, looks like Team Rudolph was involved in a little accident near the fountain!"

Eldan looked back toward the fountain and saw the dad who was pulling his kids had run into a pile of fake gifts.

"And that about wraps it up, folks! With that, our first ever Silverstone Mall Derby comes to a close. Team Frosty, ah, let me see, that would be…" The old man looked over his notes. "Mason, Benjamin, Shawn, and Autumn, please come on up. You get first pick at the prizes!"

The kids rushed up to the table and started digging through the small prizes.

"Sally, Sierra, Nathan, and Sammy, otherwise known as Team Nutcracker, you're next!" The old man cupped his hands around his mouth. "And Team Rudolph! Dear David, Tyler, Molly, and Elizabeth…whenever you're free, come on up!"

David gave a thumbs-up from the pile of fake gifts, and the kids left him behind to head to the prize table.

Eldan searched for Mason in the crowd. He finally saw the alpha with his hands on his knees, taking deep breaths near the pile of pillows that served as a comfy area for the kids.

"Dogpile!" A little boy yelled.

It wasn't long before every kid in the mall was dogpiling Mason. Most of the adults were too busy to notice, and the kids reigned freely. Eldan felt something forming on his lips. He brought his fingers to his lips, and shock sparked through his veins.

A smile? God, I really am getting soft.

"Your friend looks like he needs help."

Eldan turned and saw a young woman sitting further down the bench bouncing her toddler gently. She gave the pile of children a distant smile and looked at Eldan.

"He's not my friend."

"What?" She tilted her head. "But I've seen you two talking—"

"Then, by that logic, wouldn't that make *us* friends?" Eldan motioned between them. "In fact, wouldn't that make everyone friends if we simply were able to talk to each other and gain immediate friendship status?" Eldan's voice trailed off before he let out a sigh. "Anyway, I'm sure he can take it. After all, he's got muscles for days."

Eldan snorted as Mason's arm popped out of the pile and waved frantically.

"Oh, dear!" The young mother quickly stood and tried to rush over before she seemed to remember that she couldn't do much to help with a toddler in her arms. She passed the toddler to Eldan. "I'm sorry, can you watch her for just a minute?"

Eldan instinctively cradled the small child. "I don't—"

"Thanks, doll." The mother rushed over to the pile. "Benjamin, Tyler, stop this instant!"

Why do I always end up in these situations?

Eldan watched as parents started pulling their kids from the pile, and the tots jumped back in. *Just like that video. What was it, baby pandas?*

The toddler squirmed in Eldan's arms, and he held her up and stared her in the face. "Bet you think you're some sort of big shot, don't you?"

She gave him a toothless grin and giggled.

"What, you think I'm funny? Strange girl you are." Eldan sighed. "Bet you think I'm just gonna roll over for that smile, huh?" He looked at the pile where Mason was slowly being freed.

The toddler hiccupped and giggled, reaching out for Eldan's hair. He sighed and rested her head on his shoulder.

"Guess you'd be right…"

Mason was finally free. Eldan started patting the toddler's back and humming a little tune his ma used to sing. He closed his eyes, settled into a rhythm, and relaxed into the bench.

Okay, this isn't so bad. I got this.

Or so he thought. Eldan froze as he felt the poor toddler shudder and jerk before something warm slid down his back. He was afraid to move, lest the toddler decorate the front of his sweater, too.

"Oh, no! I'm so sorry!" The young mother rushed back over with her two sons, and she took the toddler from Eldan. "Let me get you another outfit. I'm sure one of the shops will–"

Eldan held up his hand. "No, it's fine. I can–"

Dread prickled across Eldan's skin. He spent the last of his money on gifts for Mr. Hopson and Honey Bun, and, of course, he didn't have his card on him today. He quickly pulled out his wallet and opened it. Maybe, in a bout of drunken brainpower, he'd hidden a few extra bills in his wallet. Only the faded face of a single Abraham Lincoln stared back at him.

One could only hope, right? Eldan grumbled as he snapped his wallet closed and shuddered. Baby puke did *not* feel good. He needed to come up with something fast.

"Here, let me." Mason stepped up and looked at the toddler. "You worry about getting your little one cleaned up. I'll take care of Eldan here. Gotta look out for my buddy!"

"What world are you living in?" Eldan glared at Mason.

"How about the one where you have a clean sweater and a smile on your face?" Mason held out his hand.

"Fair enough." Eldan reached out a bit but came to his senses at the last minute. With a grumble, he ignored Mason's hand and stood. "But no promises on the smile."

Mason nodded. "Fair enough." He looked at the small map nearby. "Now, I'll buy you whatever you need." He grinned and held up a finger. "On one condition."

Shit. Eldan mentally prepared himself. "What?"

"I get to pick everything out."

Eldan almost disagreed, but the warmth seeping into his back was anything but pleasant.

"Fine."

~

"I CHANGED MY MIND." ELDAN STARED IN DISGUST AT THE clothing around him. "I'll just buy some cheap-ass bed sheets and make a toga."

"No take-backsies!" Mason yelled from a nearby rack.

"Oh, these backsies are being taken," Eldan grumbled. "If I'd known you were going to choose *this* shop instead of a normal clothing shop–"

"It's either this or baby-puke sweater." Mason laughed.

Eldan grimaced and stared at the bag holding his ruined sweater. He did *not* want to feel that again. A shiver ran down his spine as cold air seeped through the thin tank top he had grabbed after peeling his ruined sweater off.

"Fine."

"Fine, what?" Mason smirked.

"New sweater..." Eldan flapped his hand dismissively. "Medium."

Mason disappeared to the back of the store. Eldan heard an evil laugh before Mason returned to the front with something behind his back. He proudly showed it off with a wide grin.

"What the hell is *that*?"

Eldan stared in genuine horror at the monstrosity in Mason's hands. It was an absolutely horrendous green, red, and white sweater covered in horrid Christmas designs. There was a fluffy, tan collar around the neck, and on the back swung a reindeer tail complete with flashy lights. But the most disturbing thing about the sweater was that there was a very pronounced Rudolph head sticking out of the chest.

"It's a sweater!" Mason proudly announced.

"Obviously! But why would *anyone* wear that? *How* do you wear that?" Eldan motioned up and down at the Rudolph head.

"It's a novelty sweater! It's supposed to be wacky!" Mason waved the sweater around gently.

Eldan groaned. "Listen, I never thought the day would come that I would outright refuse a sweater, but that…*thing?*" Eldan pointed to the sweater. "It scares me."

"It's cute!"

"It's the stuff of nightmares, Mason!" Eldan huffed. "You know they've literally made horror movies out of stuff like this, right?"

"Okay, okay." Mason put the sweater to the side. "I thought you might veto that one, so hang on a minute."

Mason disappeared to the back of the store and brought back another sweater. "How about this one?"

"Do all ugly sweaters look the same?" Eldan squinted and studied the design. It was largely the same as the last one, but it was missing the horrifying Rudolph head and the lights on the tail.

"Ugly sweaters are art! You just gotta look at the details." Mason held up the sweater, and his voice took on a serious tone. "Note the crisscross stripes with gold *and* silver glitter. And the reindeer here? Hand-stitched. Every. Last. One."

Mason positioned the sweater on a mannequin, threw his arm around Eldan's shoulders, and pulled him close. "And there." He pointed to the fluffy collar. "Each hair was arranged by hand to form the fluffiest collar you'll ever see."

Eldan bit his lip. It *was* really fluffy, almost like Mr. Hopson's fur.

"So, what do you think?" Mason crooked his arm and leaned in close. "Do we have a winner?"

"I'll try it, but no promises." Eldan sighed and ducked to escape Mason's arm. "I'll be back in a minute."

"Alright!" Mason clapped. "I'll be here!"

Eldan grabbed the sweater from the mannequin and examined it closer. *Seems warm enough. And the material isn't as scratchy as I thought it would be...* He sighed and headed toward the dressing room.

Or the dressing booth, as it would seem. *Who decided that curtains on a dressing room was a good idea?* Eldan grumbled as he pulled the curtains closed and tugged the tank top over his head and replaced it with the tacky sweater. When he finally got settled, he buried his nose in the collar. *Almost exactly like Mr. Hopson...*

Eldan turned around to look at his back in the mirror. The tail weighed down the back just enough to be noticeable, but it was cute, nonetheless. Eldan gave wiggled his hips and smirked as the tail wagged.

Okay, maybe I can deal with this. If I squint, it looks kinda like a bunny tail.

Eldan pulled back the curtain and jumped when Mason called out to him from the front, where he was talking to the old man from the races. Mason had a couple of bundles in his arms and handed them to the old man before the old-timer left.

"Oh, man..." Mason's eyes lit up. "Look at you!"

"What're you so happy about?" Eldan crossed his arms.

"That sweater! And you!" Mason made a crisscross motion with his arms. "A match made by fate!"

"So, you're saying my Fated is an ugly Christmas sweater? That figures."

"You look so cute!" a woman near the store called out.

"Cute?" Eldan buried his nose in the collar. *Cute?*

"Awww...it's so you!" another woman agreed. "I might get one for my hubby!"

"I agree." Mason beamed. "Don't get me wrong, you're

always adorable, but that sweater just, like, tripled your cute meter."

"Don't call me–" Eldan grumbled. "I am *not* cute." He stormed out of the store. He saw Mason pay for the sweater out of the corner of his eye.

Guess I'm stuck with it now. Whatever. At least it's not covered in baby goo.

～

ELDAN ENDED UP IN THE FOOD COURT AT SOME POINT. HE didn't really pay attention to where he was going; he just wanted to get away from everyone for a few minutes. Or hours.

But peace was never an option. Eldan crossed his arms as he heard a chair being pulled out across from him.

"Hey."

And of course, it was Mason. Eldan groaned. "Can I help you?"

"Just checkin' on you," Mason whispered. "Sorry. Did you want to switch it out?"

Eldan sank further into his chair and buried his nose in the collar. He had grown rather fond of the sweater in the short amount of time he'd owned it. "Nah, it's fine."

"They're right, though. It does look cute on you."

"Thanks." Eldan turned away and hoped Mason couldn't somehow sense the heat on his cheeks. He would never live that one down.

"Hopefully we're not stuck here too much longer." Mason gazed at the families down the corridor. "We might get a few minutes of peace and quiet. Looks like it's story time." He leaned against the table. "So?"

"So, what?"

"What're you gonna do when you get home?" Mason asked. "Burn the sweater, right?"

Don't sound so sad. Eldan bit his lip. "Nah…"

"Does that mean you love it?"

"No." Eldan messed with the fluffy collar. "I hate it."

"You're a bad liar." Mason quirked his eyebrow. "It's okay, I won't tell anyone. It'll be our little secret."

"What about you?" Eldan quickly changed the subject. "What are you going to do when you get home?"

Mason leaned back against the railings surrounding the food court. "Well, I ain't going home for a while. I'm here for a few more weeks."

"So, you're not from around here," Eldan confirmed.

"Nope. I'm from Texas," Mason proudly announced. "I'm a history professor at Laguna Valley University."

"That's the best University in Texas." Eldan stared in awe.

"You've done your homework." Mason nodded. "Been there for about seven years now. Wanted a change of pace this year for the holiday."

"Well, why are you here? Most people go to New York for Christmas. Hell, you could've even seen the ball drop on New Year's Eve."

"It's hard to explain…" Mason clasped his hands and rested them on his lips. "I wanted to come here because my parents wanted to, and even when they had to cancel, I felt like I needed to come here, anyway."

Mason closed his eyes and took a deep breath. "Guess it was just fate."

Fate? Eldan bristled and looked at the time on his phone. *Oh, shit, it's been a while since I took my—*

"Are you okay?"

Eldan shoved his phone back in his pocket and ran his hand through his hair. "Yeah. Just a bit tired."

Everything was not okay. The more time passed, the more Eldan felt his heat welling up. The blockers could only keep it hidden for so long. He felt like Cinderella—an unfortunate soul constantly being hounded by the march of time. How long did he have until the truth came out?

Mason settled into his chair and turned back to watch the families.

"You're watching them like they're about to burst out into a spontaneous Christmas musical," Eldan mumbled.

Mason snorted. "Nah, just…" He stared at the table for a second. "It's nice spending this Christmas with so many people. Especially the kiddos. The last few years have been kind of…" Mason shrugged. "Quiet, I guess, is the right word."

Eldan leaned forward. "No kids of your own? Nieces or nephews?"

"Nope, just me and my parents. I wanted to bring them back here, but Appa got sick, so they stayed home in Montana." Mason smiled sadly. "Lord knows it would've been anything but quiet if they had made the trip."

"So they've been here before, but you haven't?"

Mason nodded. "Right. Sure, we lived up in Maine for a bit—I think until I was three—and then we moved to Texas. But they actually met here." Mason smiled. "At a Christmas parade."

"No kidding?"

"Yeah. The same one we watched." Mason hummed. "Like I said, they would've come, but Appa got sick. So, it's just me. Usually, I go up there to spend the holidays with them, but even with their antics, it's quiet without a bunch of kids running around."

"I suppose it would be kinda quiet." Eldan rested his head on his arms.

"See all of this?" Mason threw his arm over the back of the chair and motioned back toward the families. "This is what really brings the holidays together. For me, at least." He sighed. "You look at any kid in the world, and you see that spark of magic in their eyes."

Eldan raised his head as Mason continued.

"Anyone else? Nothing. Not without a little help." Mason turned around and folded his hands on the table. "I don't know, maybe it's just me, but I'm happiest when I'm bringing joy to other people. And the magic of Christmas? It's just an extra layer of fun."

Eldan clasped his hands and swallowed as Mason looked at him with soft eyes.

"I know it sucks for you to be trapped in here with all of us, and I know how you feel about the holiday, but…" Mason gave a faint smile. "Nobody should be alone on Christmas."

Eldan's mouth went dry as he got lost in that smile. He was about to say something sassy to retain his honor, but a couple of kids wandered over and tugged on Mason's sleeve.

"Guess what, guess what?" They bounced up and down excitedly.

Mason cast aside the soft look in his eyes and became more animated. "What, what?"

"We're putting up a tree!" The kids grinned. "One of the nice store owners is setting up a tree for us!"

"Really? That's great!" Mason exclaimed. "When are we gonna decorate it?"

"We don't have anything to decorate with…" The kids slumped and looked back at the main area where their parents were. "There aren't any ornaments left in the nice man's store."

"Well, you know what that means, right?"

"What?" The kids' eyes lit up.

"That means we've gotta make our own decorations." Mason stood, new purpose flooding his expression. "And that means it's popcorn time!"

The kids cheered and ran back to their parents. Within a minute, an employee rushed over and pulled on a striped apron. He flipped a few switches and started prepping the popcorn machines as the kids ran back over.

Mason crouched to look them in the eyes. "Okay, team. I need names. I need to know who I'm working with here."

"I'm Molly!" the little girl announced.

"And I'm Shawn!" the little boy grinned.

"Alright, Molly, Shawn. Here's what we need." Mason motioned to the stores. "We need fishing line, garbage bags, sewing needles, and all the popcorn you can carry. Got it?"

"Yes, sir!" The kids shouted.

"Alright, and ya'll be careful with those needles! Now, break!" Mason clapped and stood up before turning back to Eldan. "I'll try to keep them out of your hair."

"Nah, it's okay." Eldan stood and crossed his arms. "It's fine."

"What do you mean?"

Eldan sighed and waved his hand dismissively toward the popcorn machines and then at the families. "I'll try to deal with *all this.* For a bit. So you won't have to worry about me and miss it." He averted his gaze and buried his nose in the fluffy collar.

Eldan let out a yelp when he suddenly wasn't on the ground anymore. Mason held him tightly in a bear hug and rocked him back and forth.

"Thank you, thank you, thank you!" Mason squeezed a bit, and Eldan let out a little squeak. "Oops, sorry." Mason put the poor omega back down. "I didn't break anything, did I?"

Eldan rapidly shook his head and stepped back just as the kids returned with armloads of popcorn. They filled up the tables and ran off again.

"Are you sure that won't that be too much popcorn?" Eldan stared at the tables now covered in boxes of popcorn.

"Listen, if there's one thing I've learned about life, it's that you can never have too much popcorn."

CHAPTER 5: DECEMBER 24TH

*A*s Mason hauled the thirteenth garbage bag full of popcorn to the side of the food court, he came to a striking realization. One that would haunt him to the end of his days.

You can, in fact, have too much popcorn.

"I think we should stop here." the employee called from the popcorn machines. "These poor babies have worked overtime all day."

"Alright, man. Thanks for everything." Mason waved as he tied up the last bag. "Go get some rest."

Mason sighed and dragged his hand down his face. Okay, so Eldan was right. This was *way* too much.

Maybe we can get some movies, set up a DVD player or something.

"Hey, what's with all these empty spots?"

A little girl's voice dragged Mason from his thoughts. He looked at the fountain, where Eldan was working with Molly, Shawn, and a couple other kids to make strings of popcorn garland.

"You're missing a lot of popcorn!" Molly pointed out the thread that was missing popcorn. "Do you need some help?"

"Nah, I got it." Eldan shook his head. "Carry on."

"It goes like this, mister!" Shawn showed Eldan how to string the popcorn properly. "It's easy!"

"Yep, I got it, kiddo. Thanks." Eldan's fingers threaded the popcorn easily, and Shawn went back to his own work.

Mason watched for a moment, and his eyes narrowed in suspicion. *If you already know how to do it, why are you missing so much?*

Eldan cast a quick glance at the kids before snatching a few pieces of popcorn from the bag and tossing them in his mouth. The string inched a bit from his fingers as it moved down the line of kids, woefully missing a spot of popcorn.

Oh, you cheeky little– Mason snorted. *Better hope you don't get caught.*

No sooner had Mason thought that than one of the kids turned around and caught Eldan in the act. There was no way Eldan was talking his way out of this one.

Boy, if looks could kill...

"Hey, you're eating all the popcorn!" Shawn pointed an accusing finger at Eldan.

Eldan shrugged. His cheeks were puffed out, full of popcorn, and he crossed his arms before he swallowed. "Oops."

I should probably save him before he gets mobbed. Mason shook his head before he cupped his hands around his mouth. "Hey, Eldan!"

Eldan's head shot up, and Mason pointed at the garbage bags. "Wanna help drag more supplies to the front lines? Sounds like they need–"

Before Mason could finish his sentence, Eldan was next to him ready to help out.

"Damn, that was fast!" Mason snickered. "So, you've escaped their wrath. *This time.*"

Eldan crossed his arms. "Don't look at me like that. It's

your fault we have so much. I'm just doing my part to make sure none of it goes to waste."

"What, no 'thanks for the rescue, Mason' for me?" Mason held his hand over his chest. "I'm hurt. Truly."

"You'll get over it." Eldan flapped his hand dismissively. "Come on, let's get these bags to them before they come over here and yell at me again."

"Aww, you scared of them?" Mason slung a couple bags of popcorn over his shoulder and grabbed two more in his other hand. "Don't worry, I'll protect you."

Eldan grabbed a couple bags in each hand. "Please, I've dealt with angry rabbits. Kids have nothing on angry rabbits. Have you ever seen a pissed off Flemish? Kids have nothing on that terror."

"I'll have to take your word for it." Mason chuckled as he tossed his bags near the fountain. The employee that helped pop the corn followed with a few more bags.

"All the popcorn you can grab," Eldan scoffed as he put one of his bags down. "Who was the genius who said *that*?" He raised another bag up just as a kid zoomed under it. "And who decided to give these kids sugar?"

Mason smirked. "I don't know, but I bet he's a darn tootin' kinda guy." He counted the bags and looked back at the food court. "Couple more bags. Let's go get 'em."

A few kids circled the fountain and ran down the corridors. Their laughter and squeals echoed in the large building, and Mason felt a grin tugging at his lips. It was hard not to join them, but they had a job to do. Mason slung the last few bags of popcorn over his shoulder.

"So, what does it take?" Mason cast a glance at Eldan, which was returned with a quizzical look.

"For what?"

"To make you laugh?" Mason set the last few bags on the ground and started undoing the knots. "There's gotta be something."

Eldan crossed his arms. "See, that's where you're wrong. I don't laugh–"

"Incoming!" a little boy yelled. "Target locked!"

Mason didn't hear the rest of Eldan's sentence before a flash of yellow exploded in his face. He sputtered and fell back, looking around to see popcorn scattered across the floor and fountain.

"We hit the target, Captain!" another little boy yelled out.

"Benjamin! Tyler!" The young mother cried out from across the corridor. "What are you two doing?"

Benjamin and Tyler scrambled to their feet when they saw their mother coming over. They held their arms out like wings and made plane noises as they zoomed off.

"Look at the mess you two made!" the mother yelled after them. "Come back here and help clean up, right now!"

As the young mother hurried after her sons, Mason's ears perked up at the sound of snickers behind him. He quickly turned around and saw Eldan trying to compose himself, but his red face gave him away.

No way.

"Did you just–?" Mason stared in awe.

Eldan looked away and crossed his arms. "Nope."

Mason quickly stood and looked down at Eldan. "You totally did!"

"Did not."

"Did he laugh?" Mason asked Shawn as he pointed to Eldan. "Did you hear this man laugh? This is vital information!"

"I did!" Molly raised her hand.

"Wrong." Eldan turned his side to Mason and glared at him from the corner of his eye. "I did no such thing."

"Normally, I'd roll with it," Mason started. "But I feel like I have to point out that your ears are giving you away."

Eldan hunched his shoulders, and his hands shot up to cover his ears. "I don't know *what* you're talking about."

"Ooooh, busted." Mason snickered as he flicked popcorn off his shoulders. Eldan let out a little sigh.

"Sit," Eldan commanded. He pointed to the fountain.

Mason quirked an eyebrow but did as he was told. "Yes, sir." He smirked. "Have I been bad?"

Eldan scoffed as he stepped a bit closer and reached out toward Mason's face. "No, you just have popcorn on your… everything." He started picking popcorn out of Mason's hair and tossing it to the floor. "Don't give me that look. I'll sweep it up once you're cleaned up."

"You don't have to do this, you know." Mason gave a lopsided grin. "I am perfectly capable of grooming myself."

Eldan tensed for a split second, and color bloomed across his cheeks. "I don't doubt it. Just shush and let me work."

Mason took a deep breath. Would it be wrong to ask some of the kids to throw more popcorn on him? Eldan was standing so close now, it was hard not to reach out and pull him closer. No, the only thing he could do now was close his eyes and enjoy the moment.

What I wouldn't give for a few moments with you. Just a few more like this.

"Don't fall asleep on me, big guy."

"Kinda hard not to." Mason forced his eyes open and smiled. "After all, you're being so gentle with me."

"Would you rather I be rough with you?" Eldan scowled. "Grab a handful of your beard? Force you down to my level?"

Mason flashed a flirty grin. "Too many witnesses. I'd rather find a nice, secluded spot if you want to play that way."

"You…" Eldan shuddered and bit his lip. "Let me work. Please."

Mason's eyes slipped closed again, and he focused on Eldan's unsure, careful movements. Mason inhaled sharply as he felt Eldan lean closer.

"You're absolutely intolerable, you know?" Eldan whispered. "Enough to try the patience of a saint."

"So I've been told. And yet, here you are. A saint in the flesh, grooming someone like me." A low purr escaped Mason's lips. "Even better, you haven't killed me yet."

"A surprise to everyone, I'm sure."

Mason felt one last light tug at his beard before warm fingers brushed against his cheek and jawline. It only took a second, but that one bit of contact was all it took to send a shiver down Mason's spine. He cracked open his eyes as he felt Eldan's hands brushing off his shoulders.

"There. Done." Eldan's hands lingered on Mason's shoulders for another second before he stepped back and crossed his arms. "You can stand now."

"Or, you could sit with me." Mason patted the fountain next to him. "I wouldn't mind."

Just a bit longer.

Eldan seemed to consider the offer for a moment, but before he could say anything, his attention was drawn to a few of the kids nearby.

"I can't wait to see what Santa brings." Molly carefully added more popcorn to the garland.

Benjamin and Tyler had joined the group, and Benjamin shoved the needle through a cranberry before passing it to Tyler. "How's he gonna get in? There's no chimney here!"

"Santa doesn't always use a chimney," a little girl with red hair pointed out. "Our house doesn't have one, and we always get gifts from him!"

A little boy who sat near her looked at the floor sullenly. "But, Sis, how's he gonna find us here?"

The little girl put her arm around him and swayed him gently. "Don't worry, Nathan. Santa will find us! Remember when we were at that cabin in Tennessee a couple years ago?"

"Yeah." Nathan nodded.

"He found us there, no problem!" The girl smiled brightly. "So, he'll find us here."

Eldan glanced back at Mason, and the look in his eyes said it all.

Mason grinned. "You thinkin' what I'm thinkin'?"

"Yes, and I am nothing short of horrified with myself." Eldan sighed.

"We need to call a war council." Mason stood and motioned for Eldan to follow him. "Come on."

A few other adults were nearby, and Mason waved them over.

"What's up, Mason?" a young man asked. His mate held onto his arm and a young girl held his hand.

"Hey, Caleb, Max." Mason nodded to the man and his mate. "Do you think we could have a little chat?" He nodded down to the little girl, and they seemed to understand.

"I'll take Sierra over to the kids and stay with them a moment. Take all the time you need." The pair's omega placed a light kiss on his mate's cheek before he crouched down to their daughter's level. "Hey, Sierra, baby? Think we can go hang out with the other kids for a moment? Appa needs to talk with Mason, okay?"

"Okay, Oppa." Sierra bit her lip as they wandered over to the group of kids, who welcomed her with open arms.

"Thanks, Caleb." Mason waited for the rest of the adults to come over before he took a deep breath.

"So, we heard the kids earlier. Some of them are worried about whether or not Santa is gonna be able to find us here. A little girl with red hair was doing her best to calm everyone down, but I feel like we should do something, too."

"Red hair, you say? That's our Autumn, the oldest of our three." Caleb grinned. "Always the little peacemaker. Wasn't your boy worried about that too, Sally?"

An alpha mother nearby nodded. "Yeah, my little Sammy was asking about that, too."

"And my granddaughter, Elizabeth, she's been all over the mall tonight. Looking for a way for Santa to get in is what she tells me." An old woman lowered herself to a bench and sighed. "Please tell me you have something to calm them down."

Mason nodded. "Yeah, I think we have something. It'll be a team effort, but I think we can make it work." He motioned at the half-decorated tree. "I'm about ninety-percent sure everyone here got something off layaway, right?"

"Right."

"Absolutely."

"Great." Mason cracked his knuckles. "Okay, so here's what I'm thinking. We should get a ton of construction paper, pipe-cleaners, glitter, the whole she-bang and just let the kids go wild."

"And while they're busy, we can wrap some things for them to open tomorrow!" The young mother beamed in delight and cradled her toddler close. "We can put 'From Santa' on the nametags!"

"And who'll watch the kids?" Eldan asked, looking back at the small group of children.

"Can you wrap gifts?" Mason quirked his eyebrow.

"Does putting them in trash-bags count?"

"No."

"Then you have your answer," Eldan huffed.

"Welcome to Team Craft Supervision, buddy." Mason grinned. "Anyone else who can't wrap will help watch the kids."

A few people stepped forward and headed to Eldan's side.

"Those who can wrap, come with me. We'll set up in the craft store." Mason pointed to a bright, colorful store just down the corridor. "Let's get this done!"

As Mason's group headed toward the store, the young mother passed her toddler to Eldan. "Sorry to ask again, but could you? She really likes you."

Eldan bit his lip and cradled the toddler protectively close to his body. "I'm the chosen one, huh?"

"Yep. Her name is Nikki, by the way. I hope she won't give you too much trouble this time. It would be a shame to ruin another sweater, especially one that cute." She grinned and followed the group to the store.

Mason hung back and cast a glance between Eldan and the toddler. "You gonna be alright? I can ask Rose to stay out here."

"Nah. You need all the help you can get." Eldan waved his hand dismissively. "We'll be okay out here." He gazed down at the little, sleeping toddler in his arms. "Nikki will help me keep everyone in line."

A hint of a sweet scent made Mason's nose twitch. Heat flared in his chest as he took another breath, and he quickly took a step back and headed for the craft shop. When he made it into the crowded shop, shudders wracked his body.

Marshmallows? Why the fuck does he smell like marshmallows?

❧

"MASON, WE NEED MORE NAMETAGS OVER HERE, PLEASE!" Caleb called out.

Rose held up her hand. "And some more curled ribbon for us, please!"

"I'm on it!" Mason grabbed everything they needed and dropped it off before clearing the wrapped gifts from the table. A nice pile grew in the store's corner, carefully stacked to avoid crushing the prefect ribbons and bows.

Everything was finally coming together. The kids were outside working on paper ornaments for the tree, quiet Christmas tunes played over the loudspeakers, and the gifts were almost done. Really, the only thing left was waiting for the city to roll through and get them out of the mall.

Mason couldn't help but feel a bit down. He'd really grown to enjoy being around these once-strangers and their kids, but after they got out, would they keep in touch? Probably not.

What'll happen to Eldan? Mason felt his chest tighten. *If he disappears again, I–*

Mason was torn from his thoughts as the bell above the store door jingled. One of the older women, Cheryl, pushed her way in and dropped an empty box on the table.

"Those kids can go through some supplies, let me tell you." Cheryl sighed. "I'm about worn out."

"Let me get it, Cheryl. You take a break." Mason quickly stood and led her to his seat. "What all did they need?"

"Let's see...cotton balls, googly-eyes, sequins, crayons, more yarn, the list goes on." Cheryl groaned as she sunk into her seat.

"So, anything I can bring out, right?"

"Right. Make sure you get cotton balls. That's what they really want for some reason."

"Gotcha." Mason picked up the empty box and filled it with whatever he could find. "Be back in a few minutes."

Mason squeezed through the door and took a breath. It would be a nice change of pace to be back with Eldan and the kids again. He could hear the kids babbling from his spot by the craft store.

"And then what happened?" a little girl asked.

"Well, Honey Bun is a rather adventurous little bunny, and there have been times when I've found him in places he should've never been able to get to."

Wait, that's– Mason stopped in his tracks. *Eldan?* He ducked behind a potted plant and listened.

"Yeah, just imagine walking into the kitchen in the middle of the night and finding a naughty little rabbit in the cupboard eating all the crackers!"

Mason peeked around the potted plant and saw Eldan leaning against the back of the bench, cradling Nikki in his arms. His legs were stretched out, and he was clearly relaxed around the group of kids.

Does he have an apron on? Mason squinted and saw thick, brown straps tied in a bow behind Eldan's back.

"All of them?" Benjamin asked.

"Yep. Every single one." Eldan hummed. "Now, Mr. Hopson, he's the lazy one. The best pillow you could ever ask for. He can be a bit of a butt, though." Eldan pouted. "He ate my slippers recently, you know. That's why I bought him so many toys for Christmas."

"Is he fat?" Tyler looked up from his drawing with curious eyes.

"The fattest," Eldan confirmed. "That's why, whenever I've had a bad day, his belly is the best to rest on."

A wistful smile played at the corners of Eldan's lips as he looked down at the toddler in his arms. "Isn't that right, little one?"

Wait, did he just—

Mason's mouth fell open at the sight. *He did. He just honest-to-God smiled.*

And what a smile it was. Mason clutched the box close to his body and swallowed. A smile like that could move mountains. Shit, the Devil would probably return someone's soul for a fleeting glimpse of that smile.

Perhaps that was why his smile was so rare. Mason looked again and felt goosebumps prickle on his skin.

That damn smile would be the end of him.

"Oh, is that why you called him Dr. Hopson earlier? Because he makes you feel better?" Autumn looked up from her drawing.

"Yeah." Eldan stretched out and hummed a little tune for Nikki. "I wish you all could see him. He's the best therapy rabbit ever."

Now or never...

"Sounds like a dependable guy." Mason walked over to the group and lowered the box to the ground. "Now, we requested some cotton balls?" He fished the bags from the box and held them up.

"Yay! Now, I can finish my drawing!" Autumn grabbed a handful of cotton balls and headed back to her spot.

A little boy grabbed some pink glitter and rushed back to his spot. "Thanks, Mister Mason!"

Mason stepped back and gripped the back of the bench before leaning down to whisper to Eldan, "How you holding up?"

Eldan shivered but managed to hold his composure. "Alright."

"What are they making?"

"Not sure." Eldan's ears turned red.

Ah, we got a pretty little liar here. Mason smirked before he straightened up and wandered over to the kids. He crouched down next to Autumn and looked at her drawing.

"Bunnies?" Mason smiled as she pasted one of the cotton balls on the paper.

"Yeah!" Autumn held up her now-completed picture. "For Eldan!"

"For Eldan?" Mason repeated. "Why?"

"Because he loves bunnies!"

"Really?" Mason smirked as he looked back at Eldan. "I would've never guessed."

"Didn't you notice his apron?" Nathan pointed to Eldan. "Sammy's momma bought it for him so the baby wouldn't puke on him again!"

"Isn't it cute?" Molly beamed. "I want one, too!"

Mason let out a low purr. It *was* really cute. It was pale pink and had brown bunny faces with pink noses stamped on the front. The pockets had tiny brown bows. And the straps? Well, Mason knew how the straps looked: absolutely cute as hell, all tied up in a pretty little bow behind Eldan's back.

"I love it." Mason eyed Eldan up and down. "Looks amazing on you." He purred.

"Thanks." Eldan cradled Nikki closer to his body. "Better safe than sorry, right?"

"Yeah, it would be a shame to ruin such a nice sweater, especially one with a darling tail." Mason smiled. "Anyway, I'm gonna head back. Just holler if you need anything."

"Bye, Mister Mason!" The kids waved. Eldan waved slowly and returned to tending to Nikki.

It had to be illegal to be that cute. Mason made it back to the craft store and ran his hand down the length of his face, pausing on his mouth. *What am I gonna do? Arrest him?* The very thought of Eldan cuffed sent a shiver down Mason's spine.

"You sly dog."

Mason jumped. "Huh?"

An old man by the front door cackled. "Using the kids to find out what he likes. Devious!"

"I wasn't–" Mason crossed his arms and tapped his chin. "Okay, maybe I was."

The old man used his pocketknife to curl a bit of ribbon. "So, now you know the way to his heart?"

Mason shrugged. "Suppose so."

"You don't sound too thrilled.' The old man raised his lazy gaze and held it on Mason.

"It's…" Mason scratched the back of his head. "Complicated."

The old man grunted and leaned forward, balancing his elbow on his knee. "Ain't nothin' complicated about it. Listen, you like him, yeah?"

Abso-fuckin-lutely.

"Can see it in your eyes." The old man worked on another

ribbon. "The answer is yep." He tossed the ribbon in a basket and flicked his knife closed. "Then go for it, youngster. Life's way too short to spend wondering about what could or couldn't be."

"Something tells me you've been through something like this, too."

"And what gave you that impression?" The old man cackled and motioned to the corner where a few people were still wrapping gifts. "See that beautiful lady over there with the curled blonde hair and the crystal-blue eyes?"

"Yeah?"

"That's my wife, Betty. Do me a favor, and imagine me in my twenties. Long time ago, I know. I was young, stupid, and wild. Didn't think settlin' down was my cup o' joe. Poor girl put up with me all through high school, and I just left her behind. Now, looking back…" The old man's face went sour. "You know how many years I wasted? How many years I missed out on? I could've spent them with her, but instead, I dicked around and lost all that time. And for what? A job I hated in a city I hated."

The old man flicked his knife open again and started working on another ribbon. "Anyway, soon as I realized exactly what the hell was wrong with me, and what she was to me, I packed up and came back home. Proposed to her the moment I found her again."

"Wow, and she agreed just like that?"

"Hell no." The old man snorted. "I asked her three times, and I think she only married me out of pity at that point."

"You were rather pathetic!" Betty yelled across the store.

"And you love me anyway!" the old man yelled back. "But, anyway, don't waste all that time like I did. The day will come when you regret it."

"What's your name, old-timer?" Mason held out his hand. "Need to know the name of my matchmaker."

"Bill Bradshaw." The old man stood and shook Mason's hand. "Retired auctioneer, retired Army man, and professional bullshitter." Bill smiled. "Not retired from the most recent."

"My name is Mason Shepard, and I'm a professional nincompoop."

Bill lowered himself back into his seat and motioned for Mason to take a seat nearby. Mason pulled up the stool and rested his elbows on his knees. "Is it really so simple?"

"Well, I never said that." Bill smirked and fiddled with his old signet ring. "I just said life is too short to worry." He examined another ribbon and let it fall into the basket. "Keep his attention. Figure out what he likes most. Give him a gift. Invite him to do something fun!"

Mason groaned as he wracked his brain for ideas. What could he do? Unless there was a convenient basket of baby bunnies hidden somewhere in the mall, he was fresh out of luck.

"Listen." Bill kicked back and crossed his legs. "I noticed you were asking people to try on that elf suit you got when you were getting clothes for your friend. You still got that around here somewhere?"

"Yeah, I got it in a bag somewhere around here."

"Well, did you ask him if he would try it on? He looks like he's about the right size." Bill motioned toward Eldan through the window with his knife.

Mason pursed his lips. "I don't know. I think we're lucky he's participating in the activities."

"That means something changed, right?" Bill grinned. "People change."

"That quickly?" Mason quirked his eyebrow as he looked outside toward the group of kids and Eldan. "Pretty sure he was ready to bite my head off when I gave him that sweater."

"But he still put it on, yeah?" Bill flicked his knife closed and grabbed the basket full of ribbon from the floor. "Won't know unless you ask. That's my sage advice for you."

"You sure you're not bullshittin' me?" Mason chuckled.

"I'm sure."

Mason stood and gazed out the store window at the group outside. "Thanks, Bill. For your sage, bullshit-free advice."

"Ain't a problem, young'un." Bill nodded, wandered over to his wife, and placed the basket on the table. "Now, go get him!"

~

As Mason approached the group of artists, he took a deep, steadying breath.

Okay, all he had to do was ask. It was either gonna be yes or no. No in-betweensies. A fifty-fifty chance. And even if Eldan refused, the Santa suit was still an option. If Mason had to do it himself, he would.

But I would rather not do it myself...Every Santa needs a partner.

Mason took a deep breath as he headed toward the group. A ton of paper ornaments were scattered across the floor, and the kids were working hard to finish up the tree. Eldan still sat nearby, casting absentminded glances at the old TV that was playing *Rise of the Guardians*.

Okay, now or never. Will you be my cheerful little elf? That's all you gotta ask, Mason. Be my cheerful little elf. Mason psyched himself up and gripped the back of the bench where Eldan sat.

But just as he opened his mouth–

"Took you long enough."

Mason snapped his mouth closed and looked down. Eldan was giving him a mean side-eye, but his voice was missing its usual bite. Mason lowered himself next to Eldan on the bench.

"Don't even try to say you didn't enjoy this time with the kids." Mason smiled. "You got a new sweater *and* apron out of it."

"Yeah. Toss in some new slippers, and I'm golden." Eldan muttered.

"Well..." Mason started. "I wouldn't call them slippers, per se, but I do have some new kicks for you if you're interested."

"If they're glass slippers, I don't want them."

Glass slippers? Where'd you get that idea? Mason cleared his throat. "Nah, nothing like that, but they *are* kind of flashy." He stood and motioned for Eldan to follow him. "If you would..."

Eldan stared a moment before passing Nikki to Max, and he followed Mason around the corner into a quiet corridor. Mason groaned as he leaned back against the wall.

"What's this all about?" Eldan crossed his arms and leaned against the wall next to Mason. "Something wrong?"

"Listen." Mason scratched the back of his head. "I know how you feel about Christmas, and I know you'll hate what I'm about to suggest, but you're my last hope."

"Last hope? Boy, are you in trouble," Eldan muttered under his breath. "But I'll play along. Who rustled your flock, o' great Shepard?"

"Don't worry, Moses has the flock this weekend." Mason snorted. "But this is about a little plan I cooked up. See, when we were getting you all gussied up, I found a couple of outfits, and I thought, 'wouldn't it be great if we could surprise the kids with these?'"

Mason waited for Eldan to scowl, but he didn't. Instead, his gaze fell to the floor.

"You found a Santa suit, didn't you?"

"Yeah, and it fits me perfectly. The problem is–"

"The elf suit," Eldan whispered. "I've heard you asking around about it. You're not exactly subtle, you know."

"Hey, I resent that." Mason chuckled under his breath. "You're right. I asked everyone else, but it didn't fit them. They blamed it on too many holiday goodies. I'm pretty sure it'll fit you, though."

Eldan nodded but didn't say anything. He didn't even glower at the potted plants. After what felt like an eternity, Mason couldn't take Eldan's silence anymore.

"I promise this is the last favor I'll ask of you. Whatever your answer–"

"I'll do it." Eldan's gaze shot up.

Mason felt his heart throb at the look of fierce determination in Eldan's eyes. "Really? You serious about this?"

"Don't make me say it twice."

Those few words were an absolute dream come true. Mason sagged back against the wall, tension seeping from his muscles. "Thank you so much." He slid a bit closer to Eldan and let out a low purr of relief as his eyes slipped closed.

But all it took was one muffled hum to make Mason tense up again. When he quickly turned to look at Eldan, he noticed the man had relaxed quite a bit and had a distant look in his eyes.

Mason's mind went blank as a faint scent of marshmallow made his throat go dry.

There was no way. He had to be going bonkers. *Sweet scents like that mean–*

Mason quickly cleared his throat. He had to do something, *anything,* to get his mind off that delicious scent.

"Come on." Mason pushed off the wall and turned to face Eldan. "We should do this while we have a free moment."

"Do what, exactly?"

"Well, we gotta make sure your elf suit fits."

"I thought you said you were sure it would fit?"

Mason held up a finger. "Wrong. I said pretty sure."

"Why do I get the feeling you're up to something dastardly?"

Mason grinned slyly. "Ever think that, maybe, I just wanted to see what it looks like on you?"

"What? That your fetish or something?" Eldan averted his gaze. "Do you like dressing people up?" His voice lowered. "Is that why?"

"Wow, gotta say I like that tone on you." Mason placed his hand on the wall next to Eldan's head and leaned down. "What would you say if I said maybe?"

"I'd remind you that we've had this discussion." Eldan looked up and held his gaze. "A few times now."

"And?"

"And it's either yes–"

"Or no." Mason finished, then licked his lips. "So, now, the question is, you wanna take a chance and find out?"

And there was that noise again. That maddening noise. A perfect little hum that fit a perfect little beau.

"The clothing store. I'll meet you there." Mason took a step back and left to grab the costumes.

Yep, I'm doomed.

"I don't know what I was expecting." Eldan sighed inside the booth.

"Probably something dirty." Mason looked through the nearby racks to pass the time. "How are you holding up in there?"

"This thing is tight in places."

"What kind of–?" Mason stopped himself. Shit, that

wasn't what he meant to ask. He shook his head and started over. "What do you mean?"

"I need to have a word with whoever sewed these pants," Eldan grumbled under his breath.

Oh, fudgesticks. Mason held his breath.

"Son of a bitch-nugget," Eldan growled. "This piece of–"

"Hey, leave the sons of bitch-nugget out of it." Mason walked over to the booth. "Do you need any help?"

"No!" Eldan let out a strained shout just before jingles echoed in the small booth. "Yes."

"You decent?"

"Just come in and help before I change my mind."

Mason closed his eyes and pulled back the rough curtain. "And just what sort of trouble have you managed to get into?"

At that moment, Mason found out what it was like to be completely overwhelmed by the scent of marshmallows. Definitely not an unpleasant scent, and it was strong enough to send shudders through his body.

When Mason finally cracked his eyes open, the first thing he saw was Eldan's bare back and shoulders. The elf suit and collar dangled from his arms.

The second thing he noticed was the prominent dark mark on Eldan's right shoulder, a stark contrast to his milky-white skin.

You're an omega? Shit, no wonder I– Mason took a deep breath and felt heat well up in his stomach. *Jesus...*

Mason steadied himself and bit the inside of his cheek. Hard. Anything to get back to his senses.

"What?" Eldan's voice snapped Mason from his thoughts. "Are you done eyeing me up, or do I need to start charging you by the minute?"

"Sorry. I uh–" Mason cleared his throat. "How did you manage this?" He stooped down and grabbed bits of the costume that had fallen to the floor.

"Elf costumes aren't my forte. Sue me."

Mason snorted. "As much as I would love to sue the pants off you, we don't have time for the courtroom. Just hold out your arms, and I'll fix everything."

Mason quietly worked until the costume was put together nicely. He draped the red cloak with jingle bells over Eldan's shoulders and stepped back to examine his work.

"We're missing the ears."

Eldan crossed his arms and turned toward the mirror. "Do we really need them?"

"You're not an elf without the elf ears," Mason pointed out, earning a sigh from Eldan.

"Fine." Eldan pointed to the folded sweater on the bench, and Mason moved it and found the ears hidden underneath.

"Now, what are they doing under there?" Mason grinned and grabbed the fake ears. Eldan hunched his shoulders as Mason stepped up behind him.

"Everything okay?"

"Yeah, sorry." Eldan lowered his shoulders. "Just do it."

Mason shrugged and carefully tucked Eldan's hair behind his ear before slipping the fake elf ear on.

Or trying to. Who would've guessed that Eldan was ticklish? Every low whimper and every wiggle posed a real problem for such a simple task.

Mason leaned in close and whispered, "Sensitive ears?"

Color crept across Eldan's ears and neck, but he refused to say anything.

So, that would be a yes. Mason felt his heart skip a beat. Oh, the things he could do with that info.

"Just like a wee bunny." Mason chuckled as he finally managed to slip the ear on. "Matches your skin tone perfectly, too. Looks very natural."

Eldan bit his lip and shivered as Mason slipped on the other ear, but he managed to keep his voice down, much to

Mason's disappointment. Was it such a sin to wish to hear those sweet sounds again?

Will I even get a chance again? Mason's hands slowed, and he let out a low sigh.

"Thanks for doing this. I know how much you..." Mason's voice trailed off. "Don't worry. I'll keep my promise to you."

Eldan looked over his shoulder before turning around and quirking his eyebrow. "What?"

"After this, I won't bother you again."

Mason gritted his teeth. That was what he said, right? That this was the last favor. And after they got out of the mall, that was that. He'd go back to Texas, and Eldan would–

"I don't–" Eldan ducked his head. "I don't want that."

Come again?

"I don't want you to just disappear." Eldan bit his lip and let out a shuddering breath. "Because I think you're my..."

Mason sucked in a quick breath as Eldan's scent kicked up about a hundred notches. He felt the alpha inside clawing to get out, anything to get closer to that delicious scent.

"Holy shit." Mason steadied himself. "You mean to tell me you're my Fated?"

"Are you disappointed?" Eldan hugged his arms close to his body. "After all I've said to you, and everything I've done? I–"

"You kidding?" Mason leaned his elbows against the wall and caged Eldan between his arms. "This is the happiest day of my life."

Mason sniffed, and he felt his eyes burning. He tried to swallow the lump in his throat, but it became nearly impossible as Eldan let out a quiet hum.

"Fate is strange, sometimes, but it's never wrong," Eldan whispered.

Mason chuckled as he finally calmed down. "So, you're saying fate chose me for a reason?" He grinned and messed with the fake elf ears. "I get to mess with these delightful ears forever now?"

"No. I'm never wearing these again after tomorrow," Eldan grumbled and pushed Mason out of the dressing booth. "Tough luck, bud." Eldan flashed a small smile before the curtain fluttered closed.

"We'll see, Little Elf." Mason snorted. "We shall see."

CHAPTER 6: DECEMBER 24TH – DECEMBER 25TH

"Well, it goes without saying that Winter Storm Hestia has left a chilling reminder for our city as it continues to the northeast. First responders are working hard to free those still trapped and continue to ask for your patience and cooperation."

Eldan sighed as the news report played out quietly on someone's phone. Didn't seem like anyone was getting out of the mall anytime soon. He pulled his knees to his chest and rested his chin on them.

"Can't believe we're gonna be stuck here overnight," Caleb groaned.

His mate reached out and comforted him. "I know, but at least everyone is warm, safe, and fed, right?"

That much was true. A warm dinner had been a welcome affair, even if it was just food court wraps and burgers.

Now, with full bellies and fresh blankets, everyone was finally winding down. Eldan eyed the trinkets scattered around the shop they chose to settle in. As a thrift store, it had a little bit of everything: furniture, toys, old records, and more decorations, to name a few. There had even been a box full of old bobbleheads.

Which suited Eldan just fine. It kept the kids busy for a while as the adults set up for bed. Now, he was listening closely to the low timbre of Mason's voice as he told stories to the kids. Eldan's eyes slipped halfway closed as Mason came close to the end of his tale.

Eldan shivered and reached for another blanket, then he curled up on the soft couch cushions. He was absolutely astounded he hadn't frozen to death already. He glanced quickly around the store and noticed he was the only one shivering.

Does everyone else have polar bear DNA or something? Jesus, how the hell are they not Smurfs?

Eldan pulled the blankets tighter around his shoulders and snuck a quick peek at his phone. It was a little after ten, and most of the kids had already fallen asleep. Only a few were still up, listening to Mason's stories. After sending one last text to his mom, Eldan turned his attention back to Mason.

Except now, the alpha was nowhere to be seen. Eldan pushed himself up on his elbow, and his gaze shot around the room, but he only saw a few parents tucking their kids in for bed. He sank back down on the cushions and rolled over, facing the back of the couch.

"They conked out quicker than I thought they would."

Eldan flinched as a low voice rumbled above him.

"Seriously, how do you do that?" Eldan grumbled as he glared up.

"Gotta be sneaky when you have an Oppa with ears like mine. Even the slightest noise wakes him up." Mason circled around the couch and flopped onto an air mattress in front of it. "Actually thought I was gonna run out of stories for a minute there."

"You?" Eldan scoffed as he rolled over to face Mason. "Never."

"Contrary to popular belief, I don't know every

Christmas story by heart." Mason chuckled and folded his hands behind his head.

Eldan curled up on the couch and took a deep breath. It was a strangely peaceful moment for being trapped in a mall. Quiet snores and muffled chatter came from all corners of the store, and Rose was nearby, singing a lullaby for little Nikki.

"What about you? Can't sleep?" Mason's voice snapped Eldan from his people watching. "No visions of sugarplum fairies for you?"

"The day I dream of sugarplum fairies, I'll–" Eldan paused. He didn't have anything snarky to say. Try as he might, he couldn't make any sarcastic words tumble from his lips. "Forget it."

"You should try to get some sleep. You know they'll be up early." Mason checked his phone and set an alarm. "And we need to beat them up if we want our plan to go off without a hitch."

"'m not tired," Eldan mumbled into the blankets.

"That's what the kids were saying." Mason chuckled. "Then, they passed out about ten minutes later."

"It's this damn couch. Worst couch in existence." Eldan furrowed his eyebrows and ducked his chin, burrowing into the lumpy pillow. "No way I'll be able to sleep on this."

"You're always welcome to join me, you know." Mason motioned to the other side of the air mattress. "Kinda lonely over here."

Don't tempt me. Eldan swallowed.

This whole situation was nothing short of maddening. Not only was he trapped in a mall on Christmas Eve, but he was also trapped with his *Fated.*

Why now, of all times? Why in a place like this? Eldan bit his lip. *And why the hell is he so simply perfect?*

A deep heat billowed in his stomach. As it stood, Eldan didn't trust himself not to pounce on the guy. No, it was better if he stayed on the couch for now. Eldan turned away. He needed a distraction, and the twinkling Christmas tree down the corridor was perfect. Or so he thought.

"Having second thoughts?" Eldan heard the air mattress rustle a bit. "Nervous?"

Damn it, man. Can't you let me not focus on you in peace? Eldan looked over and saw Mason waiting for an answer. He wasn't getting off the hook that easily.

You remind me of someone." Eldan whispered. "Someone who would've done all this, too." He glanced at the tree.

"Wanna talk about it? You know, since you're not tired?"

Eldan went slack and let out a long breath. This wasn't exactly the best time or place to explore his sad past, but he knew Mason wasn't going to lay off until he got an answer.

"Later." Eldan stared with half-lidded eyes at the cushions. "Later is better."

"If you change your mind, I'm here." Mason nodded and pulled the scratchy quilt up to his shoulder. "No matter what you need, I'm here."

Eldan rolled over toward the back of the couch and dragged his knees up to his stomach. "I know you are," he whispered.

A low purr sent shivers down Eldan's spine, and he kissed any chance of a good night's sleep goodbye.

Eldan woke with a shiver and instinctively pulled his blankets tighter around his body. How the hell everyone else was surviving this cold, he would never know. While everyone else slept soundly, the sound of his own shuddering breaths pulled him further into the real world, and he cringed as the cold air licked at his exposed skin.

He must have slept a little while because a glance at his phone told him it was almost midnight. The only lights on in the store were the small strings of Christmas lights that lined the walls. It was almost cozy if he ignored the fact that he was almost freezing to death. He stared into the darkness, listening to the soft snores of everyone else.

Mason was still sleeping like a log, his body barely outlined by the faint lights. Eldan couldn't help but watch the alpha. In the warm glow of the Christmas lights, he looked so peaceful, like being near him wasn't so bad after all. He was a secure and steady fortress, promising warmth and tender touches.

But one thing Eldan had learned in life was that fate was cruel.

He honestly couldn't believe fate had done this to him. There was nothing quite like an internal struggle between simply wanting to be warm and wanting to be near your Fated but being afraid to get too close.

And that was it. He shouldn't be afraid to be near Mason, but he was. All through the evening, since they got trapped in the mall, his thoughts had been his worst enemy, and it had only gotten worse the longer he was near the alpha.

What if I fuck it up? What if I hurt him?

A wave of nausea pummeled Eldan's stomach, and his eyes fluttered closed.

What if it happens again?

Mary's smiling face suddenly flashed in Eldan's mind, and he forced his eyes open and focused on the dark ceiling as tears slipped from the corners of his eyes.

Eldan's ears perked as Mason groaned in his sleep. He quickly wiped the tears from his eyes and buried one side of his face in the pillow. The one thing he was sure of was that he wouldn't be caught crying.

But when Mason rolled over, and the blanket slipped down to his hips, Eldan let out a low hum. How warm was he that he could let the blankets go that low and still sleep so soundly? Eldan sat up and pulled his sweater sleeves down to cover his numb fingers. He had a decision to make. Either he could try to hold out on the couch and not run the risk of jumping the alpha, or–

Fuck it.

At this point, the cold was seeping beneath his clothes and blankets, and his legs were trembling something fierce. Eldan rubbed his legs together, hoping to warm them up a bit before he tried to stand and hopefully not fall on Mason. That would be too embarrassing, and he'd probably have to sleep outside in the large corridors if that happened.

With a quiet purr, Eldan slipped from the couch. He tugged both of his blankets tightly around his body. He stepped over Mason's shoes before burrowing under the quilt against Mason's back.

Mason jerked forward and turned to look over his shoulder.

"Sorry. It's just me." Eldan whispered.

Mason relaxed and rolled onto his back. "I know I said I was here if you needed to talk about whatever was ailing you, but you have to admit, this is a strange way of talking." He smirked. "Not that I'm complaining, mind you."

"Shut up, I'm cold."

"Hey, Cold. I'm–"

Eldan raised up on his elbow and glared down at Mason. "Okay, first off, can I have a word with you?"

"Hm?"

"Cease."

Mason let out a throaty laugh. "Yes, sir." He shifted a bit closer to Eldan and pulled the blanket back up to his shoulders. "I'm sorry it's been such a crazy ride."

"What do you mean?" Eldan looked up with half-lidded eyes. Now that he was warming up, it was hard to stay awake.

"Kinda forced you into this whole Christmas thing."

Mason rolled to face Eldan, and his hand came up to cradle his cheek. "I should've been gentler with you."

"Do you always intentionally make things sound dirty?" Eldan whispered through gritted teeth.

"Why do you always take it dirty?"

"I–" Eldan faltered. Mason's low voice wasn't helping matters.

"Dirty boy," Mason purred as he wrapped his arms around Eldan. "Is this okay?"

Nope, nope, nope. Not okay. Eldan shivered. He was screaming on the inside, really, but he hoped his face said otherwise.

Mason relaxed his grip a bit. "Still cold?"

"Not as much…"

Eldan bit his lip as Mason ran a hand through his hair and his fingers trailed along the outer edge of his ear. In a moment of bravery, Eldan huddled closer.

"How about now?" Mason whispered.

"A little better." Eldan tilted his head back and bit back a yawn. "Sure you don't mind?"

"I don't mind at all. Not one bit." Mason rested his forehead against Eldan's and closed his eyes. "If you want, I can–"

Mason's voice faded out as Eldan focused on his lips. Even in the dim light, Eldan could see that the alpha was giving him that stupid, caring smile. Him and his stupidly perfect lips.

"Ah, fuck it," Eldan whispered.

"Wha–?"

Mason's eyes shot open just as Eldan surged forward and closed what little space there had been between their lips. He felt Mason jerk in surprise, but after a moment, the alpha relaxed and threaded his fingers through Eldan's hair.

Eldan arched his back as Mason ran his hand down the curve of his spine, pulling Eldan closer to him. Mason's lips were rough and chapped, but there was a hint of vanilla, spice, and *alpha* that kept Eldan coming back for more.

As Mason moved against him, Eldan couldn't help noticing how heartbreakingly tender he was. Almost like the alpha was just as nervous as he was. Despite that, his movements were gentle and subdued, his kisses soothing in a way words could never be.

And when they finally parted, Eldan curled forward and tried to calm his heart. Honestly, he couldn't believe he just did that, and he'd do it again if he thought he could pull back a second time.

"That's one way to warm up," Mason purred. "Let me know if you need another."

Eldan burrowed into the blankets and took a deep breath, taking in Mason's scent. "I don't think I'd be able to stop a second time."

"I feel that on a spiritual level." Mason chuckled as he curled his arms around Eldan. "Guess we should get some sleep, though. It's almost–" He looked at his phone. "Oh…"

"What's up?" Eldan whispered.

"Past midnight already." Mason sighed. "Merry Christmas, Eldan."

"Merry Christmas, Mason."

"Hey, Eldan? Time to get up, Sugar Lips."

Eldan buried his face in the soft embrace of his pillow and groaned as someone ran their hand through his hair. Sounded a lot like Mason, but he was too tired and too warm to listen closely.

"C'mon now. We talked about this. We gotta get ready."

"Just a few more minutes," Eldan mumbled into the pillow.

"You gonna make me break out the big guns?"

Eldan didn't respond. He would take his chances. Besides, five more minutes sounded heavenly. What could this guy possibly do?

Eldan felt a hand pull his shoulder and roll him back against a hard body before someone planted kisses across his shoulders. When he only opened his eyes halfway, the hand running through his hair gently pulled his head back, and the wet kisses traveled up the back of his neck and over his jaw until–

"You asked for it."

Eldan's eyes shot open, and he whimpered through gritted teeth as something warm and wet trailed along the edge of his ear, followed by the graze of sharp teeth. He jerked his shoulders up to try to cover his ears, but a hand held him in place as someone planted kisses on his exposed shoulder.

"Easy, there," Mason's low voice purred behind him. "You awake now?"

"Yeah, but did you have to do *that?*" Eldan shivered and rolled over to face Mason.

"Hey, I gave you plenty of warning. Mason placed his forehead against Eldan's and smirked. "Besides, those little noises you made were really cute."

"I'll show you cute," Eldan sneered before he saw Mason's expression and tensed. "Wait, no. Pause. Time-out." He had to get his mind out of the gutter. They had a job to do, damn it. "So, it's already that time?"

"Yeah, just a little past four." Mason sat up. "The little ones are still asleep, thankfully."

Eldan propped himself up on his elbow and yawned. "Guess you guys really wore them out yesterday."

"You look pretty worn out, too." Mason pointed out. "I wish I could let you sleep a bit more, but Bill is already set up and ready to go."

"Bill?"

"Yeah." Mason motioned to an old man who was already up and about messing with the blinds on the store windows. "The old man over there. That's Bill and his wife, Betty. He's closing the blinds so we can work in peace."

"Mighty thoughtful of him," Eldan mumbled and rubbed his eyes.

"Yeah, he's a pretty swell guy. Gave me some good advice." Mason stood. "Anyway, ready to roll?"

Eldan shivered and bundled up in Mason's absence. "That elf suit better be warmer than I remember."

ELDAN CONCLUDED HELL WASN'T ALL FIRE AND BRIMSTONE. No, Hell was icy and bitterly cold, and Hell was here in Boston.

Eldan shivered as he pulled on his gloves and shoes. The fabric was lacking any sort of cold protection, and he was pretty sure the jingle bells on the tips of his shoes were frigid enough to kill on contact.

"You about ready in there?"

"Almost." Eldan eyed the fake elf ears in his hands. "Only making a life-changing decision in here."

"It's the elf ears, isn't it?"

"Yeah."

"You don't have to wear them if they bug you, you know. You're already doing a lot for this plan."

"That's the thing…" Eldan sighed. "I want to."

"You *want* to?" There was a stretch of stunned silence. "Who are you, and what did you do with my grumpy boy?"

"Just come in and help me, you old fogey." Eldan stuck his head out between the dressing room curtains and made a face, but he didn't get much else done before Mason pushed him back and followed him into the booth. Within a moment, Eldan was against the dressing room wall, and Mason was cupping his face and covering him in kisses.

"Oh, that mouth of yours," Mason said between kisses. "It'll get you into trouble one day." He tried to slip on the elf ears as Eldan whimpered against his lips. "Though trouble seems to fit you well, especially with those cute little whimpers."

Eldan arched his back as Mason kissed his neck. "We've gotta…" he groaned as Mason crowded him further against the wall. "Stick to the plan."

"True." Mason sighed. "I'll let you go on one condition."

"What's that?"

"One more kiss."

Eldan dragged Mason's face down one last time and caught his lips with his own. It was torture parting, especially with the heat building in his stomach, but they had a Christmas miracle to fulfill.

Mason licked his lips and smiled. "Perfect." He messed with the elf ears one last time before stepping back and nodding. "Now, let's give these kids a Christmas to remember."

"Okay, places, everyone!" Sally whispered and waved her arm as she closed the thrift store door behind her. "They're awake now, and they're raring to go!"

Eldan put the last package down and positioned it *juuust* right before he headed over to Mason.

"Okay, do you remember the escape plan?" Mason asked.

"A quick sprint to the southern exit, up the western corridor, and then back to the clothing store, yeah?" Eldan went over the plan in his head.

"Yep." Mason threw a thumbs up at Bill, and the old man disappeared into the thrift store. "Get ready." Mason slung the sack full of empty boxes over his shoulder and took a deep breath. "Soon as those blinds are up–"

Mason didn't have a chance to finish before the blinds rolled up, and the face of every kid there greeted them in the window.

"Go!" Eldan whispered through his teeth.

"Is that Santa?" Benjamin's voice carried down the corridors. "And an elf?"

"They found us here!" Molly giggled. "They found us!"

Eldan grinned as he and Mason took off around the corner. They had to put some distance between them and the kids before they could slow down a bit but sneaking away was rather tricky when every step made his shoes jingle.

"I don't think I'm stealthy enough for an escape!" Eldan looked behind them but didn't see any of the kids following yet.

"Here, hop on!" Mason crouched and motioned to his back. Eldan looked to the side and saw that Mason had slung his bag of empty boxes in a nearby bathroom.

"What?"

"No time to explain, just get on!"

A piggyback ride with Santa? What would the kids say if they saw him now? Eldan sighed and quickly hopped on Mason's back, and they took off for the clothing store.

When they finally got back to the safety of their booth, Mason collapsed on the small bench.

"Shit! Hope they don't find your bag in there." Eldan sank down on the bench next to Mason and leaned back against the wall.

"They won't." Mason's breath came out in ragged pants. "They'll be too busy opening their gifts to wander around much." He stood and started pulling off bits and pieces of his Santa suit.

And, with each passing moment, Eldan found he couldn't take his eyes off the alpha. My, how life had changed. There he was, clad in a tight-ass elf suit, sitting in a cramped dressing booth, watching a sexy Santa strip. What a time to be alive.

"My, what a sinful look." Mason chuckled as he hung the large red coat on a hook, leaving him in a tight white tank top and fluffy red pants. "Tell me, what's it for?"

"You're the one who decided to start stripping in front of me." Eldan crossed his legs and threw a daring look Mason's way. "What, you want me to join you, ol' codger?"

"I wouldn't mind." Mason smirked. "But remember when I said your mouth was gonna get you in trouble?" Mason drawled.

"Yeah?" Eldan stood to challenge him.

Mason cocked his head and licked his lips as he stepped forward. "I should also warn you to be careful with what you do with those eyes, too."

Eldan's back hit the wall, but he couldn't bring himself to stop now. Two could play at this game.

"Okay, so choose your poison."

Mason froze. "Hm?"

"Blindfold or gag?" Eldan smirked. "If you're so worried about me getting into trouble, might as well cut those chances in half, right? And you can only choose one."

A low purr rumbled in Mason's throat as he caged Eldan in with his arms and started pulling at the cheap fabric of the elf suit.

"How about…" Mason moved forward and hoisted Eldan up so his legs wrapped around Mason's waist. "Neither?"

Mason pulled Eldan's hat and shoulder drape off and let them fall to the floor before he pushed back Eldan's bangs.

"What if I want to see those beautiful eyes lost in bliss?"

Eldan let out a small whimper as Mason pressed him harder against the wall.

"And then there are those delicious whimpers and keens that tumble from those sexy, kiss-swollen lips of yours."

Mason smiled against Eldan's lips before capturing them again. "Whatever would I do without those?"

Eldan gasped as he shimmied out of the snug elf top, bells jingling as it hit the floor. "And what if my eyes and mouth cause more trouble?"

"I don't mind trouble, as long as you only get into this kind of trouble with me." Mason huffed as he rocked gently against Eldan. "And, from the looks of things, it seems like you don't mind getting into trouble with me, either."

Eldan draped his arms around Mason's shoulders and took a deep breath. "This is just the sort of trouble we don't need to be getting into." He planted light kisses across Mason's jaw. "Not here, anyway."

"Shit." Mason seemed to realize just where they were. "You're right. I'm sorry." He purred against Eldan's neck before he lowered the omega to the ground. "Had to be a public space where we got trapped, right?"

"Of course." Eldan sighed as he quickly changed into his regular clothes.

"But mark my words…" Mason folded up the costumes and put them on the bench. "When we're out of here, we'll get into lots of trouble if you so choose."

"A world of trouble?"

"Absolutely."

Color bloomed across Eldan's cheeks as he locked gazes with the alpha, but a small clatter in the store zapped their silent connection in a heartbeat.

"Hello?" A little girl's voice came from the front of the store. Eldan hastily stuck his head out between the curtains, and Mason quickly started pulling on the rest of his clothes.

"Oh, there you are!" The little girl smiled when she saw Eldan. "Is Mister Mason with you?" Her eyes glimmered as she tried to peek around Eldan.

Mason grunted one last time as he zipped his jeans, and

he pulled back the curtain. "Well, hey! What're you doing here? Shouldn't you be opening your gifts?"

"We were waiting for you." The girl cocked her head and took a closer look at Eldan. "Are you feeling okay? You're kinda red."

"Fine!" Eldan said way too quickly. "Everything's fine. We're coming."

Mason snickered as he stepped from the dressing booth and crouched in front of the girl. "It was sweet of you all to wait for us. Tell me, what's your name?"

"Elizabeth." She rocked back and forth on her heels. "Cheryl's my grandmama. She said you guys would be with us soon, but when you didn't show up, I came to find you."

"Well, thanks for coming to get us, Elizabeth." Mason gave her his best smile, and she lit up. "What say we head back now? I'm sure everyone is ready to get started."

Elizabeth nodded and took Mason's hand before she gazed up at Eldan and held out her hand to him.

Eldan hesitated for a moment before he sighed and took her small hand in his.

"Your ears!" She pointed out as they left the clothing store.

Shit. Eldan's free hand shot up to his ears. Well, the plan had just completely shattered, all because he forgot to take off those damn ears.

"I like them!" Elizabeth grinned up at him. "Why didn't you show them off before?"

Eldan shrugged and bit his lip. Apparently, he didn't know how to talk to kids when they weren't drawing him bunnies. Or maybe he was still flustered after his moment with super sexy Santa in the dressing booth.

Either way, he was glad when Mason came to his rescue.

"He's one of Santa's most trusted helpers!" Mason grinned. "Because even Santa needs some help. He can let his ears show now that it's Christmas Day!"

"That's so cool! What all do you do?" she asked Eldan.

"I, uh…" Eldan swallowed. "I keep an eye on things for him. I map out the fastest delivery routes, help him keep track of his list, that sort of thing."

"And he also tells Santa who's been nice and who's been naughty," Mason said. He eyed Eldan before returning his gaze to the corridors.

"Right." Eldan nodded and averted his gaze.

They were almost back to the group, and Elizabeth toddled along, holding their hands as she walked. When she suddenly stopped, Eldan and Mason looked down at her.

She looked up at Mason. "Don't worry. I'll keep your secret."

"What secret?" Mason quirked an eyebrow.

"It's okay, Santa." She smiled. "I won't tell anyone about your secret identity."

That did it. As Elizabeth headed back to the group, Eldan stood frozen in his tracks.

"Eldan?" Mason went over and looked him up and down. "Hellooo? Did you just discover the meaning of life?" He gripped Eldan's arms. "Talk to me. I need details!"

For the first time in a long time, Eldan felt a heat in his chest that wasn't caused simply by his omega nature. No, it was a feeling he couldn't quite describe.

When he finally raised his gaze from the floor and saw the kids and everyone else looking at him and Mason, a flash of red and green on a nearby TV caught his attention. The Grinch was surrounded by Whos in the town center, just as the Christmas lights in the entire town of Whoville lit up once again.

Then, it hit him.

"What was that quote?" Eldan whispered.

"What quote?" Mason followed his gaze to the TV and inhaled sharply. "Wait, you don't mean–?"

Eldan smiled. "And the Grinch's small heart grew three sizes that day."

Mason's grip on Eldan's arms relaxed, and a huge grin broke out on his face. "And then, the true meaning of Christmas came through, and the Grinch found the strength of ten Grinches!" Mason stooped and hooked his arm under Eldan's knee and hoisted him from the ground. "Plus two!"

Everyone in the group looked up as Eldan yelped, and hoots and hollers echoed through the long corridors. Mason pressed several quick kisses against Eldan's cheek.

"I thought you two hated each other?" Tyler yelled.

Bill chortled and slapped his knee with glee. "Son, let me tell you, fate plays some strange hands, sometimes."

"Fate is what chooses your mates, right?" Nathan asked as Mason carried Eldan over.

Eldan choked a bit. This was definitely how he died—he would die right here and right now and come back as an angry spirit, cursed to haunt the middle of Silverstone Mall.

"One mate, boy." Bill held up one finger. "Only one person is your Fated."

"Ohhh." Nathan jerked his head back to Mason and Eldan. "Are you Fated? Is that why you don't hate each other now?"

Mason wrapped his arm around Eldan's waist and held him close. "Yep! We just found out yesterday!" He grinned. "Ain't that right, Sugar Lips?"

"Why that name?" Eldan mumbled.

"Because you taste like peppermint and chocolate! Do you have a better name?"

"And you said you two weren't friends." Rose giggled as she held Nikki close to her. "Sure seems like it to me."

"We're really not." Eldan grumbled as his cheek squished against Mason's chest. "I tolerate him."

"Tolerate, hm?" Mason hummed. "How soon we forget our recent adventures."

"Scratch that. I obviously despise him," Eldan grumbled as he sank into the fluffy collar of his sweater.

Giggles rang out around the group, and even Eldan cracked a smile. Behind the safety of his fluffy collar, of course.

Time passed too quickly after that. The kids were tickled pink with their gifts, and the sun was shining through the skylights over the tree. It was a moment Eldan surprisingly enjoyed, despite the fact that he really wanted a hot shower and a few moments with his little snuggle bunnies.

And my large snuggle bunny. Eldan melted against Mason's side, fatigue catching up to him. He had almost dozed off when the Christmas music playing on the loudspeakers overhead cut out with a click.

"Attention Silverstone Mall-goers. It's time to pack up your things and get ready to head home because, as of now, we are free!"

"Alright!" Some of the people stood and cheered, and the kids followed suit.

"We get to go home to Nomo!" Sammy ran over to Sally and jumped into her arms.

"Got that right, baby. Nomo's been missing us!" Sally pressed a quick kiss to his hair. "Now, let's get packed up. Go get your things."

Mason shook Eldan lightly and ran his hand through his hair. "You ready? I'm sure the employees are gonna wanna close up right quick."

"Yeah, just got a question for you." Eldan rubbed his eyes and stretched.

"What's up?"

"How do you feel about brisket?"

"I adore brisket." Mason licked his lips. "And just where is this brisket you're talking about?"

"Well, I have to introduce you to my family at some

point." Eldan smiled softly. "They'd find out about you eventually, especially with that big personality of yours."

"Oh, a trip to meet the family?" Mason's eyes glowed. "Will I be welcome without gifts?"

"Seeing how it's such short notice, I think they'll be okay." Eldan snorted. "If anything, we'll just say your presence is a gift."

"You speak so highly of me. I'm flattered." Mason put a hand over his chest and bowed slightly. "Now, let's pack up. The royal carriage awaits."

~

THE CHILL THAT CREPT BENEATH ELDAN'S CLOTHES WAS nothing compared to the fresh hell that waited for him at the end of the long walk through the parking lot.

Parked near the far edge of the lot sat a tacky yellow SUV covered in tinsel. On the front was a wreath with lights and holly berries and a red nose smack in the center. It even had large antlers sticking out from the doors.

"Oh, my God. *You're* the owner of this horrendous thing?" Eldan eyed the SUV with disdain. "I saw you drive by the shop a few days ago, you know."

"Really?" Mason's eyes lit up.

"Yeah, and I thought to myself, who the hell does that much?"

"Me!" Mason opened the trunk and placed some of Eldan's bags in the back. "I almost put lights on the outside, too, but they didn't want to work with me. So, they're back here now." Mason motioned at the faint, white Christmas lights lining the underside of the car's roof.

"Do you take critiques?" Eldan crossed his arms after he climbed into the passenger seat and buckled his seatbelt.

"Sure, shoot." Mason slammed his door shut, and the car roared to life.

105

"I feel like…" Eldan tapped his chin before he pointed to a nondescript area of the car. "That part is a bit much."

"Which part?"

"All of it.

"Ouch!" Mason let out a bellowing laugh. "Well, I suppose I'll have to ease you into this whole Christmas thing a bit slower."

"I'll let you ease me onto–" Eldan bit his lip. "Nope, forget I said anything."

"I would love to ease you onto, but last I heard, we have a delicious Christmas brisket waiting for us," Mason purred. "Only thing is, I need a destination."

"Marlborough. 1225 Bethlehem Street." Eldan turned up the heater. "And be sure to be on your best behavior around Ma!" He threw a sidelong glance at Mason.

"Who, me?" Mason returned his gaze. "Well, I'll sure try, Sugar Lips, but no promises if you keep giving me that look."

Eldan furrowed his eyebrows as Mason pulled out of the parking spot. It was going to be one hell of a holiday, that much was sure.

"Okay, so we've got Felicity. She's the momma of the household." Mason tapped his fingers on the steering wheel. "Grandmama, too, yes?"

"Right."

"And Holly is the eldest. She's married to Rudy, and their kids are Angelina and Christian if I remember correctly?"

"That would be correct." Eldan kept his gaze on the passing houses and stores. "Angelina is kinda shy, so it might take her a while to warm up to you."

"That's fine." Mason ran a hand through his hair. "Continuing on, Carol is the middle child? Single mom. Her kids are Muriel, Gabriel, and… Cole?"

"Yep." Eldan stretched his legs out as far as the seat would let him. "Hang a left here."

"Question." Mason's eyebrows furrowed.

Eldan gave him a sidelong glance. "What?"

"Is Cole the youngest?"

"Yeah, why?"

"It's just… Muriel and Gabriel are the names of angels. Why break the chain with the name Cole?"

"Shit." Eldan snorted. "Well, long story short, he *was*

gonna be named Raphael, but he kept his momma in labor for 34 hours. Now, he's her favorite little lump of coal."

"Oh, damn, son." Mason stopped at a red light and shook his head. "So, you're telling me Carol has a mean side, and I should watch out for her?"

"She's not the one you gotta worry about." Eldan tensed. "It's our dear Holly. She's the mastermind behind everything that happens in this family. Nothing happens without her knowing."

"Thanks for the heads up." Mason chuckled as he swung down a quiet backroad." God, I'm so nervous. Just think, a few days ago, we didn't even know each other! Now–"

"Hey, don't get all sappy on me just yet. Eyes forward. We're almost there." Eldan pointed down the street toward a small cul-de-sac. "I want you to take a wild guess at which one is Ma's house."

Mason slowed the car and leaned forward to look under the sun visor. While every house had some form of festivity in the front yard, it didn't take long to find the one that stood out the most. At the very back of the cul-de-sac sat a house that was so covered in Christmas lights, you could probably see it from space.

And if you somehow missed the blinding lights, all it took was a glimpse of the adorable inflatables to catch your attention.

Mason's mouth dropped open as he came to a stop in the driveway. "I think NASA would like to have a word with your mother. Should we give them a call?"

Eldan grimaced. "Depends on what kind of words."

"I'm thinking something along the lines of 'Holy shit, you're my hero.'" Mason squinted and leaned over Eldan to look out the passenger side window. "Does she even have a yard anymore?"

"Please." Eldan scoffed. "If we didn't let her completely

cover the outside, we wouldn't be able to move *inside*. She'd probably go crazy if there was even one empty spot outside."

"Another question."

"What?"

"Is that a Christmas narwhal?"

Eldan leaned forward and peered out the window. "Oh, Jesus, what the hell is *that?*"

Mason snorted. "Well, narwhals are closely related to dolphins, though they *are* classified as whales, and it goes without saying that you wouldn't want to run into one under the mistletoe. They're exceptionally horny, after all."

"You–" Eldan groaned into his hand. "I know what a narwhal is, but I'm more concerned about the army of pink death over there."

"What, you mean the twelve-foot Santa in a neon pink suit with rave sticks?"

"No, the giant flamingo statue covered in tinsel holding a margarita." Eldan pointed to another part of the yard. "The one surrounded by a small army of its brethren."

"Hey, leave them be. They're living their best life, okay?" Mason nudged Eldan's arm and smiled. "After all, it's five o'clock somewhere."

"What a horrifying world we live in," Eldan groaned as he pushed open the door and went around to the trunk. "Almost as horrifying as your car."

"Don't forget who wrapped all your gifts for you when we stopped to get gas for this so-called horrifying car." Mason held out his arms to help Eldan with the gifts.

"Unless the car is the one that wrapped everything, I don't have to be nice to it." Eldan loaded the last of the gifts into Mason's arms and slammed the trunk shut. "And if it did wrap everything, then you should take it to an exorcist."

"I ain't 'fraid of no gh–"

Mason stopped as a chill ran down his spine. He looked

up at the clear, blue sky and sighed. *Okay, mighty higher being. I'll stop.*

Mason couldn't help staring in awe at the decorations lining the path to the door. He felt a deep need to frolic through the field of candy canes, but he had a mission to complete.

When they reached the front door, Eldan stopped. "Hang on a moment."

"You okay, Sugar Lips?" Mason's arms started trembling under the weight of the gifts. "Did we forget something?"

"I just need to know that you're prepared for what lies beyond this door."

"So cryptic." Mason tilted his head to the side. "Lay it on me."

"How do you feel..." Eldan started, "About twerking bears?"

Mason jerked in surprise. "Twerking...bears? Well, I mean, if that's what you're into, I'm sure I can learn how to–"

"No!" Eldan's eyes flashed. "I meant–" The shock in his eyes slowly shifted to curiosity.

"That look tells me you're at least mildly interested." Mason waggled his eyebrows.

"Get your eyes checked, old codger." Eldan scowled as he reached for the doorknob. "Just prepare yourself for the people I call family."

"I'm ready."

No sooner had Eldan pushed open the door than he was greeted by a flying hug from three boys. They launched into Eldan's arms with such force, he almost stumbled back into Mason.

"Uncle Eldaaan!"

Eldan wheezed as he regained his footing. "Jeez, you guys got big! What have they been feeding you?"

"Is that my baby boy?" a woman's voice called from around the corner.

"Get ready," Eldan whispered over his shoulder just as a woman stepped into view, wiping her hands on a small towel.

"It is!" She gasped. "My sweet baby boy, how are you?" She pulled him down and peppered kisses across his cheeks.

"Fine, Ma." Eldan slumped and let it happen. "We finally made it."

"We?" She stopped kissing Eldan and looked over his shoulder. "Who is 'we'?"

Mason peered around the pile of gifts still in his arms. Contrary to her loud voice, she was a short little thing, about four-and-a-half feet on a good day, but she looked like she could handle anything that came her way, even a huge alpha.

"Greetings, Mrs. Noelle."

Mason contemplated waving, but as the pile of gifts swayed a bit, he threw that idea out the window. Was it possible to wave with your eyes? Maybe this wasn't the best time to try it, lest she think he was a bit kookie.

"Sorry, come on in, honey. You're carrying quite a load there!" She dragged Eldan and the kids from the doorway to give Mason room. "You didn't tell me you were bringing a friend!" She glared at Eldan before looking back at Mason.

"A lot's happened in the last few days, Ma." Eldan sighed as he set a few gifts down near the tree. "A whole lot."

Mason put the mountain of gifts down next to the tree and was greeted by two little girls peeping from behind it.

"Who are you?" one asked. "That's a lot of gifts!"

"I'm Mason." He flashed his best smile. "I'm friends with your uncle Eldan."

"I'm Muriel!" One little girl returned his smile. "And this is Angelina."

Angelina waved shyly and ducked behind the tree a bit. "Hi."

"That's Christian." Muriel pointed to the tallest of the

boys. "The one with a lot of bandages is Gabriel." She leaned forward and whispered. "He got into a fight with our cat."

"Oh, you don't mess with cats," Mason whispered back. "And I'm guessing the youngest there is Cole?"

"Yeah!" Muriel bobbed her head.

"Well, howdy-doo, Muriel and Angelina. It's sure nice to meet you!" Mason started spreading out the gifts under the tree. "Are ya'll excited to see what your Uncle Eldan got you?"

"Yeah!" Muriel came out from behind the tree. "He always finds the best things." She looked back at Angelina. "Right?"

Angelina nodded.

"Don't give Eldan's friend too much trouble, girls." a man's voice rumbled across the living room. "If he needs room to put everything, you'll need to get out from behind the tree."

"Okay, Daddy." Angelina's quiet voice drifted from behind the tree, and she kept her eyes on Mason.

Mason stood and saw a man sitting nearby in an armchair. "Rudy, I'm assuming?"

"That's me." The man nodded. "I'd stand to shake your hand, but…" He motioned to his leg. It was wrapped up in a tight cast, and scribbles covered it.

"Not a problem, man." Mason walked over and shook Rudy's hand. "Mason Shepard."

"Rudolph Engel. Everyone calls me Rudy, though." Rudy chuckled. "Don't mind my little Angelina. She's a bit shy around strangers."

Mason turned and saw that Angelina and Muriel were looking at the gifts Mason had put down. Angelina stepped back and hid behind Muriel as Mason smiled at her. Perhaps it was time to pass the ball to her part of the field.

Mason dramatically swept his eyes around the room. "Now, maybe ya'll can tell me… What's all this talk I hear about a twerking bear?"

"Oh, it's over here!" Muriel took Mason's hand and dragged him over to a small table. "C'mon, Angelina!"

Angelina's eyes lit up, and she came out from behind the tree and took Muriel's free hand.

"I wanna show him!" one of the little boys yelled as he took off toward the table. "Let me do it!"

"Christian." Rudy perked up. "Inside voice, please."

"Yes, sir." Christian deflated a bit but still hurried to beat the girls to the bear toy.

Out of the corner of his eye, Mason saw Eldan murmuring with Felicity and his sisters. While the twerking bear did its thing, he kept an ear tuned to his partner.

"I thought you weren't worried about me?" Eldan huffed.

"Are you daft?" Felicity messed with his hair. "I always worry about my babies, especially my babiest-baby."

Eldan playfully swatted her hands and fixed his hair. "So, was I hallucinating when you called me at the mall?"

"What do you mean?"

"I told you I was being held hostage by the Whos, and what did you say?" Eldan's nose scrunched up. "If you can't beat them—"

"Join them!"

Mason jumped as Christian, Gabriel, and Cole suddenly shouted right next to him. *God, I hope no one saw that.*

Felicity gasped and hid a smile behind her hand. "And it worked, didn't it?"

Eldan froze. "What?"

You didn't even glare at the tree when you came in. Not even a little bit! Don't try to hide it. I know when you're lying." Felicity held up a finger.

A woman with wavy blonde hair chimed in. "And you didn't cringe when the twerking bear started doing its thing!" She looked over and saw the kids still playing with the toy before cringing herself. "And that takes true inner peace."

"Alright, Master Oogway." Eldan scowled. "Just let me know when Carol gets back in the office."

Felicity cleared her throat. "But the biggest reason I knew it worked?" She leaned closer to Eldan. "Because his scent is *all* over you."

"Ma!" Eldan flushed deep red, and his sisters giggled and twittered excitedly.

"Don't 'Ma' me." Felicity gripped her hips firmly. "Who is this mysterious man you brought home for Christmas, and why have I not heard a single thing about him? Spill it!"

"Um…" Eldan bit his lip. "Where do I even begin?"

"Start with how you two met!" Carol pulled Eldan to the couch and sat beside him. "Was it–"

"No, wait!" a shorter woman with curly black hair interrupted her as she took her spot on the other side of Eldan. "You guys probably met at Hot Shots, right? You don't go anywhere else this time of year. Tell us about how you two became a thing!"

"Holly, wait your turn!" Carol fumed. "Maybe they didn't meet at Hot Shots?"

"We didn't," Eldan mumbled. "We ran into each other on the sidewalk when I was heading home."

"Oh, a chance meeting? My favorite!" Holly's eyes sparkled. "Was there mistletoe hanging from the shop doors? Was he singing Christmas carols on the corner?"

"No, we literally ran into each other on the sidewalk." Eldan deadpanned. "I spilled my coffee on his amazing alpha body and then I noped the heck out of there."

Mason's skin burned. "Amazing alpha body? Well, ain't that just the butter on my biscuit?"

"Oy, put the butter down for a moment, Romeo." Felicity's eyes narrowed. "There ain't gonna be no buttering the biscuits until you answer a few questions."

Eldan's eyes widened, and he reached out toward Felicity,

but his sisters held him back on the couch as she strode across the living room.

Whatever heat was under Mason's skin vanished as Felicity got closer. A sense of impending doom seemed to follow the protective woman across the room—you'd have to be a fool to miss it.

"Take a seat, *please*." Felicity motioned to a low armchair.

And it was almost too low. Mason had to carefully lower himself into it, so he didn't tip the chair back with his weight. When he finally got settled, he realized exactly why the woman chose this chair. It was so low, she could easily stand over him.

She was in control now.

Felicity leaned close and circled the chair, seemingly studying his reaction. "So, you like my boy, huh?"

"Yes, ma'am." Mason looked straight forward with a stern expression on his face. "Very much. He's very special to me."

Mason quickly glanced at Eldan and saw that he was watching intently. A grin played at the corners of Mason's lips, but he dropped it as Felicity came around the front of the chair again.

"Tell me about yourself."

"Well, I'm a history professor down in Texas." Mason stared forward, focusing on the wall above Eldan. "Laguna Valley University."

"Mhmm." Her eyes bored into Mason. "What else?"

"I enjoy movies, reading, fishing, and..." Mason paused, thinking back to one of the most beautiful scenes he remembered. "Scenic overlooks."

Felicity arched her eyebrow in confusion but shook it off. "He's my baby, you know? He's so sweet, innocent..."

She gripped the chair around Mason and leaned down level with his face. He didn't make eye contact with her. No, he was waiting for the perfect moment.

Felicity tightened her grip on the chair, and her voice

dropped to a low rumble. "How do I know you'll treat him right?"

This was it. The time was now. Mason let the bright smile he'd been holding back bloom on his face, and he raised his gaze to meet hers.

"Because he's my Fated."

All at once, the living room exploded into a bluster of high-pitched screams and laughter. Felicity, on the other hand, stood completely still, her eyes wide and her mouth slightly open.

Carol tugged on Eldan's arm. "Eldan, are you for real? Is he serious?"

Eldan nodded, and Carol hugged her little brother tightly.

"You little twerp! How long were you gonna wait to tell us?" Holly's expression tightened. "You were just gonna sit there and not tell us that your Fated was sitting right across the room from us?"

As Holly and Carol continued harassing Eldan, Mason turned his attention back to Felicity.

"My baby boy found his Fated mate?" Felicity fanned herself as she took a step back, and tears welled up in her eyes. "Oh, my…"

"Mrs. Noelle?" Mason quickly rose, put a hand on her trembling shoulder, and eased her into the chair. "Are you okay?"

"Oh, I'm just peachy." She grabbed a tissue from a small table next to her chair and dabbed her eyes. "What's your name?"

"Mason Shepard."

"Well, Mason Shepard." Felicity said. "I know my boy, and I know just how hard he can be to deal with sometimes."

"Ma!" Eldan jerked his head toward her. "I am not!"

"So, on behalf of the Noelle family, well done, Mr. Shepard." Felicity gave a small salute. "You're hired."

"Looks like I officially have permission to court you, my

little elf." Mason threw a sly grin to Eldan as he made his way back over to the couch.

"Not like you needed her permission, anyway," Eldan huffed and crossed his arms.

"What, you mean like when I–?"

Eldan flinched and held up his hand. "Stop *right* there."

"Whatever you say." Mason licked his lips. "Sugar Lips."

"You–" Eldan started to stand but was pulled back onto the couch by his sisters. "I should've left you in the car."

"This is why I always say fate has a sense of humor," Felicity twittered from her chair before she pushed herself to her feet and headed toward the kids. She ran her hand through Angelina's long, dark hair. "Food's almost ready, kiddos. Go get washed up."

Mason watched the kids run off before turning back to the couch just in time to see Holly and Carol grin. Holly waved him over, throwing a wink back at Carol.

"Hey, Mason? Come on over here for a moment. We have some questions for you, too."

"Uh, oh." Mason reeled back. "Another interrogation?"

"That wasn't an interrogation. It was an interview!" Felicity pouted. "I don't interrogate when the grandbabies are here."

"Say that again?" Rudy snorted from across the living room. "I must've misheard that entire interaction.."

"Hurry up, and come sit down, Mason!" Carol hugged Eldan's arm a bit tighter. "We don't have much time to waste."

"Okay, okay." Mason sat on the couch arm. "Ask away."

"Now wait a moment." Holly frowned. "That won't do." She pointed to where Mason was sitting. "Join us on the couch."

Carol grinned. "But there's no room! What a shame."

"I know." Holly hummed. "You know what that means, right?"

"That one of you will transfer to the armchair?" Eldan's voice rose an octave, a clear edge of terror in his tone.

"Hang on tight, baby brother."

Holly cackled as she and Carol grabbed his arms tightly and lifted him from the couch with ease.

"Mason, have a seat!"

Felicity came over and lightly pushed Mason onto the couch on her way to the kitchen, and the sisters carefully plopped Eldan down on Mason's lap. Eldan didn't have a chance to move before Mason's arms snaked around his waist and held him in place.

"Why do I always end up in situations like this?" Eldan grumbled as Holly and Carol took their spots on either side of Mason.

Carol jabbed her finger at Eldan. "Because you're our baby brother, and Mason is the first person you've brought home. Ever!"

"Yeah, as the glorious older sisters, it's our job to give you hell over stuff like this." Holly snickered. "So, tell us everything! Mom told us you got trapped in the mall last night with that snowstorm!"

"What sort of trouble did you two get into?" Carol waited with bated breath before she glanced at Mason. "Mom *did* say your scent was all over him."

Eldan coughed and sputtered. "What the hell, Carol? You can't honestly expect me to tell you stuff like that." Red bloomed on his ears. "I never asked you or Holly when you brought people–"

"Toodles? Boogaloo?" Felicity called from the kitchen. "Can you come help me with something, please?"

"Sure thing, Mom!" Holly called out. "Don't think you're off the hook yet, you two. We'll be back." She pointed her fingers at her eyes, then back at the couple on the couch before she and Carol headed to the kitchen.

"Was it true what they said?" Mason hugged Eldan tighter. "That I'm the first you've brought to the house?"

Eldan turned away and huffed, but the way his body heated up against Mason's told the alpha everything he needed to know.

"The first, eh?" Mason sighed and rested his head on Eldan's shoulder. "Well, ain't that an honor?" He leaned close and blew softly on Eldan's ear, making him squirm a bit.

Eldan jerked away and swatted at Mason. "Stop. Cease. Begone!"

"You're telling him to begone when you're the one that could easily move off of him." Rudy watched with amusement across the living room. "Oh, but it's too late now."

Before Eldan could register what Rudy was talking about, the kids came bounding down the hallway before bouncing onto the free spots on the couch. Eldan grumbled and crossed his arms as he leaned back into Mason.

This truly was a wonderful world they lived in.

"You were trapped in the mall, Uncle Eldan?" Christian gaped. "How'd that happen?"

"Did you see Santa?" Gabriel looked up with concern. "Cole was worried the kids trapped in there with you didn't get gifts this year."

Eldan's mood immediately shifted into something softer as he reached out and messed up the youngest boy's shaggy, blond hair. "Don't worry, Cole. Santa found them. They got lots of gifts, right, Mason?" Eldan looked over his shoulder, a small smile playing on his lips.

"Oh, tons," Mason confirmed. "They were happy campers."

The kids bombarded Mason and Eldan with question after question, and Eldan answered them as quickly as he could until Angelina finally spoke up and asked a question.

"Have you two kissed yet?" Angelina brought a finger to

her lips. "Muriel was wondering, too. She was asking about it earlier."

"I was not!" Muriel flushed.

Eldan tensed and chuckled nervously. "That's, uh…classified."

Oh, I'm about to turn you into a flustered mess, baby boy.

Mason pulled Eldan's back flush to his chest. He let a low purr rumble in his throat as he pressed small kisses across the back of Eldan's neck. When the omega tensed, Mason knew he'd hit the target. Now came the fun part.

Just a little turn here, and a twist here, and–

Mason threaded his hand through Eldan's locks. With a gentle tug, the alpha turned Eldan's head to the side just enough to where he could kiss those beautiful lips again and again.

"Wow…" Muriel's eyes widened.

Holly and Carol popped out from the kitchen just in time to see the show.

"Oh, my God!" they squealed. "Look at ya'll!"

Mason smirked against Eldan's lips. It had taken a bit of maneuvering, but he had turned Eldan around so he would be open for such an attack. Now, Eldan's side rested against Mason's chest, and the omega's eyes darkened as Mason came back for more.

"Ewww!" Gabriel reeled back from the couple. "Why are adults so gross?" He whined.

Eldan broke off the kiss and clutched Mason's sweater before he whispered through gritted teeth, "I will kill you."

"Nah, you'd miss me too much," Mason retorted.

"What'd I miss?" Felicity came around the corner wiping her hands on her towel. "Did a balloon collapse at the parade again?"

"They kissed!" Cole pointed to Mason and Eldan. "You missed it, Gramma!"

"It was so romantic!" Muriel piped up.

Felicity eyed Mason for a second before she smiled. "Listen, I may have given you my blessing to court him, but keep the biscuit buttering to a minimum while you're here, okay?"

"Yes, ma'am." Mason snorted.

"Now, come on, everyone." Felicity waved to her gathered family. "Lunch is ready!"

~

MASON GROANED AS HE STOOD UP STRAIGHT AND POPPED HIS back. Okay, so maybe sitting at the kid's table hadn't been the best idea after all. Adorable, of course, but not the best idea. Yeah, he was definitely gonna feel it in the morning.

Sleeping off the giant meal he'd devoured sounded amazing, but he had promised to play with the kids after lunch. The only catch was that their mittens and hats were M.I.A., and now they had to split up to search for them.

"Cmon, c'mon!" Cole tugged on Mason's hand. "We gotta hurry up and find them before it gets too dark!"

"I know, kiddo." Mason grimaced as Cole pulled a bit too hard and dull pain shot through his back again. "Where was the last place you saw them?"

"I don't know. Gramma took them when we got in." Cole crinkled his nose. "We played outside a bit before we came in, and she said she wanted to dry them off."

"So, the laundry room," Mason mumbled. "Do you know where the laundry room is, Cole?"

"Oh, through the kitchen!" Cole tugged on Mason's arm harder until they reached the doorway.

Mason was about to cross into the kitchen when Cole abruptly pulled him back.

"Kiddo, if you keep doing that, I won't be able to throw snowballs anymore." Mason winced.

"Wait, Gramma is in there. And Uncle Eldan, too," Cole

whispered before he peeked around the corner. "They're doing dishes."

"Why are we waiting out here?"

Cole didn't respond, and Mason sighed before leaning up against the doorway, listening to the drone of running water and their voices.

"You look happy." Felicity hummed a little tune, and the dishes clinked. "Don't try to lie to me. I can tell you're smiling, even without looking at you."

"I'm doing the dishes. How could I possibly be happy?" Eldan huffed.

"No, I mean it," Felicity whispered. "I haven't seen that spark in your eyes for a long time, baby. He must really make you happy."

The dishes clinked against each other in the drying rack, and Eldan let out a long sigh. "I never thought…"

"After Mary?" Felicity's voice went softer. "I know, sweetie." The constant trickle of water came to a stop. "It's been six years, yeah?"

"Mhmm."

"You gonna visit her?" A cabinet door slammed shut. "Oh, what am I saying… Of course, you will. You're a good friend, baby."

A plastic bowl popped closed, and Mason ducked behind the corner as Felicity put a load of food in the fridge. "Does he know?"

"No, he doesn't."

"He should." Felicity shut the fridge doors and returned to the sink. "Especially since he's your–"

"Who's Mary?"

Dread prickled across Mason's skin as he looked back to where Cole was *supposed* to be. Which he wasn't. No, he was standing in the middle of the kitchen like he owned the place, right behind Eldan and Felicity.

"Who's Mary?" Cole asked again. "Is she a friend?"

"An old friend." Eldan turned away and started washing dishes again.

Felicity put her hands on her hips, and her eyes flared with anger. "And what were you doing eavesdropping? You know better than that."

"Mason and I were looking for our gloves and hats. We're all gonna play outside before it gets dark!"

"Were you now?" Felicity took a deep breath. "And is Mason with you?"

Nope. Nobody here but us bears. Mason pressed himself flat against the wall. *For all that is holy, don't you do it, Cole.*

"No?" Cole chuckled nervously. "I don't *think* he is?"

Felicity sighed. "I put all your stuff back in my room, Cookie. They're all nice and clean. Let's go get them."

Mason pressed himself harder against the wall as Felicity's small steps echoed on the hard kitchen floor. When she came into the living room, he jerked his head away from her in the least suspicious way possible.

And, to Mason's *total surprise*, it didn't convince her. Yeah, nobody had ever said he was a master of stealth. Felicity caught his gaze with a small noise, and she motioned to the kitchen with her head as she led Cole down the hallway.

Roger, Momma Noelle.

Mason puffed out his chest and headed into the kitchen. Water was trickling in the sink, and Eldan was washing the dishes in silence.

"How much did you hear?" Eldan muttered over the sound of the water.

"Enough." Mason wrapped his arms around Eldan's waist and planted a couple kisses on his neck. "Sorry, I didn't mean to overhear."

Eldan shut off the water and gripped the edge of the sink. "I'm gonna go visit her on my next day off."

"I want to go with you."

Eldan sighed. "It won't be a very fun visit."

"That's okay," Mason whispered against Eldan's skin. "Whatever happens, however it goes, I'll be there with you."

"Thank you," Eldan said over his shoulder as he leaned back into Mason. "Now, go have a bit of fun with the kids before we have to leave. It's about that time."

"I'll stay with you." Mason pressed a kiss to Eldan's hair. "Besides, looks like they went on without me." He gazed out the window over the sink and saw the kids building a snowman.

"Go on. I need some time to…" Eldan took in a pitiful, shuddering breath. "I'll be okay. Besides, I still need to pack up our leftovers and stuff."

Mason sighed as he unwound his arms from Eldan's waist.

Walking away was one of the hardest things Mason had done in a while. He had gotten so used to snarky comments and grumpy grumbles that seeing this side of the omega was strange. It was painful and heart-rending, a horrible feeling that burned in his chest the further he walked without *his* omega by his side.

My omega? Mason felt his chest swell with pride. *Mine.*

The word rattled around in his head as he crossed the threshold of the living room. It felt right. It felt *so* right. It also took every bit of grit to keep him from turning around and heading right back to that kitchen to love on *his* omega more.

"Mason."

Felicity's voice snapped Mason from his thoughts. She was leaning against the wall in the same place Mason had tried to hide.

"Sorry to drag you away from your inner sanctum, Romeo, but a word, please?"

Mason scratched the back of his head and let out a long sigh. "I apologize. It wasn't my intention to–"

Felicity held up her hand to silence him. "Don't apologize.

I'm glad it worked out this way." Her gaze wandered to the kitchen. "You know, I offer to go with him every year, just so someone is with him, but he always turns down my company."

"He ever say why?"

"He always says it's because he doesn't want me to drive that far for him, but I think it's a bit more complicated than that." Felicity sighed. "He was always a bit of a loner. Until she came into his life, anyway."

"Mary?" Mason asked. "Who was she?"

"A dear friend of his." Felicity lowered herself onto the couch. "He never really was the same after she–" She cleared her throat. "Well, maybe he should be the one to tell you. After all, he's really opened up to you in such a short amount of time. He didn't even try to deny your company…"

"Ah, so that's why you didn't want me to apologize for listening in."

"Guilty as charged." Felicity waved her hand dismissively. "Now go on. The kids are waiting for you."

2512 Evergreen Avenue. This is it.

Mason pulled to the side of the road and eyed the lit-up houses lining the street. Every house had something, but the one Eldan lived in was especially lit up. He looked up and down the street until his gaze crossed over the passenger seat and a perfect, sleepy, little omega.

One thing Mason learned on the way back to Boston was that Eldan slept like the dead when he finally conked out. No matter how many bumps he accidentally hit, or how many songs he played quietly on the radio, that man *slept*. Maybe it was because the heat was on.

Mason's nose twitched as he took a deep breath.

Or maybe it was because the *heat* was on.

Fuck, it was hard to keep a clear head with that scent floating around the car. Mason's stomach twisted in knots with every breath he took. His whole body ached for the pretty little omega next to him, as if the alpha inside wanted to reach out and touch his body, hear his breath, and feel his warmth.

And it was hell because he was so close, so very warm and soft, and the taste of his lips was enough to drive a person mad. Mason groaned. Could anyone really blame him for falling head over heels so quickly?

"You look constipated."

Mason flinched and jerked his head toward Eldan. "I thought you were out."

"Wrong." Eldan curled up in the seat as much as he could. "Been awake since we passed through West Newton."

"And you didn't tell me?" Mason let out an exasperated sigh. "How embarrassing. I was having a moment over here, and you did nothing?"

"I did do something." Eldan gave a blank stare. "I watched you have the moment, and I told you you looked constipated while having said moment."

"Whatever would I do without you?"

"… dress up anymore," Eldan mumbled before turning away.

Mason quirked an eyebrow. "Sorry, what was that? Why so mumbly-grumbly?"

Eldan crossed his arms and threw a look over his shoulder. "I said you would probably cry since you wouldn't have anyone to dress up anymore."

"So you *did* like that elf costume."

"No, it was way too tight in certain places. I absolutely hated it," Eldan grumbled under his breath before his expression softened. "I just hope my snuggle bunnies are okay. They're probably worried sick about me."

"Your snuggle bunnies?" Mason tapped his chin. "Mr. Hopson and Honey Bun, yes?"

"Yep. Giant fluffy babies." Eldan stared down at the floorboard as if he were quietly contemplating something.

"Now you look constipated." Mason snorted. "What's going on in that pretty little head of yours?"

"Would you like to meet them? My snuggle bunnies?"

"Is that a trick question?" Mason shut off the car. "Hell to the yeah."

As Mason started to get out of the car, he felt Eldan's hand on his arm. He turned and saw a peculiar sight. Even in the darkness of the car, dimly lit by the Christmas lights outside, he could see a deep flush spreading across Eldan's cheeks.

"Will you stay here?"

"In…" Mason tilted his head with a smirk. "In the car? Wouldn't that make it hard to meet the snuggle bunnies?"

"No, I mean with me," Eldan mumbled. "Tonight."

"Well, consider my biscuit buttered and served." Mason let out a low purr. "You do care."

Eldan jerked his arm back. "Listen, I don't know what biscuits you're seeing, but I only want your heater. It's too cold to even be alive tonight."

"My heater?" Mason smirked.

Eldan glared. "I just want you nearby. Is that too much to ask? Because if it is, I'll just employ Mr. Hopson to be my heating pad for the night."

"Never said I wouldn't be your heating pad. In fact, I'd love to. Gives me a chance to show off my new duds." Mason smiled and reached into the back seat.

"Why are you groping around back there?"

Mason held up a bag. "Got some jammies at the mall before we got snowed in."

"Jammies from the mall?" Eldan furrowed his eyebrows.

"Why didn't you wear them when we were in the thrift store?"

"I *may* have had to make multiple trips to my car to drop off all the stuff I got. And it *may* have started snowing too hard after my fourth trip out. So, they spent the night out here in the car."

"Who the hell makes multiple trips to the car to carry their goods out?" Eldan reeled. "How much crud did you get?"

"Not enough, my little elf." Mason chuckled. "Not enough."

CHAPTER 8: DECEMBER 26TH

The night passed far too quickly for Mason's liking. He could've easily stayed up all night watching over his Fated. Lord knows he'd tried to stay awake as long as possible, but simply laying next to his perfect, trusting omega was enough to send him off into a peaceful slumber.

Now, blinding light pulled Mason from his dreams. As he cracked open his eyes, he saw light streaming in through the sheer white lace curtains covering the window. He would never understand the point of see-through curtains, but they gave the room an ethereal feel that screamed 'Eldan'.

As Mason slowly started to wake up, he noticed a heavy warmth resting against his back under the quilts. He turned over and wrapped his arms around the sizable mass. And, to his credit, he only flinched a little bit when he felt fur instead of skin. In fact, it was the fluffiest fur he'd ever touched.

Mason blinked the sleep from his eyes and pulled back the bulky blankets. From the darkness of the quilts, a twitching gray and white bunny nose greeted him. He stared at the beast for a long moment before he sighed and ran his fingers through the rabbit's fur.

"I've read about stuff like this." Mason's fatigue-laced

voice rumbled in his throat before he let out a huge yawn in the rabbit's face. "I should've known you were a rabbit shifter. What else have you been keeping from me, my cute little *Lapin?*"

The fluffy rabbit stirred against Mason's side, burrowing backward under the quilts.

"It is kinda chilly in here, isn't it?" Mason pulled the covers back up to his chest, just enough to cover the rabbit. "That's okay. I'll make sure you're–"

Mason jerked up from the bed when a loud crash came from the corner of the room. His heart pounded as he quickly looked over the area, his gaze zeroing in on a fuzzy blob on Eldan's dresser. Who dared to desecrate the sanctity of Eldan's room?

"*Honey Bun.*" Mason's eyes narrowed.

The little Lop squeaked and darted off the dresser as Mason flopped back into the soft pillows. Now that he wasn't completely dead, he realized the rabbit sleeping by his side was Mr. Hopson, not his pretty little elf.

A large part of Mason was disappointed that the cute, fluffy rabbit huddled up against him wasn't Eldan in a shifted form, but he managed to drag himself out of that infamous rabbit hole before he fell any deeper.

Mason groaned as he pulled back the covers and pushed himself to his feet. He really should let Eldan know that having the kennel right next to his dresser gave Honey Bun an all-too-convenient stepping stool straight up to the dresser. No bunny should have such easy access to ruin and destruction. Dodging the darting Honey Bun, Mason stooped to pick up the scattered items littering the floor.

This room absolutely screamed Eldan. Everywhere Mason looked, he saw bunny this and bunny that, a bunny bank, and bunny bookends. If you ever wanted to see the way bunnies were depicted throughout history, Eldan's room was the place to go.

Mason paused as his hand hovered over a small bottle. He grabbed it and turned it over in his hand—a half-used bottle of scent blockers.

That's right. He was in heat when we were trapped. Probably still is...

Mason braced his hand on the edge of the dresser and stared down at the bottle. He had heard that if Fated mates meet and don't act on their bond fast enough, their bodies would essentially give in. It was commonly referred to as an intense heat, or an intense rut, in the alpha's case.

But would he go into an intense heat even though he was already in heat when we met?

Mason chewed on his lip as an image of a totally blissed-out Eldan flashed in his mind, his pale skin covered in sweat and bite marks. His hair would be a mess, tousled to perfection as he reached his limit. A tingle ran down Mason's spine.

What a sight that would be—

A clatter forced Mason from his not-so-innocent thoughts. Honey Bun darted across the dresser again, startling Mason enough to make the alpha knock against the mirror. As he hurried to steady it, a picture hanging in the corner fluttered down to the top of the dresser and landed next to a note with his name on it.

Mason slid the letter to the side for a moment and picked up the old picture, careful to not get his fingerprints all over the glossy image. He squinted at the dated scene of what appeared to be the end of a class of some sort. An old banner in the background had the words Sycamore View High School painted across it.

There's Eldan...

Mason smirked as he saw his young mate dressed up in a fluffy coat that was about two sizes too big for him. He sat next to a few old-timers, each holding a knitted blanket or clothing. Eldan sat at the front of the group holding his masterpiece, a knit bunny.

Mason's eyes drifted to the same rabbit sitting on the bookshelf to his right before he flipped the picture over and spotted a faded number in the corner.

"Two thousand and one," Mason muttered to himself. "Lord have mercy, does that make me feel old." He sighed as he replaced the picture.

A loud thump echoed from the door as Honey Bun darted into it at high speed. After a moment of recovery, he pawed at the door.

"Alright, alright. I get it, Honey Bun. Give me a moment." Mason twisted around, scanning the room. "Now, where are my clothes, Mr. Hopson?

Mr. Hopson squeaked under the warm quilts, his snuffling and shuffling muffled by the comfy bedspread.

"That's okay. You do you, Mr. Hopson." Mason stretched. "I'm sure I'll find them eventually."

Mason, in fact, did not find them eventually. Despite searching every corner of the room, he couldn't find even a thread of his old sweater and jeans. Not even a lonely sock.

Where the hell did they get off to?

Mason grumbled to himself as he searched. He cracked open the door to the hallway, ready to search the bathroom across the way, but it wasn't long before he felt goosebumps prickle across his skin.

Papers crinkled from somewhere in the room, and something told him Honey Bun was getting into trouble again. Call him crazy, but he felt he had developed a sense for this kind of thing in his short time with the little Lop.

Sure enough, when Mason turned toward the noise, he saw the naughty Lop chewing on an envelope. The one with his name on it.

Oh, it was *on* now.

Mason assumed the position, ready to catch the little Lop.

If he failed to catch this fuzzy creature, he could never show his face at home again. His family would be forced to change their names, and he would be the laughingstock of–

The air turned thick and stale with animosity as the two exchanged glares. Then, in a moment of pure balderdash, Honey Bun darted between Mason's legs and pawed the cracked door open before the alpha could react.

"Shit." Mason's shoulders sagged. "There goes my honor."

He would have to settle for his jammies. There wasn't enough time to hunt for his regular clothes, especially not when the most important letter of his life was in the jaws of a malevolent lagomorph.

Mason poked his head out of Eldan's room. He didn't want to leave it, but his desire to read that letter gave him the strength to take the first step across the threshold. Honey Bun sat at the top of the stairs, seemingly waiting for him. Until he wasn't.

As the rabbit darted down the stairs, Mason bounded after him. He finally caught up to the Lop, who was in the living room sniffing a pile of opened gifts and bags near the Christmas tree.

Mason quickly snatched the now-abandoned letter from the rug behind Honey Bun and checked it for damage, which wasn't much except for spit and teeth marks, thankfully. His gaze wandered to the pile of gifts, and cold dread balled up in his stomach.

Wait, we didn't bring those–

"Your time is up, Demon! Begone from our house!"

Mason cringed as something hit him in the back of the head. He quickly swiveled around and saw two people in the kitchen staring at him in fright. The lady of the pair had a spatula pointed at him, and a small egg-timer rolled on the floor.

"Whoah, whoah, whoah!" Mason took a step back and held up his hands. "Hold up a moment! Time out!"

"Who are you, and what are you doing in our house?" The lady hissed at him. "Answer me before the eggs burn."

"My name is Mason Shepard!" Mason sputtered. "I'm with Eldan!"

The lady instantly lit up, and the thick haze vanished. "Oh, you're that guy Eldan was talking about! The one he spilled coffee on!"

Mason rubbed the back of his neck. "Yeah, that's me. Sorry to pop in unannounced and, uh…" He motioned down to his jammies. "Under-dressed."

"Don't worry about it, I love them." She grinned and turned back to her skillet to flip the eggs. "Are those lumberjack teddy bears?"

"On top of burgundy fleece? Hell yeah." Mason nodded. "Got 'em half-off, too."

"Ooooh, we love 'em thrifty." The lady giggled. "I'm Jenny, and this is my husband, Quentin." She motioned back to the man, who was setting an extra place at the table.

"You messed him all up, you know?" Quentin carried a few extra napkins over to the table. "Like, big time. He came home one day and was just destroyed."

Mason chewed on his lip as he took a place at the table. "The day of the parade, right? Trust me, I understand that feeling completely."

Quentin's eyes widened. "That's right! He said you were his Fated that day!"

"He what?" Jenny's mouth fell open. "He didn't tell me that!" She glanced at Mason before glaring at her husband. "You didn't tell me!"

"Well, sorry, I wasn't aware you were keeping such close track of Eldan's love life!" Quentin threw back.

Mason watched the couple bicker in amusement as Honey Bun hopped into the kitchen and sat underneath his chair.

Jenny huffed and loaded some eggs onto a plate before

cracking new ones into the hot skillet. "Anyway, we were ready to bust you. Nice of Eldan to let us know someone was staying here before he left for work."

"Seriously." Quentin pulled out his chair and took a seat. "He left for work a couple hours ago and then we heard stomping in his room and down the stairs. Downright terrifying."

"Quentin was totally convinced the house was haunted. I was about to go up and check for him because he wouldn't calm down." Jenny giggled. "I have to take care of my favorite weenie."

Quentin's head jerked up. "I thought I was your only weenie."

Jenny put plates down in front of everyone and took her place at the table. "Sorry, babe. I have a side weenie." She licked her lips and smiled. She pierced a piece of maple sausage with her fork and took a slow bite, never taking her eyes off Quentin.

"Does Eldan do this kind of stuff to you?" Quentin pointed at Jenny with his thumb.

"He'd kill me if I said too much." Mason flashed a coy smile. "With his eyes. Gently, of course."

"Oh, so he *does* show his sweet side to someone other than the rabbits?" Jenny flinched, then looked down and saw Honey Bun against her leg.

"I will not confirm nor deny." Mason took a quick bite of his eggs.

"I told you he had a heart!" Quentin laughed. "Anyway, yeah, he didn't tell us you were here. Damn near gave us a heart attack."

"Sorry, we didn't really plan on my staying over. It just sort of happened."

"Oooh, spontaneous nights with your chosen weenie are the best." Jenny grinned as she stabbed another piece of sausage. "So, tell us everything. Where did you guys have to hold up?"

"We were in Silverstone Mall with a bunch of families. We did a few sled races with the kids, a lot of crafts, and we managed a surprise visit from Santa and his favorite elf." Mason grinned.

"Wow, you guys lucked out." Jenny poked at her eggs with a sigh. "We got stuck in this awful boutique over on Greenfield Lane."

"Yeah, the owners weren't happy having campers in their store." Quentin furrowed his eyebrows. "They won't be around long with that kind of service."

"Do you remember that nice boy who fixed up my old wedding dress when it got snagged in the move? Eliseo, I think it was? I keep hoping he'll open a shop. It would be loads better than that hag on Greenfield."

"He has the talent for it, that's for sure." Quentin nodded. "Anyway, what else happened, Mason?"

"Oh, we went down to Marlborough. I met his family, got a picture of an invading army of flamingos, you know, the usual."

Jenny perked up. "I demand to see those pictures. You are excused to go get your phone, mister."

Mason pushed his chair back and bounded up the stairs with Honey Bun hot on his trail. When he got back into the room, he noticed Mr. Hopson was still under the covers, with his head on Mason's phone.

And it was buzzing. Mason's blood ran cold when he saw the picture on the screen. He dared not make any noise that would cause Mr. Hopson to move his head, lest he accidentally answer the call.

When the buzz stopped, Mason ran his fingers through Mr. Hopson's soft fur and gently pulled the phone out from under his head. He took a deep breath and scrolled through his call and message history.

He was dead. He was *so* dead.

Mason made his way back downstairs before he plopped down in an armchair in the living room.

"What's wrong?" Jenny called out from the kitchen. "Is your phone dead? I have an extra charger around here somewhere."

"No, it's very much alive, but I don't think I'll be when I make this call."

Quentin cleared the dirty dishes from the table and came into the living room. "What do you mean?"

"I currently have seventeen missed calls and twenty-three unread messages." Mason waved his phone weakly. "All from my Oppa."

"Oh, shit. Yep, you're dead." Quentin shrugged and wandered back into the kitchen. "We'll be sure to tell Eldan the bad news."

"Thanks. That's all I can ask." Mason hunched over on the couch and rubbed his neck with his free hand. This was gonna suck big time. He found his Oppa's name in his contacts and pressed the screen, then slowly lifted the phone to his ear.

When the ringing stopped, and all Mason heard was breathing, he swallowed the lump in his throat and forced a chuckle.

"Heyyy, Oppa. How are you?"

"You know damn well how I am, *Mason Malakai Shepard.*"

The sound of his full name coming from his Oppa's mouth still struck fear in his heart even to this day. Mason hesitated before he spoke up again.

"Uh oh, we're breaking out the Malakai now?"

"Don't you give me that lip," Oppa growled. "Do you have *any* idea, any idea at all, how worried we were?"

"Oppa, I–"

"Ah, ah!" Don't you say a word. I am beyond disappointed in you, letting us worry and worry. That storm rolled through Boston, and we had no idea if you were safe or not or–" Oppa's voice cracked, and he let out a choked sob.

"Oppa…" Mason whispered into the phone.

"Ah, ah. I'm not done yet." Oppa blew his nose and cleared his throat. "Would it've killed you to at least *call* on Christmas?"

Mason held his breath. The only sound in the entire world right now was his Oppa's ragged, pissed-off breathing on the other end of the phone. Where could he even begin to start explaining everything that had happened?

"Answer me, Plum."

"Sorry, I was afraid you were gonna give me the growl of total annihilation again." Mason swallowed. "Oppa, you're not gonna believe this…"

"Some reason is better than none. Try me." Oppa grunted. "I'll be the judge of whether or not it's a good reason."

Mason took a deep breath. *Now or never.*

"Well, when that storm rolled through, I ended up having to shelter-in-place at a shopping center. Silverstone Mall."

"Mhmm?"

"And I got a lot of stuff for you and Appa, and some nice new jammies for me." Mason turned on FaceTime and showed off his new jammies.

"Mhmm. Cute." Oppa leaned a bit closer to the phone. "But no matter how darling those jammies are, it doesn't excuse you from not calling us."

"I'm getting to that, Oppa." Mason sat back down in the chair. "Anyway, I met someone very important. A very special person. I daresay he's a gift to humanity."

Oppa pinched his chin for a moment before his eyes lit up. "Colin Mochrie?"

"Nah, but that would've been pretty awesome." Mason shook his head. "No, I met fate's gift to me."

Oppa's mouth fell open. "You're kidding. Are you serious?"

"Serious as a Southerner's sweet tea on football Sunday."

Mason braced himself as a scream came from the phone speakers. On the other hand, Jenny and Quentin were not as prepared, and things crashed to the floor in the kitchen.

"Who the hell?" Quentin rushed back into the living room. "Did you just accidentally watch a screamer?"

"Are you okay, baby?" On the phone screen, Appa rushed into the living room behind Oppa. "Did you get hold of Mason?"

"Our little Plum found love!" Oppa threw his arms around Appa's waist and let out a wail into his stomach. "He found himself a little Christmas elf!"

Appa settled onto the couch next to Oppa and passed a tissue to his mate. "Well, who's the lucky little lovely, and when do we get to meet them? Is that him behind you?" Appa looked toward Quentin.

"Oh, no, sir. Not me." Quentin held up his hands and backed away from the armchair. "Sorry."

Oppa tossed his tissue into a nearby trashcan. "So, where is he? Wait, is your Fated a she? When do we get to meet them?"

"My Fated is a he. His name is Eldan. As for meeting, that's the hard part. There's a lot of planning to do before I..." Mason grimaced.

"Oh, Plum, your trip..." Oppa practically deflated right there on the couch. "You gotta go back home after New Year's, right? Have ya'll talked about it yet?"

"No." Mason rubbed his hand down his face. "I know it's a horrible excuse, but I lose all track of time when I'm around him."

"It was the same for me, too," Appa mumbled. "Omegas are downright distracting but worth every moment." He nuzzled into Oppa's neck for a long moment, leaving a kiss as he pulled back.

"Sounds to me like you need to drop everything you're

doing today and go pick up your pretty little beau. Now is the time to make some plans." Oppa pointed to the phone. "And no chickening out!"

"Yeah, Mason!" Jenny called from the kitchen. Mason turned back and saw Quentin rushing to slap a hand over her mouth.

"Who's that?" Oppa tried to peer around Mason's shoulder through the phone.

"Jenny and Quentin." Mason held up the phone to show the couple in the kitchen to his parents. "Eldan lives with them."

"Ya'll make sure he doesn't have a chance to chicken out!" Oppa yelled. "We're counting on you!" Oppa settled back down on the couch. "Anyway, we'll let you start plotting. Keep us up to date. We'll help any way we can."

"Take him to that diner we told you about," Appa chimed in. "I know for a fact you haven't been there yet."

Mason quirked his eyebrow. "How could you possibly tell that from one look?"

"Your face isn't nearly as full as it would be if you had eaten there," Oppa pointed out. "The Roaring Ridgemont Eatery. Visit it!"

"I second the R.R.E.!" Jenny shouted.

"Alright, alright." Mason held up his hands. "Sounds like we're going to the diner for lunch today."

"You better." Oppa flashed a fanatic gaze before it melted into a softer expression. "Love you, Plum. Stay safe."

"Love you, too. I'll keep you updated. I promise."

Mason ended the call and wandered back into the kitchen. That went much better than he thought it would. Honestly, he had half-expected his Oppa to reach through the phone and strangle him somehow.

"So, you have to go back home soon, huh?" Quentin asked.

"Yeah. January 3rd is when I have to head out."

Jenny looked at the calendar hanging on the wall. "You don't have much time, and you know how quickly these last few days of the year go by."

"I know." Mason picked at his breakfast. "So much to go over, so little time."

"Stop moping!" This is just the beginning of the rest of your life!" Jenny balled her hand into a fist and leaned forward on her elbow. "Now is the time for action!"

"You really know what to say to calm a person down, Boo." Quentin sighed as he grabbed another drink from the fridge and sat.

"Listen, we've been married for eight years. You should know I'm more of a spur to action kind of gal." Jenny shrugged before she pushed back her chair and headed to the sink. "You can comfort him if you want."

Quentin held out his arms toward Mason. "C'mere, baby. Comfort inbound."

"Oh, Quentin, you always did know what to say!" Mason snickered as he leaned to the side and fell into a light, theatrical embrace with Quentin.

"There, there. Don't let my mean-ass wifey scare you. You are strong, you are kind, and you've got this in the bag–"

A hollow thump rang through the kitchen as Jenny whacked her husband's back with a wooden spoon. "Ya'll can cuddle all you want *after* Mason and Eldan figure out what they're doing!"

With a sigh, Quentin untangled himself from Mason's arms. "Well, I guess this is it for a while, Mr. Shepard. Remember me fondly."

Mason pushed back his chair and stared down at Quentin for a long moment. "Sorry, sweet pea, but you're just my side weenie."

"No!" Quentin gasped, clutching his chest. Eventually, he relaxed back into his chair. "Well, now that I think about it,

I'll be fine. I'm a strong, independent beta who don't need nobody."

"You say that now, but mark my words, you'll be screaming my name when you run out of toilet paper later," Jenny scoffed and tossed a few dishes into the dish rack. "Mark. My. Words."

"I would never," Quentin retorted. "Anyway, did you ever read that letter, Mason?"

"Oh, yeah!" Mason headed over to the counter where the letter, thankfully, still lay.

"What's it say?" Jenny dried her hands on a small towel. "Is it a love letter? Do we need to leave you alone for a moment?"

"Nah, not a love letter, per se." Mason stared at the paper. "It says, 'I'm off work at 1PM. Your clothes are in the bathroom across the hall. Quentin and Jenny are home, so make sure you're decent before you head downstairs. Thanks for staying with me all night.'"

"Well, he doesn't mince words, does he?" Quentin sighed. "So, this all could've been avoided if Honey Bun wasn't a little thief."

Honey Bun squeaked underneath Mason's chair as if in protest.

"Yeah, I'm talkin' about you." Quentin glared underneath the table, and Honey Bun took off up the stairs. "Anyway, we're gonna head out soon, so it'll be up to you to make sure you and Eldan get to the diner."

"No pressure there." Mason pushed his chair in and leaned against it. "Only the beginning of the rest of my life, right?"

Quentin grinned. "Right."

When people think about the hardest thing in the world, they often think of diamonds or deep, dark philosophical questions.

But to Eldan, the hardest thing he had done so far was forcing himself to leave the comforting embrace of Mason's arms. Not only that, it was *still* snowing, and he couldn't find his favorite scarf.

Was everything that had already happened a prelude of the day to come?

"Mistletoe Mocha for Gloria!"

Eldan busied himself cleaning out the old pastries and cookies in the display cases. Despite how slow the day appeared to be going, the shop around him was as busy as ever. It was complete and utter nonsense how two days around his Fated had affected him so badly. His hands were shaking, he couldn't concentrate, and every thought of the alpha made his heart flutter.

And as the day wore on, his entire body felt weighed down. Even the tin tray in his hands felt like it weighed a hundred pounds. Eldan placed it down before he dropped it and caused a scene. The last thing he wanted was to draw attention to himself. Really, the only thing he wanted was for the day to be over with so he could get back to his snuggle bunnies.

All three of them.

A few years ago, he would've thought those feelings almost nauseating. Now? Eldan took a deep breath to reset his brain and went back to his task.

"Perk up, Eldan! Your most hated holiday is done and over with!" Louie slid more trays of fresh baked goods into the display cases. "So, why do you seem so down?"

Eldan's movements slowed, and he pursed his lips. What could he say? That he wasn't feeling well? Or that he didn't sleep well? He couldn't exactly say what he wanted to, that he desperately wanted to leave and deck the balls.

"Hello?" Louie waved his free hand in front of Eldan's face. "Lookin' a bit red there. You feeling sick?"

"No, I'm fine," Eldan mumbled. "Carry on."

"Well, I still think you're looking a bit sick." Louie slid one last tray into the case and closed it up. "*Lovesick.*"

Eldan snapped awake. "No!"

Welp, if that hadn't given him away, nothing would. He had practically written and signed his confession, and there was no going back now. Eldan mentally slapped himself and prepared for the coming onslaught.

"I knew it!" Louie cackled. "So, tell me about the special human who captured your heart."

"No."

Louie jabbed Eldan's side with his elbow. "Come on, not even a little tidbit?"

Eldan crossed his arms. "Nope. Not a chance. Besides, you know me. I'm not gonna parade him around like a prized show dog. You know public displays of affection make me gag."

"Right." Louie shrugged. "So, what are you thinking about that's got you all hot and bothered in my shop?"

"I'm hot, but I am not *bothered.* Not my fault you keep it like a sauna in here," Eldan grumbled under his breath as the bell above the door jingled. "Welcome to Hot Shot–"

Eldan's voice caught in his throat. He had called it. He knew this would happen. In the entryway, a simply perfect alpha wearing a stupid Christmas sweater stood scanning the shop. Eldan resisted the urge to sink behind the counter and slink away, but the alpha spotted him before he had a chance to move.

Louie leaned closer to Eldan and let out a low whistle. "Ooooh, is that him? I remember him. And the extra chocolate."

A lot of Eldan's co-workers seemed to remember Mason, too. They buzzed with excitement behind the counter, and some of them rushed back to the breakroom to preen their feathers. Eldan quickly slapped on a disinterested mask.

Or at least, he hoped it was one of disinterest. As Mason headed up to the counter, a cold ball of dread settled in Eldan's stomach. Why did he suddenly get the overwhelming feeling that Mason was about to say something embarrassing?

Mason placed both hands on the counter and leaned forward to look into Eldan's eyes. Eldan couldn't help noticing the brief flash of heat in Mason's gaze before the alpha gave him a cocky grin.

Oh, no.

"I have come to pick up the cutest barista in Boston!" Mason announced.

Son of a–

Eldan shuffled back from the counter and scowled when he heard his co-workers giggling behind him. "Think you've got the wrong guy."

"Nah, I'd know that face anywhere." Mason grinned. "T'would be a shame if I were to forget such a cute face."

"Mason," Eldan hissed under his breath, "I still have fifteen minutes."

Louie flinched and cleared his throat. "Uh, no, you don't. You're off as of..." He checked his watch. "Thirty seconds ago!"

"What?" Eldan looked at the clock on the wall. "It was 5:45 to 1:30, right?"

"Sorry, I messed the schedule up a bit." Louie shrugged.

Eldan narrowed his eyes. "You don't mess up. You're a perfectionist. You go over the schedule *at least* four times before it's published."

"First time for everything, right?"

"Right..." Eldan scowled as he signed off the register and started weaving through his co-workers. Though they didn't say anything, he could see the shock in their eyes. Others looked on in disappointment, no doubt upset they missed their chance with such a fine alpha.

When Eldan made it to the breakroom, he flung open his locker and undid his apron. The door clicked behind him, and he didn't have to look to know who it was; the gait said it all.

"Why're you playing favorites, Louie?" Eldan pulled his dark purple apron over his head and hung it in his locker.

"Because you've been here almost four years now, and I've never seen that look in your eyes before."

"What, of despair?" Eldan scoffed.

"No. Curiosity, interest, heat–"

Eldan didn't turn around to look at his boss. He simply held his hand up and let out a growl. "Stop right there. I do *not* look like that."

"Oh, sure." Louie eased himself down into his chair and propped up his leg. "Listen, I'm old. There could be a million and one things wrong with me, but I know, sure as shit, that I ain't blind. Not yet, anyway."

"Nah, stubborn is what you are," Eldan grumbled.

"Right back at you, boy." Louie grinned as he pushed himself to his feet again. "Now, I do believe you're due for some fun."

"Fun?"

"I know it's a strange word to you, but you really should try it sometime. It keeps you young, you know?" Louie cackled. "See this leg? Happened because I didn't party enough as a young man. Trust me."

Eldan snorted and tugged on his coat. "Alright, Captain Good Times, I'll be sure to go out and have some *fun*."

"But not too much fun! Depending on what you do to pass the time, I can't guarantee we'll have enough money to bail you out," Louie said. "Anyway, I gotta head back out to the floor. Have a good time."

After Louie left, the room was far too quiet.

"Fun, huh?" Eldan closed his locker with a long sigh. "I guess even I can get away with a bit of fun."

A loud grumble stopped Eldan in his tracks. A hollow, aching feeling gnawed at his stomach. Perhaps food before fun. Eldan waited for the terrible rumble to stop before he pushed open the breakroom door.

And he got a face full of Mason's chest. What a sight that was. Eldan licked his lips and trailed his gaze higher. The alpha was giving him a stupid, toothy grin. Did he ever stop smiling?

It only took a moment before Eldan's feet were off the ground, and he was wrapped in a big bear hug right in front of everyone.

This alpha would be the death of him.

"Down. Down, boy! What, are you happy to see me?" Eldan tilted his head as the alpha's scent spiked. "I was only gone a few hours!"

"That's a few hours too many, I think." Mason lowered Eldan to the ground and reached into his fanny pack.

"You know fanny packs went out of style ages ago, right?" Eldan grumbled under his breath.

"Is that any way to talk to the man who brought you your long-lost scarf?" Mason pulled the ring of fabric out of his pack and draped it around Eldan's neck.

Eldan burrowed into the scarf as soon as he could. "Where was it? I looked for it everywhere."

"I, uh…" Mason smiled and rubbed the back of his neck. "I may have been sleeping on it. I swear, I didn't know until this morning."

Eldan was suddenly very aware of the number of people listening to their conversation, and he grabbed Mason's hand to lead him out of the shop.

"In a hurry?" Mason grinned. "Where are we going?"

"Away," Eldan mumbled. "From prying eyes." The door eased shut behind them, and Eldan led Mason down the sidewalk. It would've been a clean getaway, too, if not for the almost-demonic noise coming from Eldan's stomach.

"Worked up an appetite, did ya?" Mason dug his heels into the snow and forced Eldan to stop. "Boy, have I got the cure for that."

"I'm not hungry. You're hearing stuff."

Eldan's stomach growled again as if to protest his words. The longer Mason stared at him with that stupid grin on his face, the more heat climbed Eldan's neck and ears.

"I didn't have time to eat this morning. Too busy looking for my scarf."

"Admittance is the first step on the road to recovery." Mason looked up at the street signs and headed off. "We'll get you fixed up right."

When Mason pulled open the door, Eldan was hit with a massive sensory explosion—the warmth of the diner, the scents, and the sound of sizzling food. It all served to stoke the ungodly noise in the pit of his stomach.

Eldan licked his lips as a waitress sauntered past with a tray full of food. He didn't know how Mason knew this was his favorite place. *I don't think I ever mentioned it.*

"You're drooling."

Eldan quickly swallowed his spit and scowled over his shoulder at Mason. "Not my fault you picked my favorite place in Boston."

"Oh, shit, really?" Mason's eyes sparkled. "You can thank my parents for that. They've been recommending this place since I checked into the hotel."

"They know their food, that's for sure." Eldan crossed his arms and headed up to the small host podium.

"That you, Eldan?" a voice called out from the order counter. "Am I seeing things? C'mon, Lukas!"

Eldan perked up a bit as a waitress rushed over, dragging a young waiter behind her. Either he was new, or Eldan hadn't been there in a while. Probably a mixture of both.

"What're you doing here?" The waitress stood with her hands on her hips and a wide smile on her face. "I half-expected not to see you until it warmed up a bit!"

"I'm being forced to eat here against my will, Sienna," Eldan huffed before the slightest hint of a smile broke through his mask.

"That ungodly noise your stomach made just a few moments ago says otherwise." Mason snapped his eyes to the ceiling, and Eldan bristled.

"Listen here, you." Eldan pointed toward Mason's exposed throat. "I've had it up to here with–"

"Hey, hey, hey." Sienna giggled. "If ya'll are gonna do this, take it somewhere private. You're scaring the newbie."

Eldan flushed a furious red but simmered down after a moment. He ran his gloved hand down his face before he groaned.

"How'd you know?"

"Because you've been eating here for, what, seven years now?" Sienna counted it up on her fingers, then nodded in satisfaction. "Yeah, seven years, and you've never brought a date here!"

"You're imagining things," Eldan retorted. "I've brought other dates."

"Really? Name one. We've got all the time in the world, sweet pea." Sienna batted her eyelashes and leaned forward on the podium.

Shit, quick, random name, brain. Go!

"Don't be throwing any of those fake names or numbers out there. In fact, I'll save you some time. I know you're lying." Sienna giggled. "Your ears turned red."

Damn it, he really needed to invest in a pair of earmuffs. Eldan burrowed into his scarf and grumbled behind the thick fabric.

"Fine, I lied." Eldan motioned back to Mason. "I found him outside. I'm just feeding him as a favor."

"But I'm the one paying." Mason flashed a cocky grin.

"Shut–" Eldan started.

"Okay!" Sienna beamed and grabbed two menus from the pile before passing them to the waiter behind her. He stumbled in surprise and stared with wide eyes.

"This is Lukas, our resident newbie. It's his first day, and I have decided you'll be his first table!"

"What? Already?" Lukas fidgeted, tugging on the corner of his apron. "Are you sure about this?"

"Yep, I believe in you." Sienna beamed. "Now, remind me. What's first?" She held a hand up to her ear and leaned toward Lukas.

"Um…" Lukas clammed up and awkwardly grasped the menus.

Sienna placed her hand on his shoulder and shook it

lightly. "C'mon, ask if they want a booth or a table, you big doof."

"Right!"

"Order up for booth seven, Lukas!"

"Got it!" Lukas rushed over and gripped the tray but was stopped by Sienna.

"Slow down, you big doof. You move that fast, and you'll drop the tray and ruin all of Archer's hard work. Take a breath." She took a deep breath with him and exhaled slowly. "Now, balance, and take a step forward."

Mason watched the pair with amusement as he took a swig of his sweet tea. "She's gonna make a super-waiter out of him yet."

"That's the plan!" Sienna held up her hands behind Lukas, ready to steady anything that wobbled. "You got this, Lukas!"

Eventually, Lukas made it safely to the table and started dishing everything out. Eldan had to hold himself back. The sight of his fish and chips made his mouth water, and he was *so* ready to dig in.

"Alright, it's killing me. So, I gotta ask." Mason slid the plates down the table and unwrapped his silverware. "Where you from? That drawl stands out like a fly on a wedding cake!"

"Oh, I'm from North Carolina." Lukas set Eldan's plate down in front of him. "Bellcrest. Ya'll probably never heard of it. It's a pretty small town." Lukas tucked the empty tray under his arm.

"You kiddin'?" Mason grinned. "I've been through there a few times. Home of Prize-winning Poultry, right?"

"Surely you mean Award-winning Cocks, right?" Sienna draped her arm around Lukas' shoulders and shook him lightly.

Eldan spewed his drink across part of the table. "Excuse me?"

What was with his luck today? Just as he took a drink, someone says that shit? He grumbled as he grabbed some extra napkins and cleaned up his sticky root beer.

"Just a little play on their town greeting." Mason snorted and grabbed more napkins. "Try not to think about it too much."

"Too late," Eldan grumbled. What a waste of perfectly good root beer. Next time, he'd be sure to get it all over Mason.

Wait, bad thoughts. Bad thoughts. Eldan shook his head before he wadded up the napkins and tossed them to the side of the table.

"Eat up, little Lapin. I'll clean up the rest of this."

"What happened to Little Elf?" Eldan unwrapped his silverware and tossed a curious glance toward Mason.

"Well, do you prefer Little Elf or Lapin?" Mason grinned. "Either name suits you well, if I'm being honest."

"Pet names. Bah," Eldan scoffed. "Excuse me while I try not to vomit."

"You didn't mind pet names in the mall." Mason leaned forward, his voice low enough so only Eldan could hear. "Or last night."

"I was drunk on fatigue. I was not responsible for my lack of action toward your cutesy pet names." Eldan took a bite of his food and chewed slowly, savoring the taste. Every crispy bite was a small piece of deep-fried elation, and he melted into his seat.

"Whatever you say, Lapin." Mason took a bite of his burger and almost moaned. Eldan's hand froze, his fork halfway to his mouth.

"You look like you just had the best orgasm of your life," Eldan whispered as he slowly lowered his fork. "Are you okay?"

This time, Mason let a moan slip, and his eyes glittered. "I can see what Oppa was talking about."

"Do we have any compliments for the chef given what I heard over here?"

Sienna had wandered over to the booth in their moment of bliss. She balanced one arm on the table and placed her other hand on her hip. The look on her face was enough to strike fear into the hearts of even the bravest people.

"Oh, you heard that?" Mason chewed on his lip. "How embarrassing. Eldan was the only one who was supposed to hear what I said."

Eldan fidgeted in his seat. "You–"

"By all means, I'm sure Archer would love to have praises heaped upon him." Sienna motioned toward the kitchen. "He's right in there."

Mason stood and cleared his throat.

"Hey, Archer! I just wanted to let you know the angels smile upon you and your kitchen! A thousand pats on the head to he who made this burger!"

"Name the time and place, buddy-boy!" rang out a distant voice from the kitchen. "Except Thursday! That's poker night!"

Mason chuckled as he settled back down into the booth and took another big bite of his burger. Sienna headed off to pick up another order, and Eldan watched the alpha carefully as he picked at his own food.

There's something in his scent. Eldan crinkled his nose as a somewhat musty scent drifted over him.

"What's wrong?" Mason's voice drew Eldan out of his studies. "Are you okay? Does your food taste alright?"

Eldan sighed and put his fork down. "What's really on your mind?"

"Huh?"

"I can tell something's up. Your scent..." Eldan whispered. "So, spill it."

Mason stared at the table with pursed lips, and he practically deflated like a forgotten carnival balloon. It didn't suit his alpha. Not one bit.

"I have to leave soon."

Reality hit Eldan in the face harder than he was expecting. Despite his poker face, he felt a lump forming in his throat. Suddenly, the prospect of being separated from his Fated made him feel more nauseated than the idea of pet names.

"How soon?" Eldan croaked.

"January 3rd."

Eldan bit his lip and went slack against his seat.

"Listen, I know it hasn't been that long since we met, but fate decided a long time ago that we're meant to be together." Mason reached across the table and let his hand cover Eldan's. "Which is why I want to talk to you about everything."

"One moment." Eldan waved Sienna and Lukas over. "I need a moment to prepare."

"Yes, sir?" Lukas whipped out his notebook and flipped to a new page. "What can I get you? Maybe a nice desert?"

Eldan sighed and pointed to the small dessert menu on the table. "You read my mind. I need one of those hot fudge brownies, please."

"Do you want caramel or vanilla ice cream on top?" Lukas looked up from his notebook.

"Yes." Eldan stated.

"Um…" Lukas glanced at Sienna with concern. She gave him a thumbs up. "Okay, yeah, I can do that. It'll be right out."

ELDAN HUMMED AS HE MUNCHED ON THE PERFECTLY GOOEY, chocolatey brownie covered in caramel and vanilla ice cream. At least one good thing had happened so far today.

After all, you couldn't go wrong with anything Archer made. Mason waited patiently, seemingly gathering his thoughts as Eldan finished off his brownie with a satisfied sigh.

"Okay. Let's begin." Eldan pushed his empty plate to the side. "Where do we start?"

"Here's what I'm thinking." Mason threaded his fingers together on the table. "With the way everything is going in the real estate market, it shouldn't take too long for my place in Texas to sell."

"Or I could move down there," Eldan offered. "I mean, I don't have my own place, and I don't have a long-term job like you do."

"But your family is here, and you've still got some time left in school, right?" Mason stared for a long moment.

"How'd you know?"

"You think that I, as a Professor, wouldn't know the joyous, over-the-moon look of a college student on break? Even you have that look, Mr. Grumpy-puss. Besides, your desk gave you away."

"What were you doing going through my desk?" Eldan quirked his eyebrow.

"Hey, in my defense, you left all your books and papers out in the open." Mason snorted. "If you didn't want me seeing anything in your room, you should've strapped me down to the bed before you left."

Don't tempt me. Though Eldan scowled, he still felt pain deep in his chest and stomach. If talking about this made him ill, he probably wouldn't survive a full parting, even if only for a few days. He didn't want to be away from his Fated for long.

Even if his Fated was an infuriating, dirty old codger.

"As it stands, I'd have to make a few trips back and forth to finalize everything. A week at a time, maybe. That's if I get a place to stay here in the meantime, but I doubt I could find anything on such short notice..." Mason's voice trailed off.

"Hang on. Stand by." Eldan dug through his coat pocket and whipped out his cell phone. After a few quick taps on the screen, he brought the phone to his ear.

It was at that moment that a phone in the booth behind him rang loudly.

Nothing surprised him anymore. As Eldan listened to the people in the booth behind him fumble and curse, he slowly lowered his phone and threw a sharp glare over his shoulder.

"Jenny?" Eldan hissed through gritted teeth. "I assume you and Quentin are just here for lunch and *not* to be nosy?"

Jenny chuckled nervously before she turned around in her seat. "Heyyy, Eldan. You know us. We love this place almost as much as you do."

Quentin gave Mason a tiny wave. "So, how do you like the place, Mason? Is it everything you've heard?"

"Let's just say I'm surprised my Appa and Oppa didn't move back here the moment they found this place. I'd show you the burger I got, but, unlike my little Lapin here, I didn't take any prisoners."

"Now why are you two really here?" Eldan turned sideways in his seat to meet Jenny's gaze. "Something you need to tell me?"

"Just that you're the best roommate we could ever ask for." She sweetly smiled as she slid out of her booth and came to Mason's side. "Make room, Mason. We have some important insider info we gotta share."

"Uh, huh..." Eldan sipped his root-beer as Mason squished next to him, and Jenny and Quentin slid into his spot. "Go on, tell us."

"In a hurry, are we?" Jenny arched her eyebrow. "Well, as I'm sure you know, Eldan, Mason is an absolute delight to be around."

Eldan chewed obsessively on his plastic straw. Did everyone get some sort of pleasure in tormenting him?

"A treasure," Eldan muttered through his teeth.

"So, we're all in agreement that Mason should stay with us?" Jenny formed her hands into a steeple. "That *is* what you were calling to ask us about, right, Eldan?"

Eldan wanted so badly to be snarky, but he couldn't bring himself to give her an attitude now. She had just given him one of the best options he'd ever get on a silver platter. He hadn't even had to beg or bargain with her.

"What are you waiting for? Quentin looked at Eldan. "Ask him!"

"Do you wanna stay with us?" Eldan mumbled. "With me?"

Mason tilted his head. "You forgot to bat your eyelashes. C'mon, I know you've got those pretty lashes…"

Eldan felt heat rising on his neck, but he swallowed his pride and locked gazes with the alpha. If he had to flutter his lashes, he would damn well flutter his lashes.

"Please?"

Now it was Mason's turn to falter. After a brief moment, he leaned in and dotted kisses over Eldan's cheeks. "Absolutely."

"And that's that!" Jenny clapped. "What's next on the agenda?"

Mason let out a low whistle, going over his mental checklist. "I need to turn in my letter of resignation and find a new job here as soon as possible."

"What do you do?" Jenny asked.

"I'm a history professor down at Laguna Valley University in Texas."

"No joke?" Quentin beamed. "You're in luck, my dude. See, Jenny and I are grad students at Hornebolt University. Last I heard before break, there were a couple of openings that might interest you. You should definitely check them out."

"Is this really working out?" Mason swelled with

confidence. "So that's living arrangements, potential jobs… What else?"

Mason's phone buzzed in his pocket, and he fished it out to look at the name. "Ah, there's the last piece." He looked up and slung his arm around Eldan's shoulders. "Ready to meet the folks, Lapin?"

Eldan clammed up and let out a string of stutters until he felt Mason grip his shoulder and purr softly.

"I promise they'll love you."

Eldan took a deep, steadying breath. It was only fair. Mason had met his entire family on day one, so he could deal with meeting the parents, right?

"Quick, answer the call before I sink under the damn table."

Mason answered the call, but Eldan couldn't hear much over the pounding in his ears. *What if they hate me? What if I make a fool of myself? What if–*

"So, Appa, Oppa…" Mason turned the phone to get both him and Eldan in the shot. "Say hello to my pretty little beau."

As the screen showed two curious faces, the one closest to the phone screamed. Mason almost dropped the phone and fumbled to catch it.

"Oppa! Weren't you always the one gettin' onto me about inside voices? What happened to quiet down or suffer the consequences?"

Oppa paid Mason no mind as he glanced excitedly between another man and the phone. "Look at him! Honey, look at our Plum's mate!"

"I see, pumpkin." The other man stared into the phone with a gruff expression. "Eldan, right?"

"Yes, sir." Eldan nodded. He took a deep breath of Mason's scent to calm himself. That man may be related to Mason, but he was so scary looking! He didn't need a whiff of the man to know he was an alpha to be reckoned with.

"Well, ain't you just as cute as a button?" Oppa leaned closer to the phone to get a better look at Eldan. "I bet you're just a right angel, the way my Plum talks about you! Better be glad I'm not there. Those red cheeks wouldn't go long without getting pinched!"

"Oppa, careful. You're gonna make him explode under the pressure." Mason squeezed Eldan's shoulders.

"Oh, sorry, sweet boy!" Oppa reeled back and fanned his fingers over his chest. "I'm Hosea, but you can call me Oppa!"

"Leslie." The other, gruff-looking man piped in. "Appa."

"So, tell us a bit about yourself, sweetie!" Oppa threaded his fingers together below his chin and balanced his elbows on the table. "What do you do? Do you go to school?"

"Well, um…" Eldan clammed up before Mason gently squeezed him again. "I'm a part-time barista right now working my way through school. I'm in my last semester, studying to be a lab technician."

"And he likes cute bunnies!" Jenny called out from across the table.

"Jenny!" Eldan covered his face with his hands.

"Hey, same," Appa grunted.

Eldan spread his fingers and saw Appa duck out of sight. The alpha clicked his tongue a couple of times and came back up with a mass of snow white fluff.

"This here is Sylma Storm-Maiden. She's a French Angora, and our second baby after Mason there."

"I'm still their favorite," Mason leaned over and whispered. "I don't shed as much as she does."

"And you didn't get a cool Nordic name like she did, so who's the real favorite here?" Appa cuddled the little rabbit and kissed her soft little head before putting her back down on the ground.

"I'm hurt." Mason's head lolled over on top of Eldan's. "I'm hurt, Sugar Lips."

"What do you want me to do? Kiss it better?" Eldan

pursed his lips and glared up at Mason from the corner of his eye.

Mason puckered up, and Eldan quickly put his fingers up to block his advance. "Remember when we were at Ma's house?"

"Now that you mention it, I vaguely remember a meager death threat, but you know what I think?"

"What?"

Mason stuck out his tongue between Eldan's fingers, causing Eldan to jerk his hand back and shudder before he threw a flustered look at the phone.

"Was he always like this?"

"Not at all, sweetie. Believe it or not, he was shy and reserved growing up." Oppa snickered. "This seems to be a recent development."

"What a treat," Eldan grumbled as he grabbed a napkin and wiped the spit off his fingers.

He really hoped he didn't look as red as he felt. Why did Mason always do this kind of stuff in public? If they had been anywhere else, *not* surrounded by people–

Eldan sank down into the booth cushions a bit further. All he could do was clean himself up and *not* think about how hot and silky Mason's tongue felt against his skin.

"Anyway, that's the plan, Oppa. If all goes well, I'll be a permanent resident of Boston within a few months."

Eldan jerked his head back toward Mason. Either Mason was an auctioneer in a past life, or he had been spaced out for a lot longer than he thought.

"That's wonderful, Plum!" Oppa grabbed Appa's arm and hugged it.

Appa glanced at something off-screen, then leaned against Oppa, his lips moving in a whisper. Oppa lit up.

"Oh, that's right! Sorry, Plum, we've gotta head out. With all this excitement and all these new faces, I forgot we were meeting a few of our friends for dinner."

"I see how it's gonna be." Mason snorted. "Well, have fun. Be good, and don't go too crazy."

"Be good," Appa scoffed. "That's rich coming from the serial glitterist of Boston!"

"It was so wonderful meeting you, Eldan." Oppa's eyes sparkled. "Make sure to give us a call if our boy starts giving you too much trouble, you hear?"

Eldan nodded. "Will do."

"Love you, Plum. Make lots of memories, okay?"

Oppa ended the call, and Mason leaned back in the seat. "And there you have it. My Appa and Oppa. You did great, Lapin."

"I didn't make a total fool of myself. Hooray." Eldan weakly pumped his fist before he sunk back into the seat and leaned against Mason's side.

"So, what sort of memories are you guys gonna make?" Jenny asked. "Got any big plans for New Year's?"

Eldan felt his eyes drooping. Now that the toughest part of the day was over, he just wanted to snuggle. He felt Mason's arm snake around his back and rub his side.

"Well, whatever you guys plan, we're gonna be out New Year's Eve and most of New Year's Day," Jenny continued. "We're going to a party with some of our friends, so you'll have the house to yourself if you want a little party of your own." She winked at Mason before she placed some bills on the table.

"We're gonna head out." Quentin rose from the booth. "Don't forget to make some memories!"

As the couple left the diner, Eldan let his eyes slip closed. This probably wasn't the best place to sleep, but it was Mason's fault for being so damn warm.

Memories, huh? Eldan yawned. *Make some memories...*

Okay, here we go. Deep belly breaths.

Eldan took a deep, steadying breath. Today was the day, and he was already experiencing the tensest moment of his life. If he got caught now, he wouldn't ever live it down. Eldan dragged his body against the wall, avoiding the center of the hallway in case he had to duck into a room to hide.

From whom, or what, you may ask?

"Yeah… Yep, uh-huh…"

Mason's muffled voice drifted up the stairs, and Eldan let out a quiet huff. The alpha was making this secret mission more difficult than it should be. Every time he thought it was safe to head to the door, Mason started pacing around the kitchen again.

Eldan counted to ten, waiting for another opportunity to open up. All he needed was a simple diversion that would keep Mason distracted long enough for his plan to go off without a hitch. It was one of those times when he wished he had started training Honey Bun in the art of total distraction.

Sadly, he hadn't gotten around to it yet. He would just have to time this right. Eldan kept his ear trained on every shuffle in the kitchen as he clutched a bundle of pillows and blankets to his chest. At this rate, he would be better off heading back to his room and building a pulley system outside his window.

"Yeah, I know. I can't believe it either. What were the odds, right? If you could see his smile… It melts my heart every time I see it."

Eldan ran his hand down the length of his face and cupped his fingers over his lips. Shit, that man was *evil*. Just a few simple words, and Eldan was putty in the alpha's hands.

Or putty on the staircase.

"I'm gonna miss working with ya'll. Keep an eye on your phone, will ya? I don't plan on letting ya'll disappear from my life that easily."

A loud scrape echoed in the kitchen as Mason sat down at the table.

"Yes, that's a crude way of saying keep in touch, dingus." Mason snorted. "Anyway, I've gotta let you go. We're heading somewhere today, and I still haven't gotten dressed. And no, I am *not* sitting at the table naked. I have the 'bear necessities' on."

A loud laugh and unintelligible words echoed from the kitchen.

"Don't go making fun of my jammies." Mason snorted. "I'm hanging up. Bye."

Mason let out a long sigh and pushed his chair back, forcing pinpricks across Eldan's skin. If Mason was still in his jammies, he needed *clothes*, and his *clothes* were up—

Eldan headed back to his room as quietly as he could. He tossed the pillows and blankets back across the bed and flopped down next to Mr. Hopson just before the door squeaked open.

"Thought I heard you stomping around up here." Mason nudged the door closed behind him.

"You talk too loud." Eldan faked a grumble. In reality, his

heart was beating so fast he was afraid it might explode. "You woke Mr. Hopson up, too."

"Awww, I'm sorry. How about I make it up to you?"

Eldan flushed when he saw the mischievous light glittering in Mason's eyes. The alpha walked a few slow steps closer, then sat on the bed, sandwiching Mr. Hopson between them.

"And just how are you gonna do that?" Eldan leaned forward, his eyes glinting in a silent challenge. Every nerve in his body flared as Mason leaned closer, and he felt his eyes slip closed. Just a little bit further and–

"I'm sowwy, Mr. Hopson! I didn't mean to disturb your beauty west!"

Eldan's eyes shot open as Mr. Hopson rolled over against his leg and Mason ruffled the fat rabbit's belly. Was this man for real?

"What's that look mean?" Mason quirked his eyebrow. "Are we getting a bit jealous over there?"

Eldan scoffed and turned away. He was *not* getting jealous of a rabbit, damn it.

"I'm saving the best for last." Mason licked his lips. "It's your turn, Lapin."

Eldan's body tensed as he turned around and found himself in an iron grip. He barely had a chance to let out a small gasp before it was cut off by Mason's lips. This man was intolerable. Absolutely infuriating.

But he was a damn good kisser, that much was certain. Every touch of his rough lips and every swipe of his tongue were enough to drive Eldan up the wall.

And, of course, it was over far too fast for his liking.

"I'll give you a moment to recover." Mason grinned as he rummaged through his suitcase at the foot of the bed. "I'll be ready in a few minutes." He pressed another kiss to Eldan's hair and pulled open the door, dodging the escape of Honey Bun.

"What the fuck?" Eldan sighed as he flopped back on his bed and covered his face. "You don't get to do that and just leave, you ass…"

Eldan rolled back and forth across his bed, trying to calm his flaming nerves before he did something stupid. He came to a stop, facing Mr. Hopson, and peeked through his fingers at the rabbit.

"Don't you judge me, Mr. Hopson," Eldan huffed. "How the hell can I fight something like that?"

Mr. Hopson simply snuffed in response and cuddled up under the quilts.

"Thanks, Captain Cuddles." Eldan bundled up the free blankets and pillows before he pushed himself to his feet. With a new-found spring in his step, he took off down the stairs. He only had a few minutes to pack everything up, or this mission would end in failure.

And failure was *not* on the agenda today.

THE SNOW CRUNCHED BENEATH ELDAN'S BOOTS AS HE TOOK A tentative first step from the car, and the frigid air burned his lungs, forcing a shudder through his body. He quickly tugged his scarf over his nose and buttoned his jacket higher.

Mason, on the other hand, absolutely sparkled right alongside the glittering snow. Eldan watched the alpha frolic for a few moments before Mason turned around with a warm smile.

"Sorry. This reminds me of the woods back in Texas." Mason stared in awe. "Only we had hot snow instead of cold snow."

Eldan grabbed a couple of thermoses from the car and slammed the door. He understood where Mason was coming from. This forest never ceased to amaze him. It was an entirely different world from the cityscape of Boston, far from the towering buildings and crowded streets.

No matter how covered the path was or how dense the trees were, Eldan knew the way. But with each step he took, his heart sank a bit further, slowly getting stomped down like the snow beneath his boots.

He jumped when he felt Mason grasp his hand and squeeze.

"I'm here."

Eldan wasn't sure if that made it easier or harder. He swallowed the lump in his throat and pulled Mason through a few more snow-covered branches.

In a small clearing ahead, the sun beat down on a perfect pine tree. Tracks of all kinds circled the tree, and a peaceful lull blanketed the area.

Eldan sighed and headed to the tree, his fingers carefully brushing snow from the heavy-laden branches.

"Mason, meet Mary."

Mason tilted his head and looked at the tree in puzzlement. "A pine tree?"

Eldan snickered before his eyes fell to the snow. "Nah, Mary's not a pine tree, but she is here." Eldan reached down and hung up an ornament that was half-buried in the snow. "She never liked the idea of yards for graves. She wanted her freedom, so we planted this little sapling and spread her ashes around it."

"I see." Mason's gaze dropped to the snow around the tree, his slow breath coming out in white puffs. "It's a beautiful spot."

"So, I guess, in a way, she is the tree." Eldan gently touched an ornament that was hanging from the branches. "Looks like Miranda and Joel have already been here."

"Her family?"

"Yeah, her two kids." Eldan stared at the ornaments with a distant expression, then pointed to a clumsy ornament slathered in frozen peanut butter and birdseed, hanging low on the branches. "Looks like her grandkids came, too."

Eldan took a step back to admire their work. Scattered all over the pine tree were handmade ornaments. Dehydrated fruits and veggies, orange-halves filled with birdseed, and, pine cones covered in treats hung from every other branch, creating a huge feast for the animals.

"So, that picture on your dresser, the lady behind you…" Mason's gaze fell from the tree to Eldan. "Was that Mary?"

Eldan nodded. "Mary Weaver. Needleworker extraordinaire. Everyone in that picture was part of the To Knit, or Knot to Knit club."

"Shit, what a name!" Mason's mouth jerked into a grin as he rubbed his hand down his face. "Who came up with it? I need to have some words with them."

"Dunno." Eldan shrugged. "I don't remember who was in charge of the club." His gaze dropped to the snow. "I still have the last thing she made."

Eldan's fingers trailed over the worn yarn of his scarf.

"I knew it." A thin smile crossed Mason's lips. "I knew there was a reason you never go anywhere without that scarf."

"You mean other than the fact that I hate the cold?" Eldan asked, his voice low and joking. "Yeah, after the club let out, she draped this old scarf around my shoulders and told me to take care of it." He buried his nose in the frayed fabric and fought to keep his voice steady. "That was the last time she made it to the club."

Eldan bit back the tears as he thought back. After that day, she got sick often. She was too frail, too weathered by time. He should've noticed a lot sooner than he did. Maybe it wouldn't have hurt so bad when she–

A frigid wind rustled the trees above him, swishing them softly in the breeze. Hidden within the branches, birds sang peaceful songs. Further in the woods, twigs and branches creaked under the weight of the snow. Here, it truly was a different world. A frozen, peaceful world. Just the way Mary liked it.

"She was just like you, you know." Eldan gazed back at Mason. "Happy, upbeat. A real leader. And Christmas was her jam. You wouldn't believe the trouble we got into. If she wanted to do something, by God, it would be done."

"Why's that?" Mason asked, his mouth twisting into a smile.

"Because Christmas was her day, too." Eldan crossed his arms and smiled. "She was born on Christmas Day, 1929."

"Wow! Bet her family called her the best Christmas gift ever, right?"

"She sure acted like she was a gift to mankind, sometimes. Though it was true." Eldan's breath caught on a sigh. "And, really, the same could be said about you."

Eldan wondered if the alpha could hear his heartbeat from the other side of the tree. If his soft tone didn't give away his feelings, the rapid beat of his heart sure would.

Sure enough, as if he sensed how muddled Eldan was feeling, Mason returned to his side, took his hand, and squeezed it gently. It was a soft, silent gesture, a brush of emotion, soothing, sweet, and wordless in form, but it was all Eldan needed.

"After she died, I couldn't bring myself to join in on the festivities anymore. Not without her. I mean, how do you celebrate your best friend's birthday and favorite holiday without your best friend? I never had a reason to celebrate. Not until..."

Eldan took a deep, steadying breath.

"Not until you."

The look on Mason's face was enough to raise goosebumps across Eldan's skin. The alpha's warm, soft brown eyes seemed to glisten, and a tender smile curled on his lips. Eldan blinked rapidly before he quickly wiped at his eyes with his mittens. Damn feelings were making him squooshy.

"It didn't feel right celebrating her favorite day without her. And it just got worse as that feeling bled into the entire season." Eldan said, his lips trembling into a smile. "But blood washes out, yeah?"

"Absolutely."

Eldan let out a low sigh as Mason wrapped his arms around his waist and rested his head on top of Eldan's. Suddenly, the cold didn't seem to bug him as much. No, now it was the stares of the woodland creatures that Eldan knew were out there among the frozen foliage. A few even braved their presence to reach the food.

"Seems like we're being watched." Mason's warm breath fanned against Eldan's skin before he pulled away. "I'll keep them busy for a bit. Take however long you need."

"You make it sound like you're about to fight off a bloodthirsty horde." Eldan half-smiled before he pulled small Ziploc bags of birdseed from his coat pockets. "Here, battle rations."

Mason squeezed Eldan's hand gently before he stepped back and pulled open the bags, humming to himself. Eldan turned back to the tree and took a deep breath, ruminating over everything he wanted and *needed* to say.

"It's been a while, Mary. Sorry I'm a bit late this year. Life has a way of taking you on wild adventures, you know? I met someone, Mary. Someone very special," Eldan whispered. "My Fated."

Eldan's ears perked as Mason tried to talk to a few of the animals.

"He's a really big dolt, but I can't help noticing the way my heart starts racing whenever I look at him. It's the little things, just like you told me. Things like his scent—it tells me a story of open plains and endless skies, even though I've never seen such a place. His love for life is something else.

And the magic in his eyes?" Eldan sighed. "Maybe that's why this trip... Maybe that's why it's easier this time around."

A few birds chirped behind Eldan as he blew warm breath into his hands. He needed to wrap this up so he could get close to Mason again.

"I wish you could've met him. I know you two would've gotten along. He's the perfect mix of love, stability, and–"

Mason let out a quiet gasp behind him, and Eldan turned around and saw Mason covered in birds. They sat on his hat, his shoulders, and even in his hands before a sketchy-looking squirrel ran up Mason's back. Even then, a few brave birds remained in his large, rugged hands, eager to eat their fill of the birdseed in his palms.

"When did you turn into a fucking Disney princess?" Eldan stared in awe.

"Just now?" Mason whispered with glee. "All I had to do was make eye-contact with this cardinal!" He motioned with his eyes toward a fat, red bird sitting on his fingers.

Their quiet chirps were as soft as the fluttering of their wings as they came together as a chorus in Mason's hands. He was so gentle with those tiny creatures, and, despite his rough hands and massive presence, they trusted him so much. Mason had that effect on everyone and everything he came across. As Eldan watched the alpha, he felt his heart lurch a bit. In Mason, he saw an old past and an old friend, but he also saw a new beginning.

And that was all he needed to see.

"You know, every time I came here, I always thought I'd be ready to say goodbye," Eldan said, half-talking to Mason and half-talking to the tree.

"Are you?"

Eldan hugged his arms close to his body and shook his head. "No, I've realized something." He turned toward Mason, and his heart started beating faster. The afternoon sun shined down behind Mason, outlining him in a soft glow. It seemed that even the birds stopped their feast to marvel.

"What?"

Eldan clutched his chest and turned back to the pine tree. "I don't have to say goodbye because she's always here with me. So, this isn't a sad goodbye."

A dull pain thumped in his chest before he turned back to Mason.

"This is only the beginning of something magical."

And just like that, Eldan felt the weight of the world lift off his shoulders, and the nagging headache pinching at the back of his head vanished. He took a deep breath behind the safety of his scarf.

"I have to say, wistful is a good look on you." Mason shook half-eaten husks of birdseed from his hands before he pulled his gloves back on. "I see a dreamy look in your eyes that I've never seen before. Tender, nostalgic…" He stepped a bit closer and took Eldan's hands before pulling the omega into his arms.

"Maybe even a bit heart-rending. Makes me wanna hold you and not let you go until that heartbreak is gone."

Eldan let himself lean into Mason's body. "I wouldn't have it any other way."

Mason leaned back in his seat as the car rolled down the dark roads. By his side, Eldan sat in near silence, almost as if he were lost in thought. Not that Mason could blame him, though. It *had* been a day, after all.

But, despite how tired he looked, Eldan insisted on driving back, which suited Mason just fine. If he was being honest, he hadn't paid much attention to the path they took to get to the clearing. He'd been too busy checking out the decorations and snow. So, when it came time to leave and head back to the city, he couldn't exactly say no when Eldan requested the keys.

The trip to the clearing had been eye-opening. Finally, it all made sense. All that hurt, all bottled up, growing through the years—it was way too much for one person to handle. And the fact that Eldan had trusted him enough to take him to a place so dear to his heart? Well…

All Mason wanted now was to be near his little Lapin, to go the extra mile for him. He wanted to wrap him up, love all the hurt out of him, and be the one to stand by his side, even if the world crashed and burned.

Which led the Texan in Mason to wonder why Eldan was

taking them down dark back roads so soon after that huge-ass blizzard. As he hung onto the oh-shit handles conveniently placed above the windows, Mason squeaked, "I think we were supposed to take a right at that last stop sign, Lapin."

Eldan flinched before he regained his composure and gripped the steering wheel hard. "No, this is the right way."

"Are you sure?"

"What makes you think I made a wrong turn?" Eldan murmured.

"Because we're heading *away* from the city?" Mason gazed at the distant lights, which were glowing in a hazy hue against the dark skies. "Unless you've planned an impromptu camping trip, I think we should be heading back to the warm embrace of light."

"This is the scenic route," Eldan said as he messed with the knobs on the dashboard. As Mason saw it, that was a classic sign things weren't adding up.

"You're lost, aren't you?"

"Hell no, I..." Eldan protested. "I always come up here. Usually not in winter but ..."

And *that* made the Texan in Mason tense up like someone had just announced that the ice-cold sweet tea had run out at the 4th of July BBQ. He could handle city roads in the daytime, but uphill, shady, back roads? Hell to the no, man.

Then, it finally hit him. He'd seen this movie before. All it took was one wrong turn, and that was that. From there, a series of events started that would end poorly for the hapless characters. Namely, him, if he read this situation correctly. One quick glance out the window told Mason they were close to the top of the mountain, and he knew he only had a few minutes to try to undo whatever he had set in motion.

"Hey, uh... Lapin?" Mason asked.

"What?"

"This seems like a fine opportunity to tell you I'm sorry

for anything I may have done to hurt you. If in any way, I've ever wronged you, I'm sorry."

"Where's that coming from?" Eldan furrowed his eyebrows. "And why do you suddenly look so queasy? Do I need to pull over for a moment?"

Mason gulped. "Oh, you *would* like that, wouldn't you?" He shook his head and shuddered.

"Whatever." Eldan scowled. "I'm not cleaning up your car if you get sick, just so you know." He gripped the steering wheel and grimaced as he kept his eyes on the dark road. "Let me know if you feel like you're gonna hurl. Seriously."

"Nah, I'm fine, really. I'm just sittin' over here wondering what I said or did to make you want to suddenly off me."

Eldan arched his eyebrow, dumbfounded. "What?"

"You're taking us down a hidden back road in the middle of the night."

"It's 6:30," Eldan replied.

"The *middle* of the night, Lapin!" Mason motioned to the dark skies around them. "It is pitch black out here. What else could you possibly be planning other than offing me?"

"'Off you?'" Eldan snorted. "Sure, that was totally the plan."

"I just wanna know where you managed to stash the shovel, to be honest." Mason gazed out the window, watching as the twists and turns took them farther from the city lights.

"Can't believe I'm doing this," Eldan grumbled under his breath.

Mason leaned forward with wide eyes and a furrowed brow. "I know, right? I thought we had something special! Unless…" He cocked his head. "Is this a Noelle courting ritual?"

"What? Hell no. Can we just enjoy the ride for a moment, please?" Eldan hissed through his teeth.

"Don't think I won't fight back. Because I will."

Eldan groaned low in his throat. "Do I have to gag you? Or will you behave for a few more minutes?"

"Well, shit, I mean, I'd be down if you–"

"Excuse me?" Eldan squeaked.

"What?" Mason cleared his throat and his mind before he leaned back and locked his arms behind his head. "I mean, let's be honest, here. A gag wouldn't last long with me anyway."

Not that he had tried it, but everyone he'd ever met always said he could talk his way out of any situation.

The car slowed, crunching over snow and ice-cold gravel as the bare branches of the trees overhead vanished. Mason leaned forward and saw a dark, clear sky staring down at him, speckled with a few stars here and there.

"Well, thankfully, we are *finally* here," Eldan huffed as he stared straight ahead. "Go on. Take a look."

Mason tore his eyes from the sky and nearly bonked his head on the windshield as he leaned further forward. From this out-of-the-way spot on the mountain, between them and the distant lights of the city, hazy hues of pinks, purples, and more danced across the surface of a small lake. He could even see the giant Christmas tree on the edge of the city if he squinted.

"Oh, *now* you're speechless? Jeez…"

Despite Eldan's harsh tone, he smiled softly, watching with his wistful eyes.

Mason was barely breathing between the view of the city and the sincere look on Eldan's face. He probably had stars in his eyes, but he couldn't help himself. With all the excitement and awe coursing through his veins, he didn't give one hoot or holler about what kind of face he was making.

So when the car started lurching backward, it *may* have taken Mason an embarrassingly hot second to realize what was going on.

"Whoah, whoah, whoah, hold on there." Mason reached

out and grasped Eldan's thigh and shook it gently. "We need to take more than thirty seconds to appreciate this view, Lapin!"

"What do you think I'm doing?"

Mason's gaze darted between Eldan and the front of the car. "Pardon me for saying, but it looks to me like you're leaving!"

Eldan didn't respond. He looked back over his shoulder and backed up toward the dark road down the mountain. This time, the Texan inside was *screaming*.

"Don't tell me you're gonna try to back down this road?" Mason choked out. "My heart could barely handle coming up here!"

"Jesus, you're a mess." Eldan kept his eyes on the road behind the car. "Just give me a minute."

Mason closed his eyes as Eldan did *whatever* he was doing. When the car finally came to a stop and lurched one last time, Mason forced his eyes open. After a little pinch and a little slap, he determined that he was, in fact, not dead. He rubbed his hands down his face.

"Okay, so now we're facing this way." Mason let out a sigh of relief, almost missing Eldan popping the back hatch and hopping from the driver's seat. He watched the omega fumble around in the back for a moment in the rearview mirror. "Uh, Lapin? What's your plan, there?"

"Hang on a minute…" Eldan grunted as clanks came from the back of the car. Mason unbuckled his seatbelt and climbed out, heading around to the open hatch.

When Mason stepped around the back, he bit back a snort. Oh, this was rich. Within a few moments, he knew exactly what Eldan was looking for, but he'd never find it. Not without him. Mason crossed his arms as a slow grin spread across his face.

"Do you need help?"

Eldan didn't answer for a long moment until, finally, he

rested his forehead against the back of the seats with a frustrated sigh.

"*Please* tell me these seats go down to make more room."

"I don't know." Mason smirked. "What if they don't?"

Eldan swallowed. "Then it'll be a bit harder to follow through with the plan I originally had in mind."

"Well, considering your original plan, should I *really* tell you how to–?"

Eldan tossed a piercing, heated glare over his shoulder, growling quietly in frustration. "That wasn't my plan." His eyes softened, almost glazing over, before he turned back to his task.

Most would've been terrified of such a look, but Mason? No, that look went straight to his stomach, planting a seed of warmth that bloomed through his body.

"Oh? And what did you have planned?"

Eldan grumbled and scooted against the side of the trunk. "Just tell me how to lower these seats before the body you have to hide is mine. I'm fixing to die of shame over here."

"Alright, coming in hot."

Mason chuckled as he crawled into what little space was left, feeling the car dip as he added his weight. And wouldn't you know it? The side Eldan had chosen to sit on was right where the lever to unlock the seats was, which suited Mason fine; it gave him an excuse to get *real* close to the omega. He heard Eldan suck in a sharp breath in response.

"For future reference, the lever you are looking for is right over here." Mason reached behind a flap hiding the lever and tugged it, unlocking the seats and pushing them down. "Now, tell me..." He motioned to a pile of folded blankets and pillows near Eldan. "What sort of plan requires lots of space and comfortable items like these?"

Eldan crossed his arms and turned away, a red hue blooming on his ears.

"I see." Mason grinned. "A sleepover, maybe?"

"Yeah." Eldan groaned as he buried his face in his hand. "Yeah, totally the plan. You got this all figured out."

Mason settled down next to Eldan, stretching out his long legs with a sigh before he wrapped his arm around Eldan's shoulders. "Shame I can't sleep without my favorite jammies. You didn't happen to pack those, did you?"

Eldan flinched against him, biting his lip in frustration. "No."

"So, how shall we pass the time, Lapin? Did you bring a portable DVD player? Some fun games?" Mason whispered. "What *was* your plan?"

"I brought you out here so you could test this new hot chocolate recipe I came up with!" Eldan said it a bit too quickly as he quickly reached for two thermoses in a basket near the blankets. "But first, you have to clear out a moment so I can set everything up."

"Throwin' me out in the cold already? Just like that? That's not very loving of you." Mason grinned, and Eldan pushed against him with a frustrated hiss.

"You know, I think I liked it better when you thought I was gonna kill you," Eldan mumbled under his breath. "At least you didn't make me feel…" His eyebrows furrowed, and he bit his lip.

"Feel what, Lapin?"

Eldan didn't answer. He simply threw another heated glare as he pulled the hatch down.

"This is some nest you've made." Mason rested his chin on top of Eldan's head, enjoying the omega's sweet scent. It had taken some coaxing and a little bit of a cold breeze from the open hatch, but now Eldan sat snug and warm between Mason's legs as they stared out at the distant city.

"I figured you'd appreciate a comfy spot for your old bones."

"Wow, ouch." Mason chuckled. "I've never heard someone sound so angry while drinking delicious hot chocolate." Mason took a swig of his drink, enjoying the warm, chocolatey flavor.

"And I've never heard someone talk so much while enjoying a drink." Eldan glanced over his shoulder and licked some melted chocolate from his lips.

Melted chocolates? Mason stared into his thermos as if he would be able to see something in the dim light of the car. Better to down his drink and see for sure.

Mason tipped his thermos back, draining his drink with a few long gulps. With a gasp, he pulled the thermos from his lips. He ran his tongue over them and found melted chocolate.

"This brings back memories." Mason chuckled and licked his lips again. "Takes me back to the second time we met, where you *totally* didn't add anything extra to my drink."

Eldan flashed Mason a heated side-long glance, then he turned back to his drink. "I don't know *what* you're talking about."

The way Eldan's heart beat faster against Mason's chest said it all. Mason set his empty thermos down and leaned closer, bringing his lips down to Eldan's ear.

"Maybe this'll remind you?" Mason whispered. He curled his fingers under Eldan's chin and turned his face toward his own. "It tasted a little something like this."

Mason leaned in and captured Eldan's lips in a slow kiss, letting him taste the chocolate on his lips. He deepened the kiss, and his tongue slipped forward and teased Eldan's lips.

After a moment, Eldan parted his lips with a tremble and let out a faint whimper. He mumbled Mason's name between kisses and shivered against his body. After a long moment, Eldan broke the kiss with a quiet gasp.

"Now who's mouth is getting him into trouble?" Eldan whispered low in his throat before he looked back up with a challenge in his eyes.

"Can you blame me? I mean, look at you, all red and sweet." Mason pulled Eldan into his lap in one swift movement and wrapped his arms around the omega's stomach. "Feels like I'm unwrapping and tasting my favorite candy every time I kiss you."

Mason pulled down the neck of Eldan's sweater and grazed his sharp teeth over the sensitive flesh of his neck before glossing over the faint red lines with his tongue.

"See, I don't think you realize just how good you taste," Mason purred. "Like chocolate, marshmallows, and just a hint of spice with everything nice."

"What do you mean? That's obviously just the hot choco–!" Eldan jerked forward with a gasp when Mason's hands ran under the hem of his sweater. His rough hands trailed over the smooth skin of the omega's stomach.

"Or maybe haughty with a little bit of naughty?" Mason chuckled. He grabbed a pillow and shoved it between his back and the row of seats he was leaning against. He moved his hips further out from the seat, which gave Eldan more room to relax against his body.

"Shut–"

Eldan didn't get a chance to finish his short sentence.

"Come sit on Santa's lap for a few minutes, won't you?" Mason whispered. *"Tell me, what do you want?"* Mason had hooked his legs underneath Eldan's, spreading them apart just enough to keep the omega from moving. At this angle, Eldan was completely at his mercy.

And his merciful side had a lot of love to give.

Eldan's head lolled back against Mason's shoulder, and he stared up at the ceiling of the car for a long moment before he turned and nuzzled under Mason's chin.

"Do I really have to say it?" Eldan whispered, heat rising

from his body. He pressed kisses to the hollow of Mason's throat and scraped his teeth across the tender flesh.

"If it's something your heart truly desires, I'll know." Mason leaned back, giving him more access. *"Show me what you want."*

And slowly, sweetly, Eldan did just that. His fingers curled into Mason's sweater, clinging tightly, as if he were afraid the alpha would disappear. With every touch, every bite, Mason felt his mind going numb, like nothing in the world existed except for the soft, warm omega in his arms. He wanted to make his little Lapin melt against his body, fall into a fathomless daze, yield to his touch as if it was a lifeline to the surface.

Eldan's gaze was longing and heated, his eyes reflecting the dimmed lights hanging around the trunk. As his shoulder rested against Mason's chest, he peppered chaste kisses over the alpha's face. Then Mason curled his fingers under Eldan's chin and pulled him in again.

"I've been waiting to see that face again, ever since that day in the mall. You remember?" Mason whispered between kisses. "Took every fiber of my being to pull myself off you."

The way Eldan whimpered said he remembered well. "What, do you want, a medal?"

Mason smiled against Eldan's lips. "Nah, no clunky medals or bulky trophies. A feat that great is worthy of the greatest prize of all."

"What do you want?"

Mason rolled up Eldan's sweater and felt a shudder roll through his body. "Do I really have to say it?" He ran his fingers over Eldan's chest, pinching and rolling the sensitive, pink buds. He purred when he heard a whimper low in Eldan's throat. *"You. You're the greatest prize I could ever hope for."*

Mason lowered one hand to Eldan's jeans, rubbing small, soothing circles above his waistband before popping the buttons loose and pulling on the zipper. Eldan rested his head against Mason's cheek. A noticeable heat burned on his face.

"*Is this okay, Lapin?*" Mason asked. His hand paused above the waistband of Eldan's jeans.

Eldan whimpered and buried his face against Mason's neck. "*Yes...*"

And that was all Mason needed to hear before his hand slipped beneath the waistband of Eldan's jeans. With a careful tug, he pulled Eldan's cock from the harsh confines of his clothes. He purred when he saw just how hard it was.

"*Look at how hard you are.*"

"Don't say shit like that," Eldan hissed. "Can't believe you. You're a sap. A cliché master. Maybe even a–!"

Mason stroked Eldan's cock, forcing the omega's voice to rise an octave before he cut off his voice with a slow kiss.

"And you say such sweet things. Makes my heart soar. Just like those cute little noises make my di–"

"Don't you even say it," Eldan whimpered. "Dirty old man."

Mason slowly pulled Eldan's jeans to his knees, and the omega let them hang from an ankle. Mason spread his legs a bit further, which opened up Eldan's. As his free hand ran up Eldan's chest, he whispered against his skin, "*Would you rather I show you?*"

His free hand ran through Eldan's locks, and he pressed soft kisses to Eldan's neck and up his jawline, eventually catching his lips. Mason mumbled soft praises with each touch and gently bit Eldan's sensitive ears. While the omega was distracted, Mason pulled his jeans down just enough to free his cock, letting it rub against Eldan's ass.

"*Do you feel that? Yeah, that's all you.*"

Eldan pressed back with a whimper, his hand gripping Mason's arm tight enough to leave bruises.

"So, this is it, Lapin." Mason let out a ragged breath. A

slick substance dripped onto his skin. "Show me *exactly* what you want."

Eldan turned back with a dazed look in his eyes. It only took him a moment to raise himself slightly and push back. Mason's cock rubbed between his slick cheeks, and he mewled.

"Got it," Mason groaned against Eldan's skin.

Steadying the omega against him, Mason moved his hand down, purring as his fingers found slick. Mason pressed kisses to Eldan's neck and shoulders. He teased the omega's slick entrance, rubbing his hard cock between his soft cheeks before he pushed in, drawing a low moan from Eldan.

"*So warm...*" Mason groaned, resting his forehead against Eldan's neck. "*So slick and ready, just for me...*"

Mason rolled his hips up, drawing careless, wanton whimpers from the omega. Mason let one of Eldan's feet drop back to the floor. He stroked Eldan's cock, coating it with his own slick.

Mason slowly began moving. He ran his hand up Eldan's chest, groping and squeezing every sensitive spot as the omega arched his head back against his shoulder. With a bit of control back on his side, Eldan pushed himself up and let himself sink back down in time with each roll of Mason's hips. Eventually, a growl escaped Eldan's lips, and he glanced needily over his shoulder.

Mason pushed himself up against the back of the seats, letting Eldan's knees sink to the floor on either side of his legs. Eldan doubled over, letting his weight balance on his elbows. Mason gripped the omega's hips and pulled him down with each snap of his hips.

After a few moments, Mason snaked an arm under Eldan's stomach and pulled him up with ease. Eldan's hand gripped his own cock and stroked it feverishly. His body was soft, hot, and lustful, locked in a frenzy with Mason's. He began to push himself down harder, trying hard to hit a certain spot deep inside.

"Let me help, Lapin…"

Mason put a bit of pressure on the middle of Eldan's back. He held onto Eldan's wrists from behind as the omega leaned forward. Eldan let out a small whimper as Mason pulled out, almost to the head of his cock. Then, in one sharp movement…

Eldan's eyes widened as he tensed up beautifully around Mason's cock. He mumbled incoherent words as drool leaked from the corner of his lips.

"*Shit…*" Mason purred. "*Look at you…*" He ran his hand up Eldan's arm and pulled him back against his chest. His fingers trailed up Eldan's neck, holding him in place while he nipped the crook of his neck. His other hand moved down to cover Eldan's, stopping him from stroking his leaking cock any further.

Eldan bucked back against Mason's hips. "*Please. Please, fuck–*"

"I know, Lapin. I know," Mason whispered against his skin. "I want to burn this image in my mind, this look you have right now. Bliss, ecstasy." He rolled his hips slowly, drawing a moan from Eldan. "*Completely and utterly in love.*"

Mason groaned. Eldan's body heated about a hundred degrees. With a low mewl, Eldan pushed back against Mason's hips, and this time, Mason obliged, guiding Eldan and stroking his leaking cock.

Eldan's blissful cries made it clear he was close to his peak. He was working himself into a feverish frenzy as he slammed his hips against Mason's.

"*Come for me, sweetie…Eldan…*" Mason purred in his ear. "*Let it all out.*"

With a choked moan, Eldan sagged back against Mason's chest, his twitching, throbbing cock dripping with white ribbons as Mason milked him dry. Then, not far behind him,

Mason rolled his hips up one last time, letting out a groan as he bit into Eldan's shoulder.

After a moment, Eldan turned and nosed against Mason's neck, leaving his own marks when Mason tilted his head back. A brief fire flashed through Eldan's eyes as he pressed back down, drawing a low rumble from deep inside Mason's throat.

"Mission..." Eldan purred. "...Success."

Words couldn't convey the feeling swelling in his chest. Mason glossed his tongue over the bite on Eldan's neck, leaving kisses here and there as he rolled his hips up to draw one last reaction from his omega.

My. Omega.

"*Mine.*" Mason purred, leaning his forehead against Eldan's shoulder. "*My most cherished gift.*"

Mason shifted, and Eldan turned around and curled his fingers through Mason's hair.

"*Stay,*" Eldan whispered. "You're still–"

Mason realized what he meant. If he pulled out now...

"Alright, hang on tight, Lapin." Mason moved some pillows around and laid Eldan down so his hips were raised before he draped himself over his omega's body. "Not a drop will be wasted."

"You're such a dirty old man." Eldan threw his arm over his eyes and let out a groan. "The dirtiest."

"You were pretty dirty yourself, Sugar Lips." Mason drew him into a lazy kiss. "Was hot as hell, though." He pressed soft butterfly kisses under Eldan's eyes before moving on to his ears. "I'm so happy Fate gave me you."

Eldan heated up, letting out a mewl as he scratched his fingers down Mason's back.

"And I'm glad those seats went down."

CHAPTER 12: DECEMBER 28TH

*E*ldan stirred from his slumber. Warm light peeked through the sheer lace of his curtains. This was probably the warmest he'd ever been in his life. From his head to his toes, heat wrapped around him, making it extremely difficult to convince his body to move.

The bright rays of light drew delicate patterns across his room, and the faint shadows of the lace fluttered elegantly across his quilts. In front of him slept a gigantic, cozy wall of alpha. Eldan nestled closer to the muscled masterpiece, savoring the sweet scent that drifted from his skin.

Even in his sleep, the alpha seemed close to perfection. Not a tangle in his hair, nor a hint of morning breath. He wasn't even drooling on the pillow, for God's sake. The sunlight only enhanced his image, highlighting his rugged, tan skin and curly dark hair, not to mention the shallow bites and bruises on his neck and the scratches on his shoulders.

It would've been a beautiful sight if not for the gnawing pit of dread growing in his stomach. To most people, the morning sun was a beautiful thing to wake up to, especially if it was shining down on your Fated mate.

To anyone like Eldan, who was a barista and was *supposed* to be at work, the morning sun was distressing.

"Shit, shit, shit!" Eldan hissed through his teeth as he launched from his bed and glanced at his clock. He was so fucked. He was supposed to be at work an hour ago!

Ignoring the pain in his hips, he scrambled to pick out an outfit for the day. He was *never* late, damn it.

Mason barely showed any sign of life under the quilts, save for his quiet snores. Leave it to a clueless alpha to sleep through one of the most distressing moments of his mate's life.

Eldan grumbled under his breath as he buttoned up his coat and tossed his scarf over his shoulders before rushing to the door.

It was definitely gonna be one of those days.

ELDAN DIDN'T KNOW WHICH HIGHER BEING HE PISSED OFF, BUT everyone and everything was determined to make him later than he already was. Not only had he overslept by an hour, roadwork was blocking the usual bus route, and he had been forced to run five blocks to bypass the jam.

Exactly one hour and twenty-seven minutes late, Eldan finally arrived at Hot Shots. He was completely frazzled. And, of course, everyone noticed when he walked through the door. Even Louie smiled mockingly at his state.

And here Eldan thought he could sneak in without anyone noticing. Why the hell did he think *that* would go well? He tugged off his gloves as he stepped behind the counter, heading toward the breakroom.

"You're extremely late today." Louie grinned as he followed Eldan into the breakroom. "Rough morning?"

"You have no idea." Eldan quickly hung up his coat and

pulled his apron over his head, tightening the straps behind his hips.

"Did you have fun?"

Louie's smile was anything but pure. Eldan closed his locker and crossed his arms defensively. "Yeah, why?"

"Looks like you had quite a night, that's all I'm saying." Louie shrugged. "We were a bit worried about you."

"I didn't sleep much last night." Eldan groaned as he straightened his back. He never thought the pain would last *this* long. "Some pain in the ass kept me up all night."

'Another round, Lapin?'

'Well, sure, what's one more?'

And one more turned into two more, and so on and so forth. Eldan grumbled, flushing at the memory. The claiming bite was one thing, but the other marks? Those were just to embarrass him.

"Guess so." Louie said before he headed back out to the shop. Eldan bristled with anxiety. Did Louie somehow *know?* The voices of his co-workers pulled him from his thoughts, and he brushed his fears off as best he could before he rushed out to the line.

But when the stares continued and the snickers taunted him further, Eldan excused himself from the line and headed back into the breakroom. He looked in the mirror in the employee restroom.

What he saw in the mirror horrified him to no end.

His hair stuck up in waves in about six different places, and the dark circles under his eyes stood out against his pale skin. Even his clothes were wrinkled, despite being folded neatly in his basket the night before. Or did he grab the ones from the dirty laundry?

Either way, the sorry state that his clothes were in were nothing compared to what he saw next. Eldan's stomach lurched as he focused on his neck, homing in on the red and purple bites blooming on his throat and the crook of his neck.

He was going to *destroy* Mason. Eldan fumed as he ran his fingers over the bruises and bites, but with each mark he came across, he couldn't help focusing on the tingling beneath his skin.

These marks identified him as *claimed*. He was part of something amazing now, part of Fate's plan. How could he be mad about that? Eldan lowered his hand and gripped the edge of the sink, then he fixed his hair and scrubbed his face. He could at least make himself look *somewhat* presentable before he went back out to the floor.

When he finally left the bathroom a few minutes later, Louie was waiting at his desk, typing something on the computer.

"Finished primping?"

Eldan turned the combination lock on his locker and tugged it open with a hiss. "Why didn't you tell me?"

"Tell you what?" Louie gave him a sidelong glance.

Oh, you bastard.

"Tell you what, Eldan?" Louie swiveled around in his chair and formed a steeple with his fingers. "About the love bites?"

"Obviously." Eldan fumed as he grabbed his scarf from his locker. He draped it around his shoulders and neck, making sure it stayed flush against his skin. "I would've kept this on had I known!"

"If you ask me, that scarf of yours draws attention to your neck even more," Louie pointed out. "You wanna know what I think?"

"No." Eldan shut him down.

"Well, I'm gonna tell you anyway." Louie snorted. "Wear 'em loud, wear 'em proud! They're marks of pride, I say. Besides, you keep turning red like that, and you won't be able to wear that scarf for long."

Eldan flushed as he tore the scarf from his shoulders and hung it back in his locker. "Whatever. You keep it too hot in this shop, anyway."

"Give it time! The heat'll fade along with those love bites!" Louie called out. Eldan slammed the door shut behind him, drawing looks from his co-workers.

He returned to his place on the line, and he heard his co-workers whispering behind him.

"So, you got him, huh?"

"About time!"

Another co-worker let out a low whistle, and Eldan gritted his teeth before he forced a smile and turned around.. If this was the game they wanted to play…

"Can I have a word with all of you?" Eldan hissed through his teeth. "Come on, team meeting. Get in a huddle."

When nobody moved, Eldan flashed his trademarked angry eyes, and everyone jumped. There wasn't a soul alive who could fight that look, and Eldan knew it. When they were all good and close, Eldan wrapped his arms around their shoulders and took a deep breath.

"Cease."

With that single word, he broke the huddle and went back to stocking the display cases.

"C'mon!" a younger co-worker with long, blonde hair spoke up. "There's gotta be more to it than that?"

"What do you want me to say?" Eldan spun around, almost throwing cookies from the tray he was holding. "That we met at a bar in the Bahamas? That he took me out into the shallows on a moonlit night to show me the 'peak of the high seas'?"

"Did you?" Her eyes sparkled. "Did he?"

"No, I spilled my coffee on him and ran into a really pissed off Santa in my haste to get away. I got called a cockmuppet," Eldan huffed. That outta ruin whatever view she had of him. He turned back to his display cases and muttered, "Not romantic at all, right?"

"Are you for real?" She clasped her hands together and tilted her head. "Obviously, it was! I mean, look at your neck!"

Eldan flushed and spun around to face her. "I will end you…" He narrowed his eyes and looked at her nametag. "Lexie. Mark my words, I will–"

"Eldan Noelle!"

Oh, for fuck's sake, what now? Eldan growled under his breath. Jenny was stomping across the floor toward the counter.

And she looked even worse than Eldan did.

"Yo, what the hell, Eldan? Could you two have been *any* louder coming home last night?" Jenny glared at him.

"Jenny." Eldan took a sharp breath. "I literally *cannot* today. Do not–"

"Seriously! You guys got home at like, what, 1AM? Would it have killed you to keep it down a bit? Some of us *enjoy* sleeping!"

"If I buy you a cookie, will you shut it?" Eldan retorted.

Jenny gripped the edge of the counter so hard, her knuckles turned white. "And another thing. Do you know how hard it is to fall back asleep when your husband thinks there's a demon in the house *again*?"

"Again? What–?" Eldan shook his head and looked pleadingly at Quentin. "How do I make it stop?"

"You don't." Quentin shrugged. "An angry Jenny is kind of like the stomach bug."

"The hell does that mean?"

"Some things just have to run their course." Quentin sat at a nearby table and started scrolling through his phone, a clear signal that Eldan was on his own.

This was Eldan's life now. He was cursed to be an object

of unwanted attention simply because he went out and enjoyed life for once. How *dare* he indulge a bit?

"Well, *excuse me* for actually going out and having fun," Eldan grumbled. "I'll be sure to lock myself in the house from now on. Just leave me a list of chores and shit, so I have something to do with my endless time."

The bell above the door jingled again, and Eldan heaved a sigh of relief. Finally, someone to take the attention off him.

"Welcome to Hot Shots!" Eldan called out over the chatter and clatter of the line. "We're running a special–"

Eldan's voice caught in his throat when Lexie gasped behind him. "It's him!"

He wondered if he would wake up from this nightmare anytime soon. Maybe he'd wake up back in his room, *not* late, this time.

Sadly, when he snapped back to reality, a quick pinch did not spirit him back to his room. Instead, his alpha bounded across the shop toward him with his stupid grin and those honey-colored, love-filled eyes.

Wait, *his alpha?* Eldan swallowed. *His* alpha. Those two words were enough to cause his breath to catch in his throat and start his heart racing down the path to *Funkytown*.

"Morning, my little Lapin." A slow grin quirked Mason's mouth. "You left without a kiss this morning!"

And then he had to go and say stuff like that in front of everyone. It was enough to drive Eldan mad. But looking into those eyes, he couldn't be mad for long.

Because Mason was *his* alpha. And, judging by how proudly Mason displayed his neck, there wouldn't be a soul in the world who didn't know that little fact.

CHAPTER 13: DECEMBER 29TH

Mason never claimed to be the best wordsmith in town. Maybe in another life, he could be, but this one? That was a negative. After all, what fun would it be if he didn't push Eldan's buttons?

Because Eldan was so cute when he was angry. That perfect pouty lip, those glowing red ears… It would've been a sin *not* to aggravate him. Even the marks on his neck stood out, turning bright red when he got angry. Mason couldn't help but purr in pride.

"So, I heard you were runnin' a bit late today?" A bubble of laughter rose in Mason's throat. "Did you manage to find everything?"

Eldan crossed his arms and leaned back in the seat. "Honestly, I blame you."

"Hey, it's not like I held you against me and wouldn't let you leave." Mason's voice lowered. "As much as I would've loved to."

"Have I ever told you what a sap you are?"

"No?" Mason grinned. "Please, go into great detail. I'd love to hear everything you have to say."

"You're maddening." Eldan scowled. "Absolutely

maddening. The most infuriating, sappiest alpha I've ever had the displeasure of meeting."

"I think you meant to say 'charmin'," Mason drawled.

"Charmin'?" Eldan scoffed. "So, are you ultra-soft or ultra-strong, *darling*?"

Mason stopped at a red light, and his lips twisted up into a pensive smirk. "I'm a package deal, Lapin, don't you know?"

Eldan huffed in response. He sank down in his seat and crossed his arms. He probably wanted to get home to Mr. Hopson and Honey Bun. Seemed like it had been a rough day for his poor mate.

Mason's ears perked at distant squeals. From the corner of his eye, he saw a small park buried under mounds of snow. Kids of all ages were working on something, rolling up snowballs that were slowly growing bigger than they were.

Their amazing teamwork allowed them to lift the big spheres. Old Frosty was going to be the biggest snowman ever, easily over six feet tall.

"Why do you look like you've never seen a snowman?" Eldan's voice snapped him from his appreciation of the art.

"Well, you know me. I tried to make sandmen in Texas, but I got tired after a few minutes." Mason shook his head and let out a small chuckle.

For a long moment, Eldan's eyes bored right through him. Then, Eldan straightened up in his seat, and his dark blue eyes seemed to glow with conviction.

"Take a left up here."

"Hm?"

"Ease *into* the left lane" Eldan motioned with his hand. "And turn *left*."

"Yes, sir," Mason replied, his lips curling into a smile. "Your forceful command is my eternal confusion."

Eldan grumbled under his breath. "There's a big park down this road. Thought we could build a snowman or something? But if you don't want to…"

"Uh-uh, don't you try to back out." Mason shook his head. "We. Are gonna build. A snowman."

~

MASON COULDN'T STOP STARING AT THE HUGE PARK AROUND him. He swiveled around, half-expecting to see a crew setting up movie props and actors practicing lines. After all, this was literally a Hallmark moment. Maybe even a Kodak moment.

"This. Is. Awesome!"

Mason's gaze darted around the park. It was just what he had dreamed about from the moment he arrived in Boston. All around him, kids were pelting each other with snowballs, while others were building snowmen and making snow angels.

"The longer you stand still, the bigger a target you are." Eldan grabbed Mason's arm and dragged him toward a large tree away from the warring children. "Let me know when you're done gaping."

"I'll never stop. Not while we're still here." An uncontrollable smile tugged at the corners of Mason's lips. "So, where do we start? I'm ready to *live* a Hallmark movie."

"Well, what does one do at this point in a Hallmark movie?" Eldan crossed his arms. "Been a while since I've watched one."

"Let's see…" Mason pinched his chin between his fingers, and his eyes slipped closed. "First, there's always that awkward first meeting."

"Check." Eldan's voice softened. "Extra awkward."

"Then, by sheer coincidence, the pair meets over and over again. In fact, it's a bit suspicious how often they meet, but nobody ever questions it because it's a Hallmark movie, damn it." Mason chuckled low in his throat.

Eldan's ears glowed pink. "Check that off the list."

"And finally, there's always a kid in the mix that helps

push the pair together. Usually, one of the main characters is a single parent, and their kid gives them a push, or–"

"Watch out!" a little boy's voice called out.

"Outta the waaaaaay!" another little boy screamed.

Mason pulled Eldan against his side and jumped out of the path of two young boys flying past on their sleds. When the boys looked back for a split second, they swerved and crashed into a small bush.

"Ooooh, that's gonna smart in the morning." Mason cringed. "You okay?"

"I'm fine, but was that…?" Eldan squinted at the accident. "Wait, don't tell me those kids are from…?"

"Benjamin! Tyler!" a woman yelled. "Are you okay? I told you two to stay away from the trees and bushes!"

The boys popped up out of the snow and looked back with glee in their eyes. "Mister Mason! Mister Eldan!"

"Well, I'll be damned," Eldan marveled. "What are the odds?"

"In a city this size? I'd say that's a little nod from Fate right there." Mason stooped down and held his arms out to his sides as the boys ran over. He caught each of them on an arm, grunting at their weight before they all toppled over into the snow.

"Hey, kiddos, Rose, long time, no see!" Mason hugged them tightly as Rose finally caught up. She was carrying a bundled-up Nikki on her hip. "What're ya'll doing here?"

"Santa left us sleds at home!" Benjamin held up his brand-new, bright red sled. "We're trying them out!"

"Benjamin's lost two teeth already!" Tyler pointed to his brother's mouth. "Show them!"

"No way!" Mason gasped. "Which ones?"

Benjamin flashed a toothy grin that wasn't as toothy as it could've been, thanks to two empty spots right at the front of his mouth.

"No! Your two front teeth? Do you whithle?" Mason grinned like a madman before he whistled a familiar tune.

Eldan half-heartedly swatted Mason's arm. "If you get that song stuck in my head, I will end you."

Mason pushed himself to his feet as Benjamin and Tyler took off on their sleds. "Ah, you said that a couple days ago, but I'm still kicking."

Rose giggled, pulling Mason from his little world. "Did you two have a good Christmas?" She sat on a bench and patted the middle with her free hand before curling her arms around Nikki again.

"The best." Mason settled down on one end of the bench and threw his arm across the back. Eldan took a seat in the middle. "We drove out to Marlborough. I met his family, saw a Christmas narwhal, that sort of thing."

"A Christmas narwhal?" Rose beamed. "We're at a point in time when we're coming up with some of the strangest decorations. Why, before we got trapped in the mall, I saw the most horrifying ornaments at Walmart. Christmas poos, of all things…" Rose tended to Nikki who was squirming on her lap.

"And I bet your boys loved them, right?" Mason smirked.

"Of course. So, now we have a Christmas poo hanging on our tree." Rose sighed. She turned her attention to Eldan, and her smile faded. "Are you okay, Eldan?"

Eldan flinched. "Sorry, sorry. Just spacing out a bit."

Rose watched him for a long moment before Nikki babbled and reached out toward Eldan with her tiny hands.

"Guess she remembers you." Rose held Nikki out toward Eldan. "Would you like to hold her again?"

Eldan's shoulders tensed, and he nodded. As soon as Nikki was in his arms, he immediately relaxed, and his scent spiked just enough for Mason to catch it.

"Hey, sweet girl," Eldan whispered. "Missed you, too."

As Mason watched Eldan interact with Nikki, he couldn't help noticing the growing warmth in his chest. Seeing his mate turn from a little grump into a nurturing soul was quite alluring. Even the primal alpha inside seemed to agree, almost as if he would reach out and seize his omega, if only he physically could.

If Mason wanted to tumble down a rabbit hole into a world of madness, all he had to do was imagine Eldan with *his* baby in his arms. *Their* little baby.

"You okay over there, Mason?"

Mason clawed his way out of the rabbit hole and saw Rose giving him a wary side-eye. Eldan was still, thankfully, distracted, and Nikki babbled with glee on his lap.

"Never better." Mason cleared his throat. "Never better."

"If you say so." Rose giggled. "Anyway, Santa thought it was a good idea to leave those little sleds for my boys, and now the tooth fairy is gonna be a bit busy in the nights to come. They're growing up way too–"

Rose cut herself off and stared at two incoming shapes.

"Benjamin, Tyler, slow down! You're gonna crash again!" Rose stood and waved her arms. However, her worries were in vain as the boys skillfully drifted their sleds by the bench, throwing snow in their wake.

"Come sled with us!" Benjamin's gaze darted between Mason and Eldan.

Tyler hopped off his sled and sat behind Benjamin. "Yeah, race us! Come on!"

"What do you think, Lapin?" Mason crouched down next to Eldan's legs and played with Nikki. "Feeling up to a little race?"

"I don't…" Eldan paused. "Actually…"

After a moment of hesitation, Eldan gave Nikki a light squeeze before handing her back to Rose. He pushed himself to his feet and stretched, then grabbed the empty sled and dragged it behind him.

"Let's do this."

The frigid wind stinging his skin was the happiest slap in the face Mason had ever experienced. Never once did he think he'd be smack-dab in the middle of a high-stakes sled race in the middle of Boston.

Not only that, but his Fated was pressed tightly against his chest, and they were flying down the hills like they had practiced this a dozen times before. Mason probably had icicles hanging from his beard, but the only thing that mattered was that he was *here* in this moment with his mate.

Benjamin and Tyler were just a little bit ahead of them, and every now and then, one of them threw taunts back at the older competitors. Mason didn't have to see Eldan's face to know there was a spark of determination in his eyes. The way he controlled the sled said it all.

"How many teeth do you think Benjamin is gonna lose?" Mason asked, shouting over the whistling wind. "Place your bets now!"

Eldan leaned to force the sled in a different direction. "I'm more worried about how many teeth *we're* gonna lose if you keep distracting me!"

As Eldan raced the sled down the hills, Mason scooted a bit closer to his body and relished in the faint marshmallow scent still spiking from Eldan's neck.

"How are you holding up, Little Elf? Is your face blue yet?"

Eldan looked over his shoulder. "My body is frozen, and my need for mead is unfathomable!"

"Mead?" Mason snorted. "Why drink mead when you could, I don't know…" Mason leaned forward, right next to Eldan's ear. *"Borrow my heater?"*

"Might take you up on that offer." Eldan tensed up as Mason wrapped his arms tighter around his waist. "Wait, no, not now, you bonehead!"

Eldan tried to twist around, and the sled swerved, sending both men flying into a huge pile of snow. After a moment of recovery, Eldan popped up from the snow, sputtering and cursing under his breath.

"Damn it," Eldan grumbled before turning to Mason. The alpha half-expected an attack-lapin, but when Eldan reached up and ran his hand over his cheek, Mason tensed in surprise.

"Are you okay?" Eldan asked, his comforting touch leaving sparks across Mason's skin. A second later, Mason grabbed Eldan and pulled his mate on top of him.

"What're you doing?" Eldan hissed. "We just crashed, and now you're trying to–?" He let out a little squeak when Mason wrapped his arms around him.

"I'm just lovin' on you a bit," Mason murmured, running his hand through Eldan's hair. "We just survived a crash landing, after all."

"Not my fault. You're the one who whispered all that dirty drivel in my ears." A low growl rumbled in Eldan's throat before it tapered off, and he relaxed against Mason's body.

Mason sighed and rubbed his hand down Eldan's back. Their hearts were beating a million miles a minute, and a wistful smile tugged at the corners of Mason's lips.

"How could I resist?" Mason whispered. "Especially with that sweet, sweet scent. That's asking the impossible."

Eldan groaned as he pushed up from Mason's chest and stared down at the alpha. "This is why I can't take you anywhere nice."

Despite Eldan's angry glare, Mason couldn't help tossing a flirtatious smile at his mate. This whole dynamic was part of the fun, and even when it seemed like Eldan hated every antic, Mason didn't worry. It was a game to them now, their words a form of verbal foreplay. It was their world, one that nobody would ever understand, and that's what made it so special.

And in their world, time seemed to mimic the frozen acres surrounding them. Mason raised his hand to cup Eldan's cheek and rubbed his thumb over his mate's skin.

The sun's rays shined down on Eldan from behind, framing his body in a warm glow. His scarf had drooped slightly, and the marks on his neck seemed to stand out even more. The soft scent of marshmallows still drifted around his mate. Only now, Eldan's scent, mixed with his own, told the age-old story of two lives becoming one, just as Fate intended.

Mason stared, even as his vision burned with tears.

"Are you crying?" Eldan's voice was barely a whisper.

Mason removed his gloves, rubbed his eyes, and flashed a reassuring smile. "Ah, don't worry about lil ol' me. If you could see what I see, you'd understand."

I hope you know just how beautiful you are.

"Crying doesn't suit you." Eldan nuzzled close under Mason's chin and let a low purr rumble in his throat. "But if that's what you need to do…"

"Does crying ever suit anyone?" Mason smirked as he sniffled. "Anyway, I get the feeling we lost the race."

"Well, if *someone* hadn't shouted dirty things behind me–"

"Then we wouldn't be in this adorable situation, would we?" Mason trailed his fingers along the edge of Eldan's ear. "Totally worth it, in my opinion."

"Jesus, could your hands be *any* colder?" Eldan hissed as he jerked away from Mason's hand. "Put your gloves back on; you're gonna get frostbite."

Mason chuckled. He tugged his gloves back on just as Benjamin and Tyler skidded to a stop near them. In their haste, they threw a bit of snow over Eldan's back and into Mason's face.

"Wipeout!" Tyler pumped his fist in the air. "We win!"

"Are you two okay?" Rose called out.

Mason flashed a weak thumbs-up before he let his arm thump down on Eldan's back again. In a flash, Benjamin and Tyler were off, leaving the motionless pair in the snow.

"Maybe we can convince them to help us build that snowman," Eldan mumbled. "It's safer."

Mason snorted in response. "You kidding? They're not gonna stop until they lose all their teeth."

"Guess so," Eldan whispered. "So, does this count as a normal part of a Hallmark movie? My memory's a bit foggy."

Mason curled his arm around Eldan and sighed. "Nah, but I think I like this version better."

"Why's that?" Eldan eyed him.

"Because this is *our* version. Our story. And *our* story…" Mason pressed a kiss to Eldan's forehead. "…Is, without a doubt, my favorite."

CHAPTER 14: DECEMBER 31ST

*E*ldan wrapped a heavy blanket around his shoulders and cursed the sudden drop in temperature. He had *just* begun getting used to the whopping twenty degrees, and now it was in the single digits?

He grumbled to himself as he headed down the stairs and plopped down on the couch like an angry little burrito. Behind the couch, Jenny was rushing to and fro, going over her mental checklist.

"Alright, so you've got movies, popcorn, takeout, and lots of blankets." Jenny glanced around the living room. "Ya'll gonna be good?"

"Oh, ye of little faith." Mason dished up the takeout and set it in the microwave to warm up. "Go enjoy your party. We'll try not to burn the place down."

"Sorry it isn't hot and fresh." Jenny slung her purse over her shoulder. "Holiday evening and all…"

"It'll be fine," Eldan grumbled as he rubbed his hands together. "Microwaved Italian is still Italian."

"Mama mia." Quentin came around the corner fumbling his bowtie. "Ah, shit, here we go again."

Jenny sighed and set her purse down before reaching up to fix his bowtie. "My, my. You're doing it wrong. Hang on."

"You know, when people think of marriage, they think til death do us part." Quentin kept his head tilted up as Jenny fiddled with his bowtie. "But the real, unadulterated vows are along the lines of you're doing that wrong."

"Oh, hush. Let's not forget who falls asleep faster than I do. I could do many things to make your life miserable before you even wake up tomorrow." Jenny nodded in satisfaction and stepped back to grab her gloves. "Now, we're heading out. Don't wait up for us. We'll be staying with our friends until tomorrow."

"And who knows exactly what time we'll be home?" Quentin tugged on his gloves before he held up his wife's coat for her. "Depends on how much we drink, I guess."

"Hey, all the power to you." Mason raised his shot of peppermint schnapps before taking a swig. "Free drinks and good company? Hell yeah. Go out and live a little."

"Alright, you don't gotta tell us twice." Quentin winked. "Try not to have too much fun without us."

"With movies, takeout, *and* alcohol readily available?" Mason took a bite of his food and waved with his empty fork. "No promises."

"Just don't leave a mess in the kitchen, okay? I don't want to come home to a sink full of dirty dishes and messy countertops." Jenny eased herself into her coat. "And leave some drinks for us!"

"Yes, ma'am." Mason snorted.

As the front door creaked shut, Eldan pushed himself up from the couch and wandered over to the thermostat. It was a wonder he hadn't frozen to death yet. Jenny had the thermostat set on 70!

Eldan glanced out the window and counted down the seconds until he heard Quentin's car rumble down the road.

"Finally." Eldan's arm snaked out from the blanket

wrapped around his shoulders and cranked the thermostat up to a comfortable 80 degrees.

Mason peeked around the corner and quirked his eyebrow. "Are you sure that's not gonna be too hot?"

"Would you rather wrap me up in five blankets and–"

"And hold you on my lap while we watch movies? Yes, please."

Eldan thought for a long moment before turning the thermostat back down. "The things I suffer through for you."

"You'll only be cold for a moment, Lapin. I promise." Mason grinned. "Wrap up and get comfy. I'll bring the food out."

"WHAT A MEAL." MASON HUMMED AGAINST ELDAN'S EAR AS HE squeezed his arms around his waist. "That takeout place is to die for."

Eldan took a sip of his peppermint schnapps and shuddered as he felt the warmth settle in his stomach. As much as he hated to admit it, Mason had been right. One blanket was already on the floor, and the other was sliding from Eldan's shoulders. Alcohol and body warmth were an amazingly wonderful combination.

As the movie they were watching came to an end and the credits rolled down the screen, Mason shifted and checked his phone. "It's almost midnight."

Already? Eldan raised his head and checked the clock on the fireplace mantle. He felt cold dread in the pit of his stomach. *That means...*

"You feeling okay, Lapin?" Mason wrapped his arm around Eldan's shoulders and massaged small circles on his collarbone. "Too much to drink?"

Eldan shook his head. No, he'd had the usual amount of liquid courage, but this time itwas different. Instead of comfortable numbness and a couple hours of peace, an unnerving gloom tugged at his heartstrings.

Mason moved closer. "What's wrong?"

"When you head back, even if it's only for a few days…" Eldan's voice trailed off as he snuggled closer to Mason.

"It'll be okay. I'll call every day, I promise."

"That's not what I'm worried about." Eldan rubbed his hand down his face. Had it just gotten warmer in here?

"What's on your mind?"

"You." Eldan groaned. "You'll be gone, and your scent will fade. Even if it's only a bit, it'll fade. I wish I could bottle your scent and keep it forever." He pulled his knees to his chest and pushed more of his weight against Mason. "I don't want any more sleepless nights."

Eldan cringed at the memory of his last sleepless night. The night after he met Mason, he hadn't been able to stop himself. It had been hot. *So, so hot.* His hands seemed to move on their own at the mere thought of the daring, lively alpha.

Flustered didn't even begin to cover the range of emotions he had felt that night. How could he describe it in words? One moment, Eldan was lost in the alpha's eyes on the street. The next, he was in his room at midnight, and his body felt like it was on fire. Forget sleep. He needed more of that *delicious* alpha.

Of course, Eldan was a little nervous. Those few days without Mason by his side had been enough to drive him mad, and now said alpha was on the couch next to him as his *mate.* Could anyone really blame him for being anxious?

"I couldn't stop thinking about you either."

Eldan flinched, pulled from his thoughts as Mason's low voice whispered in his ear.

"Even though I thought I was crazy," Mason purred. "You know, your scent was *almost* completely hidden."

"Almost?"

"After the parade–" Mason started.

Eldan grimaced at the memory. "Oh, don't get me started… I was cruel. I hated myself when I saw how crushed you were, but I couldn't stop. Everything just came pouring out at once, and I–"

"Shhh." Mason pressed his finger to Eldan's lips, then ran his thumb down Eldan's jaw. "Don't worry. I know now how painful that must have been. What I said."

Eldan bit his lip before he leaned into Mason's touch. "So, how'd you know?"

"When you got all fired up, I caught a whiff. And, you know what?" He let out a low purr. "I couldn't keep my hands to myself, either."

"Shit," Eldan whimpered as Mason peppered kisses across any exposed flesh he could find.

"So, no matter what happens, or how hard it is, always know that I'll come back. I *will* be back. Because I'll always be wrapped up in you," Mason whispered against Eldan's skin. "All wrapped up in my pretty little beau."

As Mason pressed lazy kisses to his neck, Eldan felt heat take over his body, and he pushed himself from the couch before straddling Mason's waist. Maybe it was a mix of alcohol and hormones. Or maybe it was plain and simple *want*, as though his very soul needed to reach out and know that his mate was near.

Either way, Eldan couldn't stop now. Not with that dark, loving look in Mason's eyes, and *especially* not with the way his dick twitched against Eldan's ass.

Eldan licked his lips and settled down on Mason's legs. "… *It's my turn.*"

"Take it away, Lapin." Mason purred, letting his hands roam down to cup Eldan's ass. "*Do whatever your little heart desires.*"

Mason's large hands slipped below Eldan's waistband and squeezed gently as he moved with Eldan's motions. He let out a quiet rumble as Eldan peppered chaste kisses on his face. Eldan trailed his fingers through his alpha's hair, gripping and pulling his head back gently.

"I like this side of you." Mason chuckled and Eldan cut him off with a lazy kiss.

As Eldan focused on keeping Mason's mouth busy, he let out a quiet whimper. Mason's warm hands left his ass and began rolling up his sweater, then Mason dragged his fingers along the sensitive skin along his sides.

With every tease and tickle, Eldan felt his resolve slipping. He needed to get back in control of this situation, and he knew just how to do that. He wiggled his hips as he pushed himself back to Mason's thighs, and his hands fell toward his alpha's lap.

"Seems you've got a bit of a problem." Eldan reached out and rubbed the straining bulge trapped in Mason's sweatpants. He bucked his hips up at Eldan's touch, and the way Mason's cock twitched against his hand told him just how much his alpha enjoyed this whole situation.

Eldan dropped to his knees and pulled Mason's sweatpants down to his ankles, releasing the beast. As he grasped Mason's rock-hard shaft, he pressed light kisses to his cock's head.

Eldan looked up, and the look on Mason's face was enough to make shudders wrack his body. He wanted this so badly. Eldan purred as he stroked Mason's cock and the alpha's fingers gripped his hair. He had no choice but to deliver. How could he say no to that face?

Mason curled his fingers through Eldan's locks, whispering soothing praises. Eldan brought his lips to the tip of Mason's cock. He gave it an experimental lick before taking the first few inches into his mouth. He swirled his tongue around the hard shaft as he moved down it.

"Jesus... Keep doing that, sweetie."

With such kind words, how could he not go further? Eldan took in as much as he could, then moved his hand to grasp the base of Mason's cock. Eldan was in such a state of bliss, he didn't even realize when he pulled his own cock out and began stroking it in a steady rhythm.

Eldan felt Mason's dick throb in his mouth. He carefully pulled back and tucked a strand of hair behind his ear. In one swift movement, Mason pulled Eldan up and dragged him back into his lap. Eldan positioned himself over Mason's red, begging cock, which hovered just above him, out of reach.

"*Oh, Sugar Lips, you're driving me mad.*" Mason groaned. "*Eldan...*"

"You look like you want something." Eldan settled down on Mason's thighs and pushed back against his cock, getting slick all over his exposed skin. "*You want this sweet ass, don't you?*"

"*Fuck yeah.*" Mason purred, bucking his hips. "More than you could ever imagine."

"Well, let's make sure you get something off your wish list tonight." Eldan brought his arms up and wrapped them around Mason's shoulders, burying his nose in his alpha's hair. "*I will ride you so damn hard, you'll call me a fuckin' cowboy.*"

"Please, don't stop and worry on my account." Mason nipped Eldan's throat with a warm chuckle. "*Take me to the rodeo, cowboy.*"

Don't gotta tell me twice. Eldan took a deep breath, taking in Mason's spicy scent. He sank down, and his desirous moans flooded the living room. Hard, searing flesh pressed deep inside him, filling him completely. Mason gripped his hips hard enough to leave marks and scraped his nails down Eldan's hips and thighs.

Eldan kept steady pressure on Mason's chest, holding his alpha down as he raised his hips and slammed them back down. Full to the hilt, Eldan wiggled his hips, rolling them in a slow circle before he forced his muscles to clench around Mason's cock.

"That's a dangerous game you're playing, Lapin," Mason growled low in his throat. He clenched his teeth, and his eyebrows furrowed into a knot. "You're about to get yourself into a heap of trouble."

"Weren't you the one who said we'd get into trouble when we got out of that mall?" Eldan pulled himself up halfway before slowly sinking back down. "Show me just how much trouble you can muster."

Mason smirked as he wrapped his arms around Eldan and held him tight. In one quick movement, Mason was on his back, stretched out along the couch. His knees formed a support for Eldan, and he snapped his hips up in one smooth thrust, grinding against the most sensitive spot inside Eldan.

"*Oh, my God,*" Eldan hissed. He nearly doubled over onto Mason's chest as the alpha started stroking his leaking cock, rubbing and squeezing the sensitive flesh. He felt a searing heat flare through his body. Mason's eyes darkened.

"Hang on tight, cowboy." Mason grinned. He took Eldan's wrists and pulled him against his chest. "This bronco's gonna buck you hard." He grinned.

"Wait, what–?"

Eldan let out a loud moan and hung on for dear life as Mason bucked his hips up, taking his omega for the ride of his life. He was pretty sure he drooled on Mason a bit, but how could he not? How could he not lose himself when all he felt was love and want and *need*?

Mason ran his hand down Eldan's back and scratched lightly at his tailbone. A jolt ran through Eldan's body at the sensation, and Mason let out a low chuckle.

"*Still so sensitive.*"

As Eldan tried to gather the strength to retort, Mason grabbed his waist and slammed him back down, cutting off any sassy comeback he may have come up with. Eldan gasped and leaned forward, burying his face in Mason's hair.

"*We're down to twenty seconds, folks!*" announced the TV

host. *"So, grab a loved one and grab some drinks. The New Year is almost here!"*

Mason groaned low in his throat. He slowed his hips and captured Eldan's lips in a messy kiss. "Look at you. You're so fucking pretty when you're sitting on my cock." He pushed Eldan up a bit so he could run his tongue down his jawline. "Almost like you were made to ride."

"I'll show you pretty..." Eldan whimpered, leaning back and balancing his hands on Mason's knees. The new position forced him to sink further down on his alpha's cock. "When I decorate your stomach with white ribbons."

"Please do, Lapin." Mason smirked as he gripped Eldan's thighs. "I wanna see."

"Ten, nine, eight..."

With each roll of his hips, Eldan let strings of gibberish slip from his kiss-swollen lips. He leaned down and nipped Mason's lower lip, then shuddered as Mason wrapped his arms around his back. His alpha's voice came out ragged and choked and, from the way his hips snapped, Eldan knew he was close to his peak.

"Five, four, three..."

With a rough moan, Mason bit down on Eldan's shoulder and buried his nose against his neck. Three ragged thrusts later, he pulled Eldan down one last time and held him in place as his cock pulsed inside him. A warm heat shot up deep inside Eldan, and he snapped his blurry eyes closed as his body spasmed, shooting white ribbons across Mason's stomach.

"Happy New Year!"

Pops and cheers echoed from the TV as the crystal ball dropped. Eldan listened as fireworks exploded in the neighborhood, and he turned to look at the bright colors through the curtains.

Mason panted as he stared at the screen. "That was perfect. Happy fuckin' New Year!" He ran his hands through

Eldan's sweaty locks. "Look at you, though. You didn't get bucked off once. I think you might've found your calling."

"Yeehaw…" Eldan smiled weakly into Mason's neck and nipped at his skin. As Mason shifted beneath him, he bit down a bit harder than he planned, making Mason purr.

"Careful. Don't want to set off the bronco again, do you?"

"Okay, listen. Even if I *wanted* to get off you right now, I can't. My ass and legs are sore. So, cease with that hip movement, sir."

"Right, right." Mason sighed, pulling Eldan's thighs further up his sides. "That tends to happen when you stay in the saddle too long."

"Ha, ha," Eldan hissed as he relaxed against Mason's body. "And you would know, eh, Texas?"

"You know it." Mason watched the fireworks for a moment. "Guess this means we'll have the best luck in the coming year."

Eldan quirked an eyebrow. "Why do you say that?"

"You haven't heard the old wives' tale?" Mason scooted back against the armrest, pulling Eldan with him. "They say you have to kiss someone at midnight for good luck in the new year. But how great will our luck be since we…"

Eldan waited for Mason to finish his sentence, but when his alpha simply stared at him, he waved his hand in front of Mason's eyes.

"Hello? Since we what, 'Charmin'?"

"Wow, not gonna stop me this time?" Mason purred. "You always try to stop me when I'm about to say something dirty. I was gonna ask how great our luck is gonna be this year since you just rode me into oblivion."

"We're gonna be the luckiest fuckers in Boston," Eldan declared. "Pun totally intended."

Mason reached over and grabbed of the blankets from the floor and tossed it over Eldan, wrapping him up like a sexy little burrito.

"Aww, look. We made a mess all over the rug, man..." Mason's gaze dropped to the rug.

"What?" Eldan panicked. He swiveled around to see the rug. It was a nice rug. If he had gotten anything on it–

"Kidding." Mason patted Eldan's back and trailed his fingers down the curve of his spine. "Though we did come close. Pun also intended."

Eldan whimpered as Mason moved again. "We'll have to roll through here with some blockers if we don't want to get 'the look' from Jenny, though."

"Hey, she just said not to make a mess in the kitchen. She said nothing about the living room." Mason took a deep breath, as if he were savoring the scents around the room.

Eldan slumped against Mason in defeat and let out a ragged sigh. "This is why I can't take you anywhere, you know."

"On the contrary," Mason said. "I'm suitable for every event. You just gotta know how to use me. Give me the right costume, and I can become anything."

"The only costume I want you to wear right now is your birthday suit." Eldan breathed against Mason's neck and rolled his hips back against Mason's cock. "You're hard again."

"Can you really blame me when I have the prettiest omega sitting on my lap? And with all these scents floating around the room?"

Eldan pulled Mason up into a sloppy kiss.

"Might as well double our luck for the year." Eldan pulled back the cover and rubbed against Mason's cock. "I'm ready whenever you are." His eyes flashed in a silent challenge. "Old man."

"*And that was* Imagine the Future *by Ruben O'Doral. You're tuned into 98.3, The Watch. Coming up next we have—*"

Mason hummed to himself as another song started up on the radio. Fate must have smiled upon him when he woke up this morning. Not only had he managed to dodge traffic all the way from Baltimore, but he was finally heading home. For good, this time.

After a few weeks of negotiations, his house in Texas had finally been closed on, and everything was packed up and ready to ship whenever he and Eldan found a place of their own. For now, Mason had a few suitcases stuffed with clothes and some of his favorite movies. That oughta keep them busy until September rolled around. Then, Mason could start his new job at Hornebolt University.

Mason took a deep breath of the fresh air flowing through the open window. The Charles River shined brightly in the corner of his eye as he sped down the interstate, weaving through the cars ahead of him. After a few more turns, he arrived in the heart of Mission Hill. He was one step closer to home.

All around him, the streets were bustling with life. People crowded the sidewalks. Mason felt a twinge of nostalgia as he passed by small shops and parks. March in Boston was a strange new sight, especially after seeing nothing but snow and ice for months. He kind of missed the frozen little world, but it was pleasant seeing the recently frosty buildings and streets bursting with color.

A startling, but pleasant transition, to be sure.

Just like a certain grumpy boy. Mason chuckled to himself. In the past few months, Eldan had opened up, revealing his true colors, now that the sun finally warmed his skin. *Just like a little flower.*

"Broadcasting live from witty-whacky Woburn, this is The Watch. Coming up next, here's Philippe Celice in I Wanna Build a Life With You.*"*

Wonder what he's up to right now? Mason's mind wandered as he slowly worked his way through the busy streets. *He doesn't know I'm gonna be back today.*

When he had talked to Eldan that morning, his mate had no idea he was already in Baltimore, just a few hours away from Boston. Mason had risen early and covered a lot of ground in the wee hours of the morning. Now, he was back home a full day early, and he fully expected his Lapin to attack him as soon as walked through the front door. He might even get friendly greetings from Honey Bun and Mr. Hopson if he was lucky.

"Think back to your special someone, folks. You know that look in their eyes when you give them a gift? Lucinda McKinney describes that look in her new hit single, When Love Comes Knocking.*"*

Mason whistled along to the tune, tapping his fingers on the steering wheel in time. When the song slowed down, Mason paid a bit more attention to the lyrics. Despite the happy beginning, it told a long, heart-wrenching story about a couple throughout the years. It beautifully compared their lives and relationship to the flowers they always brought home.

Eventually, the story ended happily, but that didn't stop Mason's eyes from burning. Mason rubbed his cheeks after he pulled into a free spot by the sidewalk. He couldn't help himself. Her beautiful voice had struck a nerve, damn it.

Mason sighed and pulled down his visor to freshen himself up. He only flinched a little when he saw how red and puffy his eyes were. *Shit, now he's gonna think I'm high on something.* Mason grabbed a tissue from the console and blew his nose, trying to make himself feel a bit more human after that heart-breaking song.

"And I thought these would look great on Granny's table for Easter."

A woman's voice and the jingle of a shop bell grabbed Mason's attention. He looked out his passenger window and chuckled to himself. What were the odds he would end up parked in front of a florist after that song? He climbed out of his car and slammed the door behind him, then he pulled open the shop door with a grunt.

When he stepped inside, he was hit with a burst of color, even more colorful than the spring decorations hanging around Boston. The arrangements adorning the shelves were absolutely gorgeous, and not a single bud was out of place.

"Hey, welcome!" A young woman peeked over the shelves at him.

Mason walked around the shelves just as she off-loaded a vase from the box she held against the shelf. The arrangements were decorated with small balloons and curled ribbons. They were mostly lillies and tulips, most likely set aside for Easter.

"Hiya!" The woman grinned as she balanced the empty box on her hip. "Are you looking for anything special today?"

"Howdy. Got a bit of a question for you. What would you

get for someone who's been the most loving, understanding mate while you were gone on a series of trips?"

"That's oddly specific." The woman giggled. "Come with me and give me the details. We'll see what we can do."

She waved her hand toward a small table with chairs in the corner of the shop and headed off, barely waiting for Mason to catch up.

"Where do I begin?" Mason chuckled.

"By taking a seat in the consulting chair." The woman patted a chair as she walked by and took a seat across the table. "Hi, I'm Sophie, and I'll be your guide today. Now, tell me everything."

"Well, Sophie, here's the deal." Mason steepled his hands in front of him and leaned forward. "Get this, I met my Fated in December, right before Christmas–"

Sophie gasped and clapped her hands. "Congrats! Tell me more!"

"I couldn't have been happier." A smile formed on Mason's lips. "But I was only here for a couple weeks before I had to head back to the real world. And the real world was down in Texas."

Sophie's face fell, and Mason rushed to reassure her. "Don't worry! Nothing bad came of it. No, on the contrary, a whole bunch of opportunities popped up."

Mason leaned back and stared at the ceiling. "I moved in with him, I met his family, and we made lots of memories before I started making trips back home to tie up some loose ends."

Sophie twisted her lips as she thought. "How long were these trips? And how much time in between?"

"Gosh, most of them were a week long. The drive down took longer than most of my business there. Most of the time, I stayed a week and a half to two weeks before I headed out again."

"Okay, so that comes out to..." Sophie hummed as she

tapped her finger on the table. "Five trips? Maybe six? At least one month's worth of trips."

"Sounds about right." Mason nodded.

"So he's patient, that much is certain." Sophie grinned.

Mason laughed. "For putting up with my shit? Yeah. Anyway, this trip was the last one, and I heard a song on the radio, and–"

"Oh, no. Don't you even *start* talking about that song. Soon as it starts, I start bawlin'.'"

"Hey, I already did my crying." Mason pointed to his eyes. "But, yeah, he has no idea I'm coming home today, and I figured it was fate that I ended up stopping in front of this shop after that song ended."

"Sounds to me like this is an uber-special order. We need to pass you along to the professionals!"

Sophie stood and motioned for him to follow. She led him to the front counter where a young man sat. He was scribbling, his head hunched over a sketchbook, deaf to the world.

"Sawyer, we got a live one." Sophie motioned to Mason. "To sum it up, he had to make a series of trips after he met his Fated. Now, he needs something special because this was the final trip. Also, his mate has no idea he's coming home today." She winked at Sawyer before she turned back to Mason. "Sawyer here'll take care of you. Take care!"

Sawyer nodded as he swiveled around on his stool. "Well, as you've already heard, I'm Sawyer. I'm the owner of this place." Sawyer held out his hand.

"Mason. It's a lovely shop you have here." Mason shook his hand and smiled brightly.

"Thanks." Sawyer positively glowed. "Now, after hearing Sophie's lovely summary, I've already got something in mind, but do you want any flower in particular?"

Mason scratched the back of his head and smiled bashfully. "I don't know nothin' about no flowers, I'm afraid."

"Hey, that's okay because I'm ready to build something that will blow your mind." Sawyer swiveled around and flipped to a clean page in his sketchbook. "Let's get started."

∼

"It's perfect." Mason stared, raising and lowering his head to see every detail. Oranges, purples, and pinks popped out at him, but a bunch of yellow flowers caught his eye. "What are those?"

"Asiatic Lillies." Sawyer trailed his fingers along the long petals. "They symbolize a celebration of new life."

"New life? You know, I like it." Mason pulled his wallet from his pocket. "How much do I owe you?"

"Usually, for a bouquet like this, it's about forty bucks." Sawyer closed his sketchbook and swiveled around. After a long moment, he quirked his eyebrow. "But, for you, it's on the house."

"What? You're kidding me. No way, man, you can't give your stuff away. Not with this kind of talent."

"I can, though." Sawyer smirked. "See, the wonderful thing about owning my own business is that *I* make the decisions, and *I* say you get this one for free."

"Man, I hope Fate smiles on you. You're an angel, you know?" Mason stared with half-lidded eyes at the beautiful bouquet before he perked up. "I'll be sure to recommend you and your shop."

"Thanks a ton. I'd really appreciate it." Sawyer clasped his hands. "Anyway, I hope your mate enjoys that."

"I'm sure he will. Thanks again, Sawyer." Mason took a long sniff of the flowers before he turned and headed to the door.

Sophie was near the front windows, arranging a display of completed work. Mason looked over his shoulder at Sawyer and saw the man was busy with another customer.

"Hey, Sophie?"

Sophie turned around with a wide smile. "Hey, what's up?"

"I have a secret mission for you." Mason passed her a fifty from his wallet. "Go out and buy yourselves some lunch or something. He won't take this from me."

"Yeah, that sounds like him, alright." Sophie snickered. "I'll make sure we get a good lunch tomorrow. Thanks for stopping by."

"My pleasure." Mason nodded as he stepped out into the warm, spring air.

Just one more short drive, and he'd be home.

～

As Mason pulled down the road to Jenny and Quentin's place, he noticed they weren't home. It was to be expected, though. With finals right around the corner, they were practically living on campus for their last semester.

Mason couldn't help noticing the open windows as he pulled to a stop in front of the house. He'd wanted to surprise Eldan, but those windows might throw a wrench in his plans.

He'd be damned if he didn't try, though.

Please don't let the alarm go off. That's all I ask. Mason pushed the door shut slowly and let out a sigh when he didn't see Eldan staring out the window. *He must be busy or something.* With the bouquet firmly grasped in his hand, Mason headed to the front door and smoothed back his hair.

Maybe he still had a chance of surprising–

Mason didn't have a chance to reach for the doorknob before the door burst open, and a figure came flying at him. He spread his arms and caught a soft body, taking steps to steady himself.

"Hey, you're early! Welcome home." Eldan wrapped his arms around Mason's neck, nuzzling into his rugged skin.

"Whoah there, how'd you know it was me? I was as quiet as humanly possible!"

Eldan took a deep breath. "Caught your scent through the window." His fingers curled around the back of Mason's shirt. "Not as sneaky as you think."

Mason snaked his arms down to Eldan's thighs and pulled him up, so Eldan's legs wrapped around his waist. "Yeah, well. I never claimed to be a ninja." Mason kicked the door shut behind him before heading to the living room and settling down on the couch. "Remind you of anything?"

"You seriously think I could forget the incident at Silverstone Mall? Please." Eldan scoffed and straddled Mason's lap as the alpha settled down. "What do you have there?"

"For you and your limitless patience for my shit." Mason held up the bouquet with a dreamy smile.

Eldan took the flowers and studied them, giving them a slow sniff before he threw his arms around Mason's neck again. Mason snickered as he felt his mate pepper kisses over his cheeks.

"I take it you like them?"

"Love them," Eldan whispered between kisses.

Mason squeezed Eldan's thighs with a low purr. "What've you been up to while I've been gone? Been knitting some more animals?"

"Animals, clothes, blankets, you know." Eldan sagged against Mason's chest for a moment before scrambling to reach something in the armchair. "One of the guys at work and his mate are expecting a boy soon." He held up an adorable, knitted moose, complete with an ugly sweater.

"And this..." Eldan unfolded and held up a purple and yellow blanket speckled with green. "One of the older ladies at work wanted something for her newest grandbaby."

"What about that one?" Mason pointed to a gift bag overflowing with bright tissue paper.

Eldan reached out, grabbed the bag, and dangled it in front of Mason's face. "Why don't you open it and find out?"

Mason quirked his eyebrow and took the bag. He painstakingly pulled out every individual piece of paper. He knew it would drive his mate crazy, and he was right. Eldan practically vibrated with excitement as Mason drew things out.

When the last piece hit the floor, Eldan hummed. A cute little bunny stared at Mason, and he pulled it out of the bag.

"This looks like the one on your bookshelf."

"Another attempt, yeah." Eldan rested against Mason's chest as he studied the rabbit. "I wanted to get it right this time."

"Perfectionism kicking in? You could probably do this for a living, you know." Mason purred. "Because anything you make is cute."

"Does that blessing extend to things *we* make?" Eldan whispered and raised his head.

Mason's eyes widened. "What do you mean?"

Eldan shifted and pulled his tank top over his head before he guided Mason's hand to his shoulder. "Feel for yourself."

Mason's mouth fell open. *Hot, swollen mark? You're kiddin'.* He carefully turned Eldan's shoulder to his side and confirmed his suspicions when he saw the dark purple mark.

"You're…we're…" Mason stuttered before his voice broke. "Oh, my God, I'm gonna cry. I'm already crying. Look what you've done to me." He ran his hand down his face before settling it back on Eldan's shoulder.

Eldan grinned and relaxed as Mason's hands moved to his back, rubbing up and down over every muscle and mark. "So? What do you think? Will the blessing extend to *our* work?"

"Are you kiddin'? They're gonna be *the cutest*." Mason

buried his nose in Eldan's neck and took a deep breath. "Our best work yet."

"Guess this means we'll need to look for a house with a bigger yard." Eldan snickered.

"But at least we won't need a bigger car, right?"

"Right."

I gotta ask, though…" Mason started. "How loudly do you think Oppa's gonna scream the moment we tell him?"

"The exact moment?" Eldan pinched his chin and twisted his lip. "Probably loud enough for the neighbors to hear. The ones three streets over, too."

Mason kicked back, and Eldan snuggled up against him as a cool breeze flowed through the living room. "You know, that sounds about right."

Mason absentmindedly rubbed his hand over Eldan's mark. Everything he had ever wanted had come to fruition. It was all falling into place, and he couldn't be any happier.

"I found a nice place over in Wayland." Eldan swiveled around, most likely looking for his phone, but he settled on sneaking Mason's from his pocket. He scrolled down before he returned the phone to Mason. "Lots of space, good location. Closer to Ma, too. Not to mention, the price is great."

"Wow, that's a beautiful house." Mason flipped through the pictures. "I love the outside of it. Imagine all those big trees in the fall. Imagine the leaf piles!"

"I'm more excited about the craft room." Eldan dragged his finger through the pictures, skipping a few until he stopped on a picture of a large craft room lined with shelves. "Look at that space. I could make so many things in there."

"Sounds like you've got your heart set on this one." Mason grinned. "Maybe we can go see it soon?"

"Yeah, they're taking appointments." Eldan reached forward to touch the screen, but it changed, and Oppa's face popped up.

Mason snorted and stared at the screen. "I swear that man knows when we're talking about him." He grinned as Eldan tugged on his tank top. "Okay, prepare your earholes, Lapin. We're about to find out if Oppa can break the sound barrier. Ready?"

Eldan settled down next to Mason again. "I'm ready."

EPILOGUE

December 25th

"*B*ut as Santa promised, Frosty returned every year with the magical Christmas snow."

Eldan listened to the TV in the living room as *Frosty the Snowman* finally came to an end. To his credit, he only cringed a little as memories of his nightmares from years ago haunted the back of his mind.

He shook off the thought and turned back to his current task: getting breakfast ready. He juggled the pans skillfully, as if he had gone through years of rigorous training in the Ramsay Cook Camp. Yes-sir-ee, he was a mean, lean, cookin' machine.

Eldan flinched as he felt a kick in his stomach. Okay, maybe not *lean* anymore, but he could still make a mean stack of pancakes, damn it. He ran his hand down his stomach and curled it around his growing belly. Seven months was no joke. He was *round.* Rotund, even.

But that was perfectly okay.

"These pancakes smell yummy, don't they?" Eldan cooed, feeling a kick in response to his touch. "I know. We'll eat soon. Maybe."

Eldan glanced at the clock on the wall. It was already 8:47 AM. Really, it was a surprise he was the only one up, especially given the day.

Except the baby... Eldan sighed. He only had to get up to pee like five times in three hours. At this rate, he'd have to live in the bathroom by the time he hit nine months.

Although, maybe last night was the reason Mason was still asleep. After all, his mate had been up well into the night putting together toys, long after he himself had passed out.

Maybe last night was the reason Mason was still asleep. After all, his mate had been up well into the night putting together toys, long after he had passed out.

A sudden pop from the skillet forced Eldan from his thoughts. He pulled the crispy strips of bacon from their pan and flipped the last pancake in another. Satisfied with its golden-brown finish, he tossed it on top of the large stack.

Another kick made him stagger forward. He gripped the counter while he recovered. "Jeez, girl, you've got some legs on you," Eldan wheezed. "You that hungry?"

The kicks calmed, and Eldan let out a sigh. At this rate, Mason wasn't going to wake up before she bruised his abdomen. It was about time to take matters into his own hands.

Eldan reached up, grabbed a cup from the cupboard, and poured a cup of coffee fit for the gods before he padded up the stairs in his worn out slippers.

As Eldan nudged open the bedroom door, he felt a wad of fur brush against his legs as it flew out the door. A slower, much larger wad of fur hobbled after the flash, snuffling as it padded past Eldan's legs.

With a sigh, Eldan quietly shut the door and waddled to the bed before taking a seat, taking a moment to relish in the comfort of the soft pillows and blankets, After a moment, he held the steaming cup of coffee below his mate's nose.

Mason snorted and brought his hand to his face, rubbing his tired-looking eyes. Though no matter how rough he looked, his eyes still lit up as they focused on Eldan's face.

"Mornin', Mr. Claus." Eldan set the cup of coffee on the nightstand before he leaned over and kissed Mason's forehead. "Made you some coffee. I know you were up pretty late putting all those toys together."

"Yeah, I'm running on about two hours right now." Mason stretched and rolled toward Eldan, snaking an arm around him, before looking at the closed door. "Still asleep?"

"Yeah, like a log." Eldan sighed as he curled his arm around his belly. "This one, however…"

"I heard. You were up and down all night after I came to bed." Mason snorted. "You're probably just as tired as I am."

Eldan's lips curled into a smile, and he nodded. "Some nights are worse than others. It was just bad luck that one of those nights happened to be last night."

Mason pushed himself up and reached for his coffee. He took a long sip. "Yeah, I'll say. Maybe she's just excited. It is Christmas, after all. Hell, *I'm* excited, and I've experienced Christmas 36 times now." Mason snickered. "Thirty-seven if you count today."

"Depends. How old do you want to feel, codger?" Eldan grinned.

"Hold that thought." Mason finished his coffee in a flash and was seemingly invigorated by the warm drink. It was almost scary how quickly he could go through a cup of coffee, but Eldan just rolled with it. They had a big day ahead of them.

"Say that again now that I've had my coffee." Mason quirked his eyebrow in a challenge.

Eldan leaned forward with a smirk. "Do you feel lucky, old man?"

A slow smile spread over Mason's face as he grabbed the edge of the comforter and pulled it over Eldan, wrapping his mate up in a cocoon before showering his face with kisses.

Eldan squirmed against his restraint but kept a sharp, defiant tone to his voice. "Is that all you got?"

Mason pulled Eldan close and sagged back against his pillow before yawning in Eldan's face.

"Ewww, morning breath." Eldan crinkled his nose. "Is that your final form?"

"Yeah, my ass is getting cold."

It was only then that Eldan realized Mason was buck-ass naked since he had used the comforter to restrain him.

Eldan flushed deep red before he buried his nose against Mason's shoulder. "Go get dressed, fool. And, as much as I would love a show, we need to get this party started." Eldan motioned to his stomach. "She's had a hankerin' for pancakes for a while now."

"Sure thing, Lapin." Mason rose from the bed and headed to the dresser. He pulled on an old set of burgundy flannel pajama bottoms.

"Can't believe you still have those." Eldan groaned.

"Hey, don't judge. They're a classic!" Mason waved his hands around his legs. "And they're super warm."

Mason turned back to the dresser and dug around for the top. Eldan slipped from the bed and snuck up behind him, wrapping his cold arms around Mason's waist from behind. He rested his head against Mason's back, leaving nips and kisses as his breath warmed Mason's skin.

"Well, ain't you in a lovey mood today?" Mason whispered as he swayed a bit, moving him and Eldan in the world's laziest dance.

"Just lovin' on you a bit. We have a bit of a day ahead of us." Eldan ran his hands up Mason's stomach and felt a shudder run through his mate's body.

"I'll never get over this. How come your hands are not blue?" Mason grabbed his hands and held them to warm them up a bit. Suddenly, a cry rang out from a room down the hall.

Eldan smiled against Mason's skin. "And there he is. I'll go get him. You finish getting ready. Breakfast is on the table whenever you're done."

Mason smiled adoringly, and Eldan untangled himself and stepped back, heading for the door.

Time to get this party started.

~

ELDAN CURLED UP AGAINST MASON IN FRONT OF THE WARM fire crackling in the fireplace.

The morning had flown by, and their little boy, Tannon, had already torn through all his gifts like a tornado. By his side sat a little knit rabbit, the same one Eldan had redone three years ago.

Mason rested his head on Eldan's, watching as Tannon tried to play with every toy at once.

"Three years already," Mason mumbled. "A whole lot has changed, hasn't it?"

Eldan squirmed as he pulled a blanket tighter around their shoulders. "I mean, if you want, I could always act like a scrooge again for old time's sake."

"Nah, I think your Ma would have some words for me if you suddenly reverted back to hating Christmas, especially since we have a Chrimmas-lovin' little rugrat now, and another on the way."

Eldan curled his arm around his belly, and Mason's hand moved to rest on top of his.

"Is she up and moving?"

"Yep." Eldan relaxed against Mason's body. "Definitely a lot more active than little Tannon was. I think we've been watching too many sports recently. She's been kicking my bladder like a soccer ball."

"Watch out. We got an MLB in there." Mason grinned.

"A major league baseball?" Eldan tilted his head. "You mean to tell me I'm giving birth to the world's first human-baseball hybrid?"

"Major League Baby," Mason whispered under his breath.

"Oh, my Godddd." Eldan groaned as Mason ran his hand over his baby bump. Mason's hand was warm on his stomach, and Eldan bit his lip.

"Are you Major League material, Eve?" Mason cooed. "I bet you are." He smirked and placed a kiss on Eldan's stomach just as Tannon toddled over with a new toy.

"What you got there, Tannon?" Mason lit up when he saw what it was. "Look at that! Ain't that cool?" Mason picked up Tannon and put him on his lap. "What is that?"

"Bo-bot!" Tannon babbled.

"A robot? Oooooh." Mason snuck his hand around and pressed a button, making the robot's eyes flash. Tannon beamed as the head started spinning around and flashing.

Eldan gingerly rubbed his hands over his belly, feeling their little girl kick in response to his touch. He had thought it was a sweet, quiet moment. Then, he felt the world's hardest kick hit him from the inside out.

"Oof! Looks like you felt something there." Mason cringed. "Hell, I think I felt that one all the way over here."

"Yeah, I think she's training for a marathon in there."

"That means she's working up an appetite! And by she, I mean you." Mason's eyes glinted. "I'll take that as a sign that it's about time to head over to Gramma's and stock up on the good stuff, yeah?"

Mason balanced Tannon on his hip and messed with the toddler, tickling his chubby little belly before he pushed himself from the couch.

Eldan grunted as he tried to get up from the overly plush

couch, then he sagged back against the back. He swallowed his pride. "I, uh, may need assistance."

"I got you, Lapin. Hang on tight." Mason reached down and pulled Eldan to his feet. He drew his mate flush against his body with ease, despite balancing a squirmy toddler on his other hip.

It was one of the hottest things Eldan had ever seen.

"I think you're the hungry one." Eldan smirked.

"Yeah, I'm a hungry man. Hell, they named an entire TV dinner brand after me!" Mason chortled. "Besides, you'd have to be crazy to pass up good home cooking."

"Not gonna argue with you there." Eldan sighed. His eyes trailed up to Mason's face as they started burning with tears.

He couldn't help it. The scene in their living room was something straight out of a storybook.

There stood his gallant mate, a toddler on his hip, with a twinkling tree behind him. The fire crackled and glowed beside them, and two fat rabbits were curled up next to the warm hearth. They were about to head to his Ma's house for Christmas lunch, and even Mason's parents were gonna be there this year.

Really, it was everything Eldan had ever wanted in life, even if he hadn't known it before. Maybe, after all these years, this was the story that told what happened when a scrooge fell for St. Nick?

After all, it was *their* story, and it was entirely based on true events.

"You okay, Lapin?" Mason shifted Tannon on his hip before wrapping his free arm around Eldan's waist.

"Don't worry about me. Trust me, it's just the hormones. I've never been better, love." Eldan sniffled. "Never better."

AUTHOR'S NOTE

I hope you enjoyed the adventures of Eldan and Mason!
Please be sure to check out the other couples in my series!
They're dying to meet you!

Omegas of Boston series – M/M Romance, Mpreg, Fated Mates, Low Angst, and Sugary-Sweet Goodness!

1. **Starry Skies for My Omega. Lukas McGuire and Owen Atkins.**
2. **Forget Me Not, My Dear Omega. Sawyer Okura and Colton McGuire.**
3. **All Wrapped Up In A Pretty Little Beau. Eldan Noelle and Mason Shepard.**
4. **(TBR) Tailored to You. Eliseo Agramonte and Abraham Gillespie.**
5. **(TBR) A Road Trip with My Mate. Archer Moody and ??? :)**

To keep up with new releases and updates, please join my group on Facebook!

MARIANNA FORREST'S FOREST OF FANCIES

If you want to be the absolute first to know about upcoming releases, events, and more, please sign up for my newsletter!

If you're looking at the e-book version, you can click this link to go straight to my site!

MY NEWSLETTER

IF YOU'RE CURRENTLY STARING AT A
PRINTED VERSION OF THIS BOOK, YOU
CAN CHECK IT OUT AT:

> forestoffancies.com <

EXCERPT

Excerpt from my first book: Starry Skies for My Omega

"Stay back. Stay away from me," he tried to growl at the stranger, sounding much less threatening than he had planned. He scooted to the side, trying to get away from the man, cringing as his shoulder hit a solid pile of stacked crates.

"I won't hurt you. I just want to get you out of all this garbage and glass," the stranger said in a husky voice. "Please let me help you."

Lukas winced as pain shot through his legs. If he decided to run, he wouldn't get far on his own.

"Fine. Okay."

Lukas took a deep breath before he felt himself being gently pulled up. He didn't sense any hostility from this alpha. He took in more of the man's scent, a heady, intoxicating blend of pine, spices, and…Wait.

He froze at the exact time he heard the alpha take a deep breath. He looked up and saw the alpha's eyes darken for a split second as if he was in a trance before recovering his senses.

"Come on, bench isn't far." The alpha's voice was rough, breathless.

The man helped Lukas limp to the sidewalk outside the alley, slowly lowered him onto a bench that was haphazardly pushed against the rough brick wall, and stood next to him, arms crossed.

"So what's an omega like you doing walking the streets at night without some form of protection?" the alpha asked, raising his eyebrow.

Lukas once again leaned his head back against the wall, warily side-eyeing the man, before saying, "The dog protected me, didn't it? And I got a good bite on that guy's hand too."

The man looked amused before replying, "Yeah, it would seem you two are cut from the same cloth."

Lukas groaned as he averted his gaze.

The man looked elated. "You must be Lukas. Archer called ahead and told us to expect you."

Lukas looked puzzled before asking, "Us? You and those other people?"

The man shook his head, "I work for Mr. Yorke. Got hired a couple weeks ago. Archer called not long ago and said to keep an eye out for, in his words, 'an angry little omega with a fighter's spirit.' Those other people were just patrons of the bar who heard the commotion."

The man bent next to Lukas and leaned close to his ear, a low voice slipping from his lips. "He also said you might get in trouble on the way. I didn't really understand what he meant at first, and then that scent of yours caught my attention. Then it all made sense."

The silky voice of the alpha so close to him made Lukas shudder, and he felt his cheeks get hot as a low purr followed the stranger's final word.

Lukas leaned his head back against the wall and watched through half-lidded eyes as the lips of the alpha curled up in a smile. No telling what this guy was thinking if he had picked up on the same thing Lukas had.

Pulling his hat over his unruly hair, Lukas opted to study the man subtly from under the brim as he rested. The alpha stood in the light of a nearby streetlamp, keeping a sharp lookout around them.

He seemed to be in his mid-to-late twenties and had a fierce look about him, but Lukas felt safe around him. The man had shaggy dark red hair, bright silver-blue eyes, pale skin, and a killer smile. He wore the sleek, vintage, black and white uniform the Shattered Gate Bar was known for. His rolled-up sleeves revealed intricate tattoos and small scars.

Lukas thought back to his dreams. *Great, so I'm a psychic now? Perfect.*

Sirens echoed in the distance, ending Lukas' idle thoughts. After a few seconds, the man turned and offered a hand to Lukas.

"Come on, let's get you into the bar. We need to get you patched up. That is, if you'll let me."

Lukas nodded and took the alpha's hand. The man carefully put Lukas' arm over his shoulders and wrapped his arm around Lukas' waist to support him. He turned his head back to the alley.

"Mimosa, come on, girl!"

The dog ran right up to the man before walking next to Lukas, effectively cutting off any escape if he decided he would rather take his chances on the streets. Oh, this alpha and his dog were quite the team alright.

Not that he would try to walk out on the street by himself again right now. Nah, he was quite content being plastered up against the side of this alpha.

Lukas looked up at the man before asking, "So, who do I have to thank for my heroic rescue?"

The alpha looked surprised before replying, "Oh, uh...

Owen. Owen Atkins. Nice to meet you. Though I wish it could have been under better circumstances."

Lukas laughed quietly.

"Agreed, Oh-uh Owen."

Owen gave Lukas a look. "Okay, Meep."

"Meep?"

"Hey, if you're going to call me Oh-uh Owen, I am within my rights to call you Meep since that's the first tangible noise you made after that asshat ran off." Owen grinned.

"Fine. Tonight has been embarrassing enough. Thank you, Owen," Lukas whispered.

Owen looked down and smiled. "No problem, Lukas."

www.ingramcontent.com/pod-product-compliance
Lightning Source LLC
Chambersburg PA
CBHW070923190726
48292CB00004B/1085